Pirates in the White House
and
Terrorists under Lake Erie

RICHARD ONDO

iUniverse LLC
Bloomington

PIRATES IN THE WHITE HOUSE AND TERRORISTS UNDER LAKE ERIE

iUniverse books may be ordered through booksellers or by contacting:

iUniverse
1663 Liberty Drive
Bloomington, IN 47403
www.iuniverse.com
1-800-Authors (1-800-288-4677)

ISBN: 978-1-4917-1017-3 (sc)
ISBN: 978-1-4917-1019-7 (hc)
ISBN: 978-1-4917-1018-0 (e)

Library of Congress Control Number: 2013917933

Printed in the United States of America.

iUniverse rev. date: 10/11/2013

PROLOGUE

PAST NOVELS REVEALED Richard Stern's passion to be a bounty hunter. He lives in a small Village of Fairport Harbor next to Lake Erie and partially surrounded by the Grand River. Only eight miles away to the east is the Perry Nuclear Power Plant. The plant had been a target of Al Qaeda operatives in the past.

The name Al Qaeda translates to 'the base.' Were they establishing a base in Lake County, Ohio? That was on Stern's mind.

Terrorists don't give up easily. They are driven by a radical ideology. Richard Stern has quite a memory or an uncanny sixth sense. His powerful dreams reveal bits and pieces of Al Qaeda plans. His dreams paint a savvy picture of the enemy. Canada is only a two hour trip across Lake Erie. Stern always thought this will be the route the terrorists take to attack the nuclear plant.

Stern faced danger because of his haphazard attitude in following leads to the enemy. Through great luck he managed to stay alive mostly because of a female FBI Agent Monica Micovich. While guarding Stern she dropped her guard and allowed Stern to seduce her. Her uncharacteristic affair with Stern was a career mistake. In a one night stand the sperm met the egg and nine months later, she delivered a son, Michael. She was devastated not by delivering a son, but from her miscue in allowing Stern to take advantage of her.

Over the years Stern's revelations through dreams gave reasons for the FBI to use Mr. Stern's incredible paranormal suggestion. He became an informer for the FBI, but his affair with Miss Micovich put cold water on his FBI role.

Cleveland FBI Supervisor Cliff Moses gave Stern the heave ho. Moses was Agent Micovich's mentor. He wasn't going to put up with Stern's recklessness.

Monica Micovich was desperate to find a husband and father for her son. Michael. He's six years old and ready to start school. She started to trust handsome Agent Bill Wright, an opportunist, a ladies man. Philander is the term pinned to Mr. Wright. He was a ladies man.

When Miss Micovich found out her fiancé was cheating, the engagement was off. She enjoyed his love making and that would prove to be a calamity and a mild gift down the road.

Agent Micovich renews her ties with Mr. Wright. It may have been loneliness or his masterful performance in bed. She didn't learn from the first encounter.

A lover's quarrel brews between Agent Bill Wright and a new character. Agent Monica Micovich has contenders taking center stage. She will have to fight for her man or (men). The difficulty for her is deciding. Is there a lucky man she will marry? Is he the handsome Agent Bill Wright or the zany, unpredictable amateur bounty hunter, Richard Stern? It should be an easy decision. Her decision comes with consequences. She is a jealous woman. Trouble is ahead for Agent Micovich. Her will power is really tested.

Agent Micovich is spearheading a drive to find the perpetrators of 'Fast and Furious." The gun-running operation in Mexico involves terrorists moving guns north to Middle America. The plot is much bigger than gun-running. Pirates in the White House (Department of Justice) are disturbed by Agent Micovich's tenacious work.

Much has happened in the last six years. In this story Richard Stern and a host of old and new characters line up for action. Finding the enemy is the bottom line for Richard Stern. He was after FBI reward money, but many factors stymied his operation. He could use a secretary, but never gave it much serious consideration until he met Lindsay Wagner.

Richard Stern isn't finished doing what he does best, meddling and finding trouble. He adds a supporting person in Miss Wagner. Lindsay is a fast learner. She became wrapped up in Stern's operation. Together, they find out a secret terrorist plan almost by accident.

The enemy has a new expedition on the Great Lakes. It's very cunning.

Miss Wagner doesn't realize she was working for a terrorist in Santee, California. Stern stopped at a restaurant where Lindsay works. This was their first meeting. She meets Mr. Stern for the second time in Lake County, Ohio by coincidence. Stern offers a secretary job to the pretty and shapely Miss Wagner. He asks her to be his secretary.

Having an employee was unusual for Stern, especially an attractive female. The law of nature changed the job description, employee and secretary. It happened. An office romance started brewing. Close quarters for two opposite sex adults made it happen.

They didn't waste time in spite of their age difference Lindsay had a couple secret promises. Her purpose was to take control. She wanted to help Richard break free of his alcoholic habit. She doesn't hold back. She goes all the way. She rides Stern and forces him to decide between sex and booze.

Richard and Lindsay teamed up and steamed up the office. Together they work to cash in on an FBI reward. Stern's experience and luck keep them from getting killed. Unfortunately, Lindsay Wagner does suffer serious consequences.

This story isn't about politics as you will see. It does shine like on the last two presidents that spend freely. Too many wars and too many bad decisions rack up a heavy federal deficit.

Terrorism is running rampant. The Middle East, Egypt and Syria are on fire. The enemy is in our country. For all we know they might be setting the forest fires in the western states. In this story terrorist are again planning to blow up a nuclear power plant. This is what the enemy calls 'unfinished business.'

AMERICA SWIMMING IN LIES AND BRIBES

THE TERRORISTS WERE sitting in the dining room of the Oasis Club in Santee, California. A new plan was put on the table. While seated in the Oasis Club restaurant, Abdul Mahdi says "The previous leaders made mistakes. We're going back to Lake Erie. My uncle in Detroit has bought a research vessel in Astoria, Oregon. He wants me to test it out and add a submersible that can be load inside the ship. The idea is to act like college researchers, test out the vessels, and sail to Panama, up the St Lawrence Seaway to Lake Erie, and dock in Toledo and Sandusky, Ohio. He's buying another ship in Detroit. It needs work, so I will be going there after I finish work in Oregon."

Mr. Akmar Mehsud, the Great Lake regional leader, says, "Some key work will take place under the water. We will be attacking during the night. Our target is the Perry Nuclear Power Plant in Northeast Ohio on the south shore of Lake Erie. I don't want to raise suspicion so we'll first train on the Columbia River in Astoria, Oregon and then move the operation to Lake Erie. You already know Abdul Madhi's uncle bought the vessels and he's buying another that will be a tourist yacht for the wealthy gamblers. The ladies that he hired to works as entertainment girls will do anything to make a paying customer have a good time. Do you know what I mean?"

The terrorists are all over America. In 2010 Stern was concerned by the number of terrorist attacks across America. In 2011 he travels across America to find the enemy. His observations are correct. Al Qaeda and homegrown terrorists are in San Diego and crossing the border from Mexico. More attacks are attempted in New York City and a horrific attack at Fort Hood, Texas. Months later Richard Stern journeys to Portland and Astoria, Oregon. He keeps traveling to find the next piece of evidence.

He would eventually journey to San Diego for the third time on a tip from a border control officer, Agent Lopez. During this travel, he meets a woman, Lindsay Wagner, who would alter his life. They didn't know it at the time. Fate would bring them together again.

On another front our government is waging a war against the TEA PARTY. Could it be the enemy is in Washington DC and has turned the Internal Revenue Service into police dogs to target certain people, certain organizations?

The story begins after Richard Stern hires a secretary, Lindsay Wagner. She knows Richard is a conservative Republican, bounty hunter, and wrapped up in the Tea Party.

Richard Stern asked, "How can the Tea Party fight the IRS, when the IRS is supposed to be unbiased?"

His foxy secretary, Lindsay Wagner, entered the office at the right time to intercept Stern's question.

"You're the one that's biased." She said.

Stern went on to explain the political rules. Many politicians made their job of getting reelected as their primary duty. It seemed like 'we the people' were getting shafted by the smooth talking politicians time after time. Fortunately, the Tea Party movement came to the rescue in the election of November 2010.

"Lindsay, Tea Party Americans can't be bought. It's a growing voting bloc. You can call us the enemy of the Democratic Party. After the 2010 election, now I'm guessing; the gloves came off. We're being suppressed. The Pirates in the White House decided to do anything and everything to halt the rise of the Tea Party's voice in America."

The Democratic Party officials were bummed out. They thought the Tea Party would fold up and vanish. Steps were put in place to stymie and circumvent the Tea Party effort.

Stern was right, it didn't happen by accident. The Tea Party had to be crushed. The Tea Party was up against the most resourceful and corrupt administration ever born to high office. High government officials made it their duty to coach the IRS into a bias against the TEA PARTY. The truth was slowly coming out, like pulling teeth. Most high ranking official in the government were clamming up. IRS official were using the sentence, 'I don't know.' more often. Even the White House press secretary was stepping on egg shells. His job was becoming increasingly difficult.

Lies lead to Pinocchio statements. Eventually, one whistle blower starts passing the truth serum. A mild panic evolves into a full scale cover up. The truth can't hide by saying 'I don't know.' It's revealed. They know the law was broken and they won't incriminate themselves, so she and he take the Fifth Amendment. Even that was bumbled. The White House was filled with people that had no memory. They had the 'I don't know' disease. It was spreading to other government departments.

Richard Stern had a clear mind on how the country was being manipulated. He couldn't convince Lindsay that voters were being bought. Most working Americans saw how low income voters were being legally bribed. The party in control and with the most power could use food stamps, unemployment checks, and free cell phones as a means to lure voters to vote for their side. It was a masterful plan.

Could it be said that taxpayers' dollars and union dues were being spent for political reasons? Why is the government advertising in Mexico, an easy way to apply for food stamps in America. The goodness of America gets better thanks to Uncle Sam's government employees. He's dishing out the goodies. It's not a homerun. No, it's a grand slap in the face of real workers. More unemployment benefits are extended. Was it for political reasons? If so, it was a perfectly planned operation. Want free money. See Uncle Sam, he's got your check.

Richard Stern says, "It's the Pied Piper maneuver, Lindsay. When people rely on the government to survive, they rarely lose their government check. Well, they won't lose it, unless it's under their work boots."

Richard Stern and Lindsay Wagner are an odd couple. They aren't a perfect match in age or complexion. She's beautiful and he's past his prime. Richard is a Tea Party member and Lindsay is a Democrat. He tries to convince her of the dubious ways the White House staff operates.

Stern says, "We are getting dumped on. The smell is coming from the White House. It's right in front of the Tea Party noses. Instead of crap, it's lies and bribes. Free healthcare, ha, ha that's a lie. The Democrats even know that."

Lindsay wasn't about to change. She cringed when he said that.

She exclaims, "You're a Tea Party believer. I have a strong desire to be with you, so I will respect your position. We'll still get along, even if you're wrong."

Lindsay was right about her strong desire and Richard had a feeling she would see his way one day.

Stern hired Lindsay to do some of the ordinary secretarial work and learn the operation of his camera equipment. He was hoping she would become a shutter bug and help him with some bounty hunting duties. She took on the task of learning in a hurry.

After Lindsay left with his camera to take pictures of Lake Erie boaters, Richard contemplated his next series of steps. He'd work with Lindsay and explain his real reason for using her talent. She had evident of terrorism and never realized it. As he worked with her, she started to understand. Over time Richard and Lindsay became true partners and accumulated much evidence about the enemy.

He turned on the TV to watch the next turn of events. The TV reporter said that the Internal Revenue Service would oversee (enforce) the healthcare laws at the expense of regular workers and small businesses.

It was reported that IRS officials were swooping down on one side of the political spectrum before, during, and after the election of 2010. Naturally, the Pirates in the White House didn't know anything about this corruption. Tea Party members were the target of political mischief authorized by IRS staff. Justice wasn't being spread evenly.

Lindsay left with his camera and missed the TV interview. It was the point he was trying to explain.

Richard says, "Lindsay, you left to soon. You missed the news. They're corrupt."

CHAPTER 1

PIRATES IN THE WHITE HOUSE

S LOWLY AMERICA WAS being whittled down by the people elected to govern her. The face of America was changing. Properly said, America was undergoing a slap down at the direction of White House executives.

The Democratic campaign strategy was a masterful plan that kept the president in office for a second term. They knew he was guaranteed the black vote. The big concern was getting his supporters to cast their vote(s) in some cases, especially from low rent voters. In the end both Blacks and Hispanics did vote in mass. There was a simple reason for this turn out, goodies for everyone. Democrats enticed the lower middle class, non-workers, and the poor with free stuff.

Campaign organizers recruited voters by offering government subsidized goodies. People receiving so much free stuff they couldn't resist the temptation, (cell phones and government handouts) to vote for the Democrats. It was like cheese to a mouse. The 'D' ranks swelled and the fix was all but certain. Of course, mission accomplished, the president was reelected.

Republicans on the other hand didn't fare as well. Their fickle message of 'hard work will bring America back' and 'you'll succeed' didn't work.

People receiving easy money (unemployment and welfare checks) from the government had little incentive to find a job in a soft economy. Why work when the government was handing out free money? All the noise about education and hard work fell on deaf ears.

Mr. Richard Stern turned to his new girlfriend, Lindsay Wagner. He was in a state of shock after the evening election results were tabulated. The president beat the Republican challenger.

The Tea Party conservative lamented, "Lindsay, the citizens have spoken. They want free stuff and unemployment checks as far as the eye can see."

"Hey, Richard, I voted for Democrats and President Obama. I don't have a full time job. I'm one of the poor persons. You know; we have to survive."

Richard says, "There are pirates in the White House, Lindsay. They're robbing the country blind and the working people can't do anything about it. The working class is getting stiffed. The president doesn't care about the military, small business, or big oil."

She bristled at his statement, "You don't get it. People want programs for protection. Some people aren't as lucky as you."

The discussion was taking a turn. Richard knew about arguments with women. The outcome wouldn't be good for him, but he persisted.

Richard replies, "Lucky, can't you see what's happening. The politicians, and I mean the pirates in Washington DC, are stealing our freedom. Big government is ruining this country. I mean the EPA, Internal Revenue Service, Department of Education, I could go on. They're methodically taking control of your life and mine. Wake up, Lindsay."

He tried to make a point. As he watched her reaction, the outcome was clear.

Lindsay shook her head. She couldn't get past his stubbornness. He was too wrapped up in the Republican Party and the Tea Party. He was just too proud or lucky to see the other side's point of view. She had to have the final word.

She says, "I need an unemployment check for now. I'm a Democrat. They're for the underdog. You can't see that."

Richard had a comeback answer for that, but he zipped it. This time he knew better. He was coming around to a point of view about Lindsay and women. She's usually right on heart felt issues as were women in Stern's past.

Lindsay and Richard found each other by chance. Stern had just broken up with Sharon Marchuk. At first he was deeply in love with Miss Marchuk, but that feeling fizzled out over time. Family, money, and most of all one bad habit killed the romance. Sharon had enough and they parted.

Richard's old flame, Brenda Clark, was still calling from time to time. She too dumped him for similar reasons, only Brenda still had the hots for Mr. Stern. She was a cougar and found young bedfellows more exciting. Stern couldn't figure her out. She was a successful woman. At times they worked together and shared the same bed.

It was always the booze; he couldn't or wouldn't stop the habit. Every relationship was ruined by booze. Maybe Richard planned it that way. Halfheartedly, he would admit his track record with women was a bit dicey. Love and lost lovers was a social albatross for him. He was a likeable guy when off the sauce.

He dated wonderful women. The stream of ladies was as long as the Columbia River. They were all Christian ladies. He met gorgeous girls and married a couple, Carla, Diane, Rita, Jamie, Bonnie Clark, her older sister, Brenda, Karen, Sharon, and there were others. When would he settle down?

He always thought Princess Sharon would help him stay sober and she tried over and over. They came close to tying the knot. She was virtuous. She boosted his life as a Christian. She gave him a King's Bible as a means of teaching him to turn to God when temptation struck. That was a big help.

Sharon mostly saw the good in people. She also saw incredible things happen during their courtship. Supernatural things happened around her man. They witnessed flying objects and white dots floating in the air. She thought it was Nana, her mother or angels. It was mystic. Were they spirits? The floating objects were spooky. He would say she was dreaming of those things, although he also saw them.

Richard could quote her. 'You have some things flying around you.' He wasn't surprised. Paranormal activity was the best way to explain it. Sharon's quote was, 'the devil is at work.' They were around when he blacked out or passed out.

She urged him to attend AA meetings and tried being a wife, all unsuccessfully. She knew he had to do it on his own, if he really wanted her. She told him to go see a doctor, a mental health specialist or enter a rehabilitation center. Stern saw many doctors. Even the FBI came into the picture.

Doctors thought a serious auto accident had loosened some deep childhood memories of conditions at home or places he had visited. Stern enjoyed one simple explanation from a doctor. It was as good as any. The simple explanation was a bit off course.

The medical doctor said, 'Your paranormal manifestations are unseated in the prefrontal cortex of the brain after binge drinking.'

That wasn't exactly a simple answer. Stern could only nod his head and agree. Mystical anomalies came calling when he was drinking.

Stern amazed an FBI Agent. Agent Ron Roman got an ear full when Stern supplied information to him during a visit to the Cleveland FBI office. What seemed like a concocted story from a half intoxicated man was quite revealing. Stern told the agent that the Perry Nuclear Power Plant was a front-burner terrorist target. Roman didn't buy into a man's half boozed up idea, but kept the accusation in the back of his mind. He took notes and didn't forget the interview nor did Mr. Stern. He thought he was a bit bold to converse with an FBI agent, but chalked it up to being half drunk and psychic.

Agent Roman realized Stern's prediction did indeed materialize when he and his partner went to the scene of a crime in Lake County. The drama really unfolded when the FBI agents discovered a plot in Perry, Ohio. Several women were killed in an explosion close to the nuclear power plant. The clairvoyant man called Richard Stern had to be shadowed by the FBI. Agent Monica Micovich was called upon to study the informer. She took on the identity of a librarian to obverse his actions in Blasdell, New York. Then all hell broke out near Syracuse at a truck stop when she had to save his life.

FBI Agents Ron Roman and Bill Wright tapped into his visions a number of times. When Stern started feeding information about terrorist plans, Roman and Wright started following his leads. His dreaming experiences contained vivid revelations of America's enemies. They used his tip to confront terrorist in Parkersburg, West Virginia. He became a paid FBI informer and was told to forget about being a bounty hunter, but he didn't take advice very well. His contact with the FBI became a lightning rod. Agent Micovich found that out in a number of ways. She ended up carrying his child.

Another Stern fault with women was the fact that he didn't stop 'to smell the coffee' as Sharon would say. He couldn't settle down. He'd launch his own investigation at the drop of a hat. He was always traveling, chasing a dream. Tracking down the bad guys was a passion. On occasions she went with him. They traveled to Dayton, Gettysburg, Columbia, SC, and Washington DC for a Tea Party Rally.

All this craziness dawned on him to start writing chapters of his adventures. The moving around, drinking and doing foolish things was the last draw for Sharon. The crash and burn romance caused him to write abundantly about his ghostly tales.

When Lindsay arrived on the scene, he had amassed quite a bundle of chapters.

"Lindsay, I've been writing about some unusual event in my life. I'll let you see some interesting chapters one of these days. Right now I'm writing down the president's pitfalls."

"Oh," said Lindsay, as she knew what was coming. "I know the Republican Tea Party guy is going to trash the president."

"No, I'll say this. The pirates around him are pulling his strings. The people he puts around him are feeding him lies. It's happened to many presidents I'm writing about this. I'm going to put it together and sell it."

Lindsay says, "That's good. Then you can pay me a normal wage."

Richard stuttered, as if holding in a thought, "Ah, Hollywood is going to call. You'll see. One of these days we might have to move the operation to LA. You stick with me, princess."

Lindsay says, "Honey, you're a real dreamer."

Richard replies, "You don't know how prophetic you can be. You'll see; my dreams can draw a picture of the enemy. We'll find them and the action that follows, well that might be nerve wracking. Do you think you can handle it?"

She says, "Time will tell."

CHAPTER 2

TRACKING A TERRORIST

THE RELATIONSHIP WITH Lindsay would be different than his previous ones. At least Mr. Stern thought so. He met Lindsay in Santee, California when the friction of his drinking was putting a cold chill between Sharon and him. He'd stop drinking for months and resume. She was deciding to end their relationship and Stern knew it. Then it happened, the proverbial shoe dropped. He told her he was drinking again. The final drink, the final phone conversation broke them apart.

Almost simultaneously, an email message came across the computer. A friend in San Diego tipped Stern about a person that seemed out of place. Border Patrol Agent Don Lopez gave a small hint in the description of a Middle Eastern man, while on a security check. The email was meant to entice Mr. Stern to return to California. Agent Lopez became suspicious of a man. In a message he pointed out a man's nervousness.

Email from Lopez: <u>Richard, Lopez news, Middle Eastern man, nervous, call me.</u>

Stern called his friend. The conversation was intriguing enough. Agent Don Lopez says, "Does the name Abdul Madhi ring a bell?"

Stern had a terrorist file with plenty of information on the Madhi clan. Lopez couldn't supply the amateur bounty hunter with much detail, only bits and pieces of his involvement with Abdul Madhi.

"Lopez, that's enough. After this conversation, I'm coming your way. I'm going to do some profiling when I arrive. I know right where to look. See you soon."

Stern was heading for San Diego. It was time to switch identities. From umpire to bounty hunter, he had a mission. Lopez supplied him with enough information about a so called nervous Middle East man, who claimed he worked in Santee.

Stern met Lopez for the very first time in San Diego at a shooting range. Lopez could see Stern was no marksman. Lopez offered a few handgun tips. They became good friends when he learned Stern had an avid interest in border protection around the Great Lakes and tracking terrorists. A good bond was made when Stern revealed his connection to the FBI.

In their second and third meetings Lopez took Stern into the high ranges south of San Diego and very close to the Mexican border. It was rugged terrain, four wheel drive country. On the trips Lopez carried his personal sidearm, a Glock 23 pistol and a field radio. All of this made Stern nervous. The radio cackled on and off with reports of illegal border activity.

Lopez pointed out the signs of illegal crossings. Toilet paper and clothes littered the manmade paths. Communications between border agents passed back and forth. Agent Bravo signaled Agent Echo from far away on mountain tops. Using Lopez's binoculars, Stern could see many border agents and their trucks. After sixty minutes a stand down signal, for 'all clear' was radioed.

Stern was out of his environment. He wanted no part of Lopez's job.

He taught Stern about disguises and the travel routes illegal aliens take to enter the United States. He pointed out a tunnel to a warehouse. It was built under the border fences. Homeland Security agents discovered the tunnel and ended that illegal entry.

Now it was time for a new adventure. Stern's Southwest airliner landed in San Diego and he rented a midsize auto. It was a thirty minute drive to Lopez's home. With greetings and handshakes exchanged the topic quickly switched to terrorists. Lopez explained a man named Abdul Madhi had crossed the Tijuana border legally, but was well off his destination. He was stopped for suspicion of trespassing. He had the proper papers to travel and work in Southern California, so the agent had no reason to hold him, but he did act nervous, like he had something to hide. Lopez did a thorough check of his backpack and ID. He wrote down the guy's name, underlining <u>Abdul Madhi. He works in Santee, as a restaurant operator.</u>

The agent knew Stern's reputation from listening to him describe his bounty hunting exploits. Agent Lopez often had to laugh at the number of times Stern bumbled his way to success. The one that really got to him was when Stern pissed his pants while confronting the enemy in Oregon. From what the agent could gather getting into trouble was Stern's primary achievement.

Lopez says, "Now you're profiling people. That'll get you into trouble."

Stern replies, "I'm doing the same as you."

"Richard, we train all the time. For example I know how to speak Spanish. I fit in with this territory. You are out of your zone."

He tried to warn Stern about dealing with hardcore criminals.

"Keep your distance my friend."

Lopez was having second thoughts about informing Mr. Stern as he tried to discourage the amateur bounty hunter.

"I think you're better at informing the FBI about troublemakers."

Richard says, "That's true, Lopez. I made some good money that way. You know I've got to gather the evidence first. I'm learning the process. Crime is being perpetrated all across the country. I try to pick up their trail just like you. The piece of the action I'm after is the FBI reward check. You know I'm on the right side of the law."

Lopez emphasizes his concern.

"Just be careful my friend!"

Stern was too proud. He had a winning streak and he had plenty of facts about terrorists worming their way into America's society. They would set up shop using fictitious businesses. Mosques were a favorite hideout. He had volumes of papers on the subject. He wanted to reassure his friend that he was up to the challenge.

With a degree of candor and confidence he addresses Lopez's concern.

He says, "Be careful, you're starting to talk like my FBI friends. I'm careful. If I'm going to make any big money, I have to take a chance once in a while. My ultimate goal is to land a big fish. I mean right now; I'm just nosing around. Only God knows if I'm doing right. You supplied me with a tip. Maybe it'll pay off."

The name 'Abdul Madhi' was enough for Mr. Stern. The Madhi clan was huge. He tangled with this group before. They were into many businesses from the Middle East to North America. When Stern looked up the full name in his notebook computer, there he was, picture and all. He was captured in Babil Province south of Bagdad during the George W. Bush era. He was released for lack of evidence linking him to Saddam Hussein's Revolutionary Guard. He traveled to Detroit in 2008 on an education visa and transferred to San Diego State. The typed notes ended, but below the type was an asterisk. It said, *was studying marine propulsion. Ties to relatives— Madhi Bank in Detroit.

Stern had garnered enough bounty hunter experience where he could do surveillance on his own without being detected. He had the camera equipment to shoot long range pictures.

Stern traveled down dead ends before. This suspect might not be the same Madhi, but he was a person of interest. Lopez wouldn't have called if he didn't have suspicion.

Richard says, "The Madhi Brotherhood is big, Lopez. It seems like every time I research one of these guys, well, something interesting happens."

Lopez says, "This guy told me he works in Santee City outside of San Diego. He said he's a restaurant operator. His hands, they were shaking. I think this guy was hiding something, but I couldn't detain him for clean hands."

Stern says, "If I find Mr. Madhi, I'll birddog him. He might lead me to bigger fish."

Stern knew where to start. He went to where the Muslims gather. As it always seemed to happen, Stern's hunch paid off. He picked up Abdul Badi Madhi's trail at an Islamic center in San Diego.

He found a location well away from the front of the center. The weather was unusual. It was overcast with a slight drizzle falling. Normally San Diego was balmy. The weather threw a curve in Stern's surveillance operation.

He had his camera ready to get a close-up picture of anyone fitting the profile of Madhi. After an hour a man appeared. He looked like the suspect, but Stern wasn't sure. With his camera at the ready, he failed to zoom in. He couldn't get a clear picture. The guy looked like Madhi, but he used an umbrella to shield his face. Stern was sure about his identity when he climbed into a late model black BMW parked near the mosque. The race was on.

Stern could hardly keep up with the suspect's car. Eventually, the man traveled to Santee City. He parked at the Oasis Club. It was here at the Oasis Club where Mr. Stern met Lindsay Wagner for the first time. Her brush with Mr. Stern would be a memorable one.

Lindsay Wagner's adventure was about to start. She never meant to have crazy things happen, but weird things happen when Richard Stern is around.

CHAPTER 3

OASIS CLUB

Lindsay Wagner's story was simple. After working at a factory and saving enough money for enrollment, she entered San Diego University where she met her husband. She didn't graduate, but moved to Santee, California with hubby and found work quickly. The job wasn't earth shattering. Waitressing was an entry level job, but she moved up fast to become the top hostess at the Oasis Club.

Hosting at the restaurant afforded her the chance to meet new people. This was something she wanted to do, because her husband was in trouble again. He failed at San Diego State and scored a second DUI. Their shaky marriage was tumbling. She wanted things to work out, but a woman usually knows the truth.

The Oasis Club was where Richard Stern stepped into her life, although only momentarily.

Stern followed Madhi into the restaurant and watched him bypass the hostess. He sat at a dining table well off to the rear of the club.

Lindsay greeted Mr. Stern as he walked up to her. Stern smiled and made a point to admire her professional look. Profiling was the first order of business for Mr. Stern. He made a quick assumption. She was unmarried, beautiful, late 20's or early 30's and he noticed a diamond ring was on her right hand along with a mark on her wedding ring finger.

He asked for a seat to view the dining area and see her at the same time. After a short while Stern scribbled a note for the hostess. She was very attractive. He tried to stay focused on Madhi. With note in hand he walked over to the hostess and offered it to her.

"Keep this."

Somewhat startled, she looked up without saying anything.

Peering at the note, it read: <u>Watch out for the man with the turban in the back of the dining area.</u> Stern winked and cocked his head in the direction of the suspect. So unusual, she thought. Lindsay found Mr. Stern to be a bit intriguing and funny at the same time. She didn't want to burst his bubble.

He returned to his seat without seeing the expression on her face. Lindsay smiled and thought this was some kind of a joke. Her impression of Stern was simple. She thought the middle aged guy was just trying to flirt.

Lindsay paid a little more attention to Stern. He had a couple scars on his face, like a mobster. Guys hit on her once in a while. She thought this guy was trying something new. Other patrons were coming in, so she folded the note and stuffed it in her pocket.

Abdul Madhi looked like he was ready to eat when another turban topped person joined him. Stern watched as the new person laid cash on the table in front of Madhi. This opened Stern's eyes. He wished he could hear the conversation.

Besides watching Madhi, Stern had his eyes on the hostess from the time he entered the restaurant. Being a man with a romance on the rocks, he wanted to meet new friends, but he had two things going at once. One, he had to tail the suspect and two, he wanted to meet her.

Madhi got up to leave after wadding up the cash and putting it in a chain linked wallet. He was heading out the side door.

Lindsay found out the jokester wasn't kidding. As Stern was leaving to follow the suspect, Lindsay and Richard exchanged some fast talk. He was in a hurry. The fact was he had to move fast. To Stern she seemed more exciting and attractive. This was probably a onetime opportunity. He'd have to pull out all the stops.

In a muffled voice he said, "I'm a bounty hunter."

"No, really? She asked."

"Yes, here's my card. I know it says I'm a photographer, but I also work undercover. Sorry, I have to go. I trust you. You don't know me, honey; keep this a secret. I really gotta go."

Lindsay was smiling. She was more intrigued and didn't know what to say or whether to believe him. Was he just a crackpot?

Lindsay was about to speak, but she didn't know what to say and Stern was on the move.

"See yah," said Stern.

Lindsay responds, "Au, au, good luck!"

Lindsay had enough problems with her alcoholic husband. She wasn't in the mood for meeting a new friend, although she thought Mr. Stern was certainly interesting and funny.

She wondered. Why is he following Abdul? Lindsay did think Abdul was a bit secretive. For one thing, he was driving a pretty nice car. A dishwasher or a cook's salary couldn't amount to much. She thought maybe Abdul Madhi was more than a dishwasher. Lindsay had a feeling that Abdul was into something illegal and now this bounty hunter shows up. She harbored that feeling for a time. Fate and the future would provide more clues.

The trail went cold for Stern as he tried to keep up with the BMW. The traffic in Santee was too much for the Ohioan. He fell behind. He banged on his steering wheel when a trolley car split the chase even more. He drove around for a short time until he found Mission Gorge Road. The Oasis Club was on the main avenue. He thought he may as well go back to the restaurant and check out the hostess.

As he entered the club he saw Abdul Madhi. He was back. This time he was wearing an apron that had the words 'Oasis Club' splashed across the front. Stern hung his head in dejection. Disappointment crossed his face like a curtain falling on a stage.

Stern whispered like he was talking to Lopez, "That's why his hands were clean, Lopez. He's a dishwasher."

Reality sunk in. The mission was turning out to be a failure. Maybe it had to be scrubbed. However, something didn't fit. Why is he living in Mexico? How could he afford a BMW?

Stern started putting two and two together. Agent Lopez was duped by Abdul Madhi. He was no mechanic. He made some mental notes. Madhi probably just said he was a mechanic to sidetrack the border agent. The question was, why? Did Lopez hold back something?

Thoughts ran through his mind. Why is he driving a forty thousand dollar BMW?

At the same time wanted to formally introduce his self to the hostess, but a new girl was in her place. Then Stern realized if the hostess returns, she'll think he was a fool for chasing a dishwasher. The hostess was likely laughing at him. Stern imagined her eyes watching him. Bounty hunter chases the dishwasher.

Stern had a bunch on his mind and was totally embarrassed. He left the Oasis Club in a hurry before Lindsay could see him. He jumped in his rental car and drove to the airport.

Stern told the car rental attendant a half truth.

"I've finished business here."

What Stern didn't realize was his bounty hunter business was just starting and Lindsay would add a new dimension to his case.

He sent a text message to Lopez. In a few words he noted <u>the Madhi case went cold. I'm leaving</u>. The plane ride back to Ohio was a bummer. He felt like an ass for wasting $800.00 bucks on a long shot.

Lindsay eventually became the business liaison for the restaurant's party center. After eight months in the restaurant business, the owner said the economy changed. He was closing the business. Lindsay Wagner was out of a job. A few weeks after leaving, she read on the internet that the old building and restaurant was sold.

She took a county job as food service assistant manager for the county jail. For a time life was good again. Her marriage ended with a divorce, but she was making a fair living. She rented a decent place. Although not making big money, getting back on her feet after the divorce was a big deal. Time flew by for Lindsay.

California's economy was hurting and Lindsay's job didn't last. Just as she was getting her act together, more bad news arrived. The tough times forced a belt tightening. It was a big blow when the news came. The county had to cut the staff. She lost her county job. Lindsay blamed Governor Arnold, the Republican. Dejected she was. After working six months for the county, she was unemployed again, however, good news was around the corner. She found relief quickly even though it was outside of California.

A job search turned up a food service opportunity in Northeast Ohio. She moved to Lake County, Ohio after applying for a Food Service job at the Lake County Jail. She had the experience and got the job. Although the work was only part time, she figured it would lead to better things. Unfortunately for Lindsay, bad luck was back. After seven months on the job she was let go. The Lake County Commissioners had to cut expenses.

She said farewell to Deputy Dallas Young and Detective Jack Donahue. Detective Donahue just happened to be interviewing a suspect and heard Miss Wagner was leaving.

"Sorry to hear the bad news, Miss Wagner," said Detective Donahue.

She gave a few hugs to new found friends and walked away with tears in her eyes. She couldn't catch a break. The bad news wasn't over. Once in the parking lot, her car, the Lindsay mobile, had a flat tire. Then everything hit her, she started to cry. All the bad news fell like a forest timber. She stood sobbing by her car.

At that moment Mr. Stern pulled into the parking lot to see a woman crying. He was going to buy a used firearm from a small gun shop, called Best Firearms. The gun shop sat next to the county jail. When he saw the woman and the flat tire, he pulled next to her and rolled down the passenger side window. He didn't recognize the hostess. As if he didn't know, he asked a stupid question.

"Miss, what's wrong? I mean can I help you?"

She looked up to see the face she had seen in the past. She wasn't entirely positive and held her tongue. Studying his face, she thought it's the funny guy. He was the bounty hunter.

"I was just let go from my job." She cried. "I'm always getting pink slips, now this."

"No big deal with the tire. I'll change it for you."

Taking charge Richard says, "The jack and spare are in the trunk."

Now she recognized the voice. She remembered the scars on his face. It all started coming together.

Lindsay says, "Thanks mister, I remember you. I met you. You're the bounty hunter."

Stern got a little paranoid. He was caught off guard by her statement.

"No Miss, I'm an umpire and a high school referee. Maybe you saw me when I was working a game, probably when your kid was playing."

"No, you were in Santee, California at the Oasis Club. That's where we met."

The statement was right on the money and Stern knew it. He was shrinking in embarrassment for chasing the cook. He asked another stupid question.

"How do you know I'm a bounty hunter?"

Lindsay says, "You are. You told me so."

He hedged. "Maybe," says Stern.

Lindsay says, "I was the hostess at the Oasis Club. You passed me a note that said you were watching a man wearing a turban. By the way he was our dishwasher and he cooked occasionally."

Stern had to fess up. She nailed him. Everything was in the open.

Richard says, "Yes, I know. I found out for myself. I actually came back to see you, but you were gone."

"You came back?" She asked.

"Yes! And I found out about the dishwasher. I mean—holy mackerel! I made a fool of myself. When I saw him with an apron on, I said, oh boy! She's going to think I'm stupid."

Lindsay says, Nah, that place attracted all kinds of people. Besides, guys do weird things, like follow dishwashers. I saw lots of stuff at that restaurant. Abdul worked there for as long as I. We were all let go. The place closed."

It really hit him. He remembered how beautiful she was. How she was dressed. It was a great vision In a French trance he thought se rappele, Oh, how wonderful to remember the hostess. Now, here she is. He was captivated and forgot about buying a pistol. That was the original purpose of his trip to Painesville.

"Well, you were funny," said Lindsay.

Richard snapped out of it. He wanted to be Sir Lancelot.

"Let me help you. I'll change the tire. This is no big deal. You put the tears away."

"Thank you, sir."

Richard says, "You know I wanted to stay at the restaurant and talk with you."

Her spirits picked up a little. How fortunate she was to meet this man again. It was quite timely. Stern was equally happy to see her again and confess his foolish chase.

"I'm Lindsay Wagner," she said with a smile.

"I'm Richard Stern. Lindsay, that's a nice name."

She says, "That was my grandma's name.

They chatted for a while as he changed her tire.

Lindsay says, "I worked at the jail part time in food service. Now I'm out of a job again. I don't usually cry, but I'm so dejected. You understand don't you?"

"Absolutely, I've been there."

Lindsay was a bit long winded and talked about California and her divorce. Richard told her a couple of stories about Lake County and said he was divorced a couple times.

Lindsay asks, "Why were you following Abdul?"

Richard didn't want to answer the question. If he answered directly, it might hinder his chance at getting to know her. His ambitious mind was churning. He had an idea.

"Tell you what. I can answer that question, but . . ." said Richard.

He didn't finish. The pause was a giveaway. She could see he was thinking.

Richard says, "But, geez, it's sort of a secret. I mean I can tell you. After I get this tire changed, please join me for coffee and maybe have something to eat at the Pizza Parlor across the street. I'll tell you more about Abdul Madhi, if that's his real name. There's something strange going on. I feel it. He might not be just a dishwasher."

Lindsay sparks Richard's interest with a comeback statement.

"It's kind of weird you were following him, but I'm not surprised."

"Why's that?"

"His weird friends would stop once in a while. They were Middle Eastern guys with beards, talking in Arabic. Not that I think they're ah, weird. But you know, I can sense, something. You know, like danger!"

"This is cool, Lindsay. I want to hear what you've got to say."

Lindsay says, "They always asked to see Abdul, kind of like, right now. I mean they never caused trouble. One of them was always watching me. I just felt nervous when they came around. I'd tell Farouk, the owner; 'Abdul's friends are here.'"

Lindsay had a concerned look on her face. She went on to explain some detail.

"It was like Farouk had orders to get Abdul when his friends showed up. He'd get Abdul and never interfere with their business.

This is what I mean. It was like the owner was taking orders. It was strange for that reason."

"Maybe, they all think alike, you know. I guess I shouldn't stereotype."

Richard says, "Wow, you're doing it, Lindsay. You may not realize you have a talent for sizing up people. You're profiling them. This is interesting. I'd like to hear more."

He pointed to the restaurant across the street. His suggestion was to have lunch there.

"It's open; the tire is changed, it's coffee time, please at least have a coffee with me."

She hesitated for a moment and then felt relieved about meeting someone nice enough to help and she kind of knew him. They sort of had something in common.

"OK, I'll buy. You helped me. I know the owners. They'll want to hear my sob story." "Good deal," says Richard.

Lindsay says, "That's the least I can do."

Stern put the jack in the car and brushed his hands together. As they walked across the street Lindsay vented her frustration. She hammered the Ohio governor as being the same type of person as the movie star governor in California.

"Governor Arnold."

She put her two thumbs down in a disapproving gesture.

She says, "He's a terminator alright. They can kiss my you know what. They're both bad acts and they're for the rich guys. I mean Republicans."

Richard cringed a bit when he heard that.

"Geez, Lindsay, now tell me. How do you really feel about them?"

Richard could honestly say one thing about Lindsay. She wasn't a Republican. The time was definitely not right to tell her he was a conservative Republican and a Tea Party member.

"Lindsay, I know one thing about you so far."

"What's that?"

"You're a Democrat and you speak your mind."

Lindsay says, "That's two things."

"Right, but I really want to hear more about Abdul Madhi. That name has come up before, with one exception. The letters in his name are reversed. Madhi can be spelled Mahdi."

Richard was all ears as Lindsay spoke. She had some important information for the bounty hunter that seemed to match the notes he already had.

Lindsay says, "OK, I know he left for Michigan after the Oasis Club closed. He has relatives in Detroit. I think he said they own a bank and a marina."

This was too coincidental. Stern's mind was churning. The thought about the lucky chance of meeting Lindsay in Northeast Ohio, this was God's plan. It had to be part of God's plan. It was time for Richard Stern to gather more facts about Abdul Madhi and Lindsay.

So much was on his mind. This was a golden opportunity. How would Lindsay react if he told her all the details of his past? He had an idea which could include Lindsay Wagner.

CHAPTER 4

LUNCH TIME AT THE PIZZA PARLOR

L UNCH AT THE Pizza Parlor would be a perfect place to bring up the past. The Pizza Parlor started out as a Charley's hamburger joint in Painesville, Ohio. For Stern, if memory served him right, it was a high school gathering point. He told Lindsay he used to stop at the place when he was a teenager.

He says, "My friends, Fox, Nutty, and Blade, they worked at the restaurant, but he couldn't recall when it turned into a quaint Italian restaurant.

Lindsay says, "I can tell by the names; they must have been top food servers."

"Yes, they were cool guys. You could get an extra burger in the bag once in a while. It was probably just a mistake."

Lindsay says, "Oh, I'm sure of that."

The flashbacks of high school and navy life stopped and started. He didn't want to become absorbed in his life. The main topic had to be Lindsay.

In front of him was a Princess. So suddenly, flashbacks filled his mind. The thoughts of high school majorettes, Ohio State cheerleaders, and other princesses, they were coming to him in waves. She was unknowingly doing this to him. Certainly, it wasn't intentional. Too many fond memories, he had to shake it off.

Some kind of magic was in the air.

Richard knew one thing. He really took a shine to Lindsay. As they entered the Pizza Parlor's side door, he noticed a table at the end of the dining area. It was a pretty good spot for an ice breaker meeting. The timing was late enough to avoid the lunch crowd. He pointed to the open table.

"Let's grab that spot."

Lindsay said she had become good friends with the owners, Dave and Beverly. She wanted to share the unlucky news of her layoff with them.

"Maybe they'll hire me."

Richard says, "You'll find a job in no time. In fact I'm considering."

Lindsay says, "Oh, there's Dawn."

Dawn waved as she waited on another table.

She says, "I'll be right there."

Richard missed the chance of asking Lindsay the big question. Would she consider a secretary job? That was on Richard's mind. He'd like to have Lindsay join his one-man operation. She had the qualities of other female girlfriends—beautiful, educated, and maybe a good cook. On top of all that was the fact that she may have worked side by side with a real terrorist. That fact could end up being a big payday.

Stern had a long list of former girlfriends. None of them were ever employees. Every woman found something special inside Richard's heart. If only he had resolved his idiosyncrasies, most likely one of them would still be at his side.

Lindsay took over the conversation as Richard daydreamed about a way of asking her to work for him. How could he sound authentic? He could hear her talking about food and tried to listen to her. He knew the Pizza Parlor had great food. That was only secondary to his concentration.

Excitedly, Lindsay says, "Dawn will be right over."

She continues, "They serve real Italian food, not just pizza. It's the best. You'll like it, everybody does. You're probably a pizza guy."

Richard confesses, "Actually, I've only had pizza here. Well, maybe I had an Italian sub a long time ago. They won't know me."

"Well, they'll know me. I'll introduce you to the owners."

Richard figured he better stick with small talk for now. He was making up his mind on what to do. The more he thought about it, the better it was. Getting Lindsay to work for him would really be a good fit. His approach had to be right. He never had an employee and maybe a new girlfriend at the same time.

Richard says, "I've never been in a county jail. How's the food?"

"It's not nearly as good as the Pizza Parlor's food."

Dawn Brown, the manager and Joy Maready, the cook, were on duty while the restaurant owners, Dave Loparo and his wife were attending an afternoon Chamber of Commerce meeting.

Dawn says, "Hi, Lindsay."

"Dawn, I hate to start out this way. I've got some bad news. I'm fired. No, not really fired, but they laid me off on a count of cut backs. Downsizing, rightsizing, they all say that, when their letting you go. It was the same way in California."

Dawn says, "It's a bad economy, Lindsay."

"Yeah, right, it's bad news for Lindsay. It's bad all over. I have no luck," says Lindsay.

Richard says, "You've got luck, bad luck. Oh, Lindsay, I'm sorry, that was bad timing,."

Lindsay says, "Save the sorry, Richard."

Dawn saw the new guy with her which sparked some interest.

Dawn asks, "Who's your friend?"

"Dawn, I met my new friend and he's not exactly new. I want you to meet Richard Stern. I met him awhile back in California. Isn't that weird?"

Joy came from the cooking area when she heard Lindsay's voice.

"Joy, this is Richard Stern, he's a bounty hunter."

Richard says, "Ah, no, that's not quite right. She means, ah."

Richard stopped Lindsay at that point by signaling 'no' with a wave and a finger to his lips. He put out his other hand to offer a handshake.

He interjects, "Bouncer, no, not really, I'm a photographer and sports official from Fairport Harbor. Bounty hunter is like a nickname. I work for high schools, well, mostly middle schools. I work games in Painesville, Mentor, Perry and Madison. Really, I'm all over the three surrounding counties. I'm dumped like goose poop, you know what I mean. Today, I'm a tire changer."

Lindsay says, "Richard came to my rescue. I had a flat tire and he offered to change it for me. He's a good Samaritan."

"Awww, that was nice of you," said Joy.

Joy noticed Beverly.

"You're back," says Joy.

"Lindsay says, "Richard, I wanted you to meet the owner. This is Beverly Loparo. They've been here for twenty-something years."

"Twenty-eight, we're going to retire one of these days. Dave's just parking the car. He'll be in shortly." says Mrs. Loparo.

Dawn asks Richard, "Are you two having something to eat?"

"Sure," says Richard. "Good food always helps to cure the bad news."

Joy says, "Look Mr. Loparo is back."

Dawn introduced Dave to Richard and clued him in on Lindsay's' plight.

Dave says, "Sorry to hear the bad news, Lindsay."

Beverly says, "She's going to get over it, Dave. We'll serve them up some real Italian food and she'll start feeling better."

Dave says, "Darn, Lindsay. We don't need any help right now. Wish we could help. Right now the economy is bad. Dawn will take your order."

Dawn handed out two menus and left. The subject was already served up by Mr. Loparo. A job for Lindsay was on Stern's mind. This was perfect timing.

"I'm really amazed that I'm sitting across from you, Lindsay. I can't believe this incredible coincidence."

She replies, "Well, I recognized you before you realized who I was."

"You know, Lindsay that is a special quality in a person. Profiling is something a bounty hunter has to do in order to track the right people. There must be a thousand things you encountered while working at the Oasis Club. Focus on Abdul Madhi, do you remember anything he may have done that was strange."

Lindsay described some of the things that Richard pointed out. The car he was driving was way beyond his means. At times cash was openly divided. He'd leave and come back at odd times. She thought he had more freedom than other employees.

"Farouk Aziz let him leave the restaurant almost all the time."

It was apparent to Richard that Lindsay had a great memory. She told of other incidents.

For a bounty hunter, this was a great quality in a person.

"One time his friends came and huddled outside. The parking lot was empty. I watched them from a tinted window. One of them had an olive colored wetsuit draped over his shoulder. By their expressions I could almost hear them say something about buying more of them. They saw me watching. It was like I shocked them. I interrupted something."

Richard was watching her intently. She had eyes and ears for detail. However, he didn't want to just buy into her story.

Richard says, "Olive color, I mean like a sand colored wet suit. That sounds like military equipment, not something a young diver would buy."

Lindsay continues, "They immediately moved away when they saw me. That's what I mean. Something was going on with that bunch. I mean we're almost in the desert. Cowles Mountain separates us from San Diego and the Pacific Ocean. I guess you could say that was strange. I mean wet suits in the desert."

"Well, maybe not," said Richard. "He may have just bought it from an army surplus store. It is fascinating that you witnessed all this and put it in your memory bank. Plus you think he was showing it off and maybe wanting to buy more."

Lindsay wanted to make a point and she didn't hold back.

"Hey, I know when people are hiding something. He held up four fingers, like signaling. I'm telling you; they were acting funny."

This was the woman for Richard. He liked her style. Something he needed in a secretary. She would bring the profiling element to his team. It was time to ask her; he needed this woman. By all measures, she had the right instincts, a personality, inquisitive, and the heavenly looks.

They ordered and ate lunch. Chatting along the way, time was flying by. Richard tried to seize the moment. Since they were getting to know each other Richard felt it was time to ask.

"I'm still interested in Abdul Madhi. You said he was going to Michigan, but before I continue, let me say this. You have so much talent. I have to ask you. I could use some help. Would you be willing to work as a secretary? Part time, I mean; I'd like you to handle some of my clerical work, like bookkeeping, filing papers and do some research. Research, I mean go to libraries. That's where I find a bunch of interesting facts."

She asked, "You're offering me a job?

One hour ago she was out of a job and now she's about to be hired by a bounty hunter. This was crazy. Was he serious? Lindsay pondered a moment.

He says, "Let's have one more coffee and I'll tell you more about me. There are some things you need to know. My gray area is the life of an informer for the FBI, but I want to hear about you."

Lindsay was pretty happy about her turn of events. By her very nature she liked to meet new and interesting people and this guy was an unusual character.

Chapter 5

Lindsay's New Career

A DISCUSSION ABOUT LINDSAY'S future took center stage. Maybe she was just a victim of circumstances. It was a sign of the times. Losing jobs by way of hard times seemed to fit the portfolio of many well healed Americans. Her education was pretty good, even though she didn't finish college. If Stern was looking for credentials, he could say this. 'At least she had a good work ethic.'

Everything she told Richard about her marriage was an opposite image of him. She was well liked, a hard worker, but didn't find success for one reason or another. On the other hand Stern could step in a pile of dog poop and come out smelling like a rose.

She was always employed and this opportunity was something of a God send. The exception was pretty straight forward. This time she wanted to collect some green from Uncle Sam and work under the table.

The conversation between the two was an oxymoron.

Richard says, "I've made some of the best mistakes in my life. I'd blunder chasing the enemy and then walk away with cash."

Lindsay says, "I'm thinking along the same lines. The government has screwed up my life time after time. They're always talking about green this and green that. Well, I'm going to take some of their green."

Politically, Lindsay and Stern were opposites, but their differences of opinion could complement each other in their work. She voted for the president and he voted for Mitt. Looking at her he could say, she did things right and didn't win. He did things wrong and it turned out right.

During the candid conversation, Richard had already mentioned a few reasons for adding a secretary. If only to work a few days a week, it would help him keep track of the businesses.

Lindsay was starting to realize a temporary opportunity was staring at her, but it could turn out to be a golden goose. He seemed like he needed someone to run his day to day affairs.

She asked, "Part time, now that does mean a cash job, right? Remember, I mean I'd like to collect; unemployment. Well, you know how things are. If I can collect unemployment for a while, that would make a difference. I have rent to pay and I might have to move."

Nearly everyone knew the economy was in the tank. The president and his side show of pirates were doing all they could to steal the wealth of unborn Americans. Paychecks were shrinking. The pirates in the White House had run up the national debt farther than any administration.

Presented with this question, Stern felt comfortable paying her with cash. It could work for him. If she wasn't working out he could terminate the agreement. In reality he wanted her. He thought his woman was not only perfect; she probably would cook and clean the house.

He never had a female employee. In his mind a simple white lie never hurt, so Stern said a Pinocchio.

"Cash, that's no problem. Of course, I'll have to figure out the details, like hours and days. I'm not a rich guy. This is only a minimum wage job. Drop by my studio, well, it's actually my home. Is tomorrow OK?"

"Well, yeah, since I don't have a job now, but I should think about this."

Richard added, 'It's tax time, I'll be doing bookkeeping and secretary work that you could be doing. Well, you think about it tonight. Let me know in the morning."

Stern was confronted with an over-promising situation. Questions were rumbling through his head. Did he offer her a job because he felt sorry for her? Was the real reason that he was attracted to her? Does he really need a secretary?

After drinking two more cups of coffee and chatting about school, jobs, and travel, Stern offered an apology. He wanted to come clean about his life. Certainly, there was an element of danger with the job.

"Lindsay, I want to let you know. I've been in some tough situations and people were after me. Realize this, I'm an amateur bounty hunter and travel often. I've run into some shady characters. Plus, I'm not sure I can pay you on a regular basis. My big income rests with catching or reporting on terrorists. The FBI pays me through a crime stopper fund. I've been lucky in the past. They pay big money if the results are good."

Lindsay says, "My dad worked with me to learn street life. He wanted me to be safe when he wasn't around. That's why he would coach me. I can shoot a gun. Wow, you catch terrorists. That is really wild."

Richard says, "I'm more of an informer. I supply the FBI with tips."

She asks, "Why would I be in danger?"

Stern had to answer without lying. He wanted to be truthful. At this point he came to admit more of his history. He didn't want to hold back.

"I've been in some hairy situations. I'm no hero. I drink too much and that has been a problem for me. The FBI saved my ass a few times. There is so much to tell."

Lindsay could see the strain of the past. She understood much of what he was saying.

She says, "Go on, you can say it."

"Well, for many reasons, I'm an alcoholic or recovering from alcoholism. Sometimes I drink to see the light. That might be a cop out. A priest, Father Pete, he's the pastor of St. Anthony's Church in Fairport. He has given me encouragement to quit drinking. For one reason or another I mess up. Darn if I don't have piles of reasons. I haven't figured it out yet."

She understood the words he used to explain his helplessness. It's a disease. She had plenty of experience on the subject and could probably help him.

Richard said more of the bad. He had wives and girlfriends that dumped him. He was gushing some of his mischievous ways. The conversation was turning into a confession.

He continued, "I have a son, Michael. I had a drunken affair. FBI Agent Monica Micovich is his mother. That's whole other story and I don't want to go there. Oh, I could tell you so much, but I've blabbed enough. I want, well let's drop it here."

Lindsay says, "You've been pretty honest so far. That's a good sign."

Lindsay could see the strain or worry in Richard's face. After listening to his adventures, she didn't hesitate about taking the job, whatever it paid.

Lindsay says, "I can help you. I know Father Pete. Since you're a Christian, you have the basics of being a good person. Try to act that way and all will work out the way God intended."

Richard says, "Yes, I've always believed that. Let's put that aside for now. We need to concentrate on the job. The work is really semi part time. I have to stress that, because it's in the first phase. I'm working on a new case. It has something to do with a cruise ship, but at this time, I can't tell you much. I mean. Are you interested?"

Lindsay expediently replies, "Yes, I am, I'm interested. I mean this is like detective work."

Richard says, "That's right. If I'm gone for say, two weeks, then you won't have much to do and you won't be making much money. Maybe I built this job up because of you. I'm sorry if I over spoke."

Lindsay says, "No, no you didn't, I've got the time now. Don't worry. The money isn't that big a deal if I'm collecting unemployment. I mean I still have rent to pay. That's going to be my big problem."

Richard admits, "I've never had a female employee. I'd have to adjust to you. Now this is only part time. I don't think I could afford a full time person unless we find a person of interest.

Lindsay isn't completely sold on the job. She's a little hesitant.

She says, "I don't know, but I want to say yes. I just got laid off. I might collect unemployment for a year maybe two years. Only God knows the future. If things don't pick up, this country is going to be for sale. I worry about moving. I can't afford to stay where I'm at."

With that being said, Richard had a brainstorm.

"You can rent from me. I have a big house. Some rooms upstairs could be converted into an apartment. You can have the whole upstairs. I can consider that as a way of paying you."

Lindsay says, "Well, my lease is up next month. Let's see about tomorrow, maybe everything will work out. I need to think about this."

Richard says, "Good, think about it, you'll be like a crime fighter."

She goes on, "My dad, rest his soul, was a police officer. He was gunned down by drug smugglers. It happened in a suburb of San Diego in Chula Vista.

Richard cuts in, "I'm sorry, Lindsay. That's so sad. I don't know what to say."

"I'm over the hurt. Dad and Mom were always fighting. In a way God settled their marriage problems. Dad was a drinker and that sometimes caused him to be rough with her."

Richard says, "I know all about those marriage problems."

Lindsay says, "I guess you can say I've got a police background. That's why this job would be so interesting. Dad taught me to be street smart. Of course, now look at me. I'm almost on the street."

Richard says, "No you're not."

She says, "I know it's not that bad. I mean I was working at a couple county jails, but I keep losing jobs. Even if they were only food service position, I did learn a lot about people. I know the difference between plain old goof balls and hard nose criminals. I've met some real weird O's."

Richard says, "OK, so now you know what you're up against. The job is about tracking people. One thing I have to bring up. There can be danger, but don't let that scare you off. Your job is pretty straight forward. You'll be doing some internet searching for me, usually hunting for leads about terrorists and smugglers. I'll teach you to find links. These people are all over the country. One thing they have in common. They all leave trails."

Lindsay asks as if she's still unsure, "I want to believe you. Do you really make good money as a bounty hunter?"

"Listen, I work many jobs. I'm an amateur bounty hunter and an informer. You have to have a sixth sense. That's how I got into this. The FBI hired me a few times and I've made some serious money following people. I don't know if they exactly hired me. That might be a stretch."

Lindsay asks, "Have you killed anyone?"

"No! It's nothing like that. I find out things and give the information to the FBI. I also write suspense stories for magazines. You probably saw short stories in the Reader's Digest. I like to do things like that. And, I'm a photographer, referee, and umpire. I've worked for many local schools. I keep the bounty hunter stuff a secret by doing other jobs. It's an identity cover. You'll see the whole operation tomorrow. That's if you come aboard."

Lindsay says, "Today started out to be really stressful. Now it feels better, but I'll have to sleep on this one. You really have me thinking; this job could be fascinating. I mean I kind of know already. Actually, I'm really excited."

She could feel the vibes. The job was a ground floor opportunity, detective work using the internet. Even if it was only a small time operation, it sounded cool. She found a job and she didn't have to go job hunting, which was something she dreaded. On top of that she didn't say yes, so she could always back out.

They exchange phone numbers and finished their meeting.

Richard said he was doing his best to recruit her. He'd pick up the tab.

As Lindsay and Richard walked from the Pizza Parlor, Richard asks if she'd want him to get the flat tire repaired.

He says, "There's a gas station one block down the street. Bartone's Service Station, I can take the tire there. I know Mike, the owner. He's into Little League Baseball, a nice guy. He sponsors teams all the time. I've probably umpired a game or two when his teams were playing. He'll have the tire ready in no time. Plus, I can still go to the gun shop.

Richard was doing everything he could to convince her. He could sense her desire and reluctance, so he tried to add a little extra incentive to sway her.

Lindsay asks, "Are you sure? I don't want to hold you up."

Richard replies, "Everything's right here. Nothing has changed for me except I might have found the right person for a job."

As they walked across Erie Street she asks, "Do you like guns?"

Richard pointed to the small firearms store. "I'm going to check out some handguns at Best Firearms. My older brother, Jerry, started taking me hunting when I was ten years old. I got out of hunting and gun, but I'm starting to like handguns more and more. I still have time to buy a pistol. I want to get another handgun or two before the politicians ban them."

Lindsay remembered seeing the owner of the little firearms store a few times. He was about thirty-five, around her age. The subject of firearms made her all the more interested in the job and Richard Stern. Her father used to take her to the pistol range and let her take some target practice.

Lindsay says, "Thanks for everything, Richard. I'll call you tomorrow. I'm leaning your way. This might be the best job for me right now. Oh, ah, one more thing. You may as well know. I carry a pistol."

Surprised, Richard utters in a high pitched voice, "You carry a concealed weapon!"

"Really, I do."

At that point she cupped her hands as if ready to fire a pistol.

Lindsay says, "Yep, I have a permit to carry. I can't bring it to the jail, but I don't work there anymore. You won't mind if I carry a gun will you?"

"Lindsay, you're the right person for this job."

The last bit of information put the icing on the cake. Stern had to hire this girl.

He says, "I can put the tire back on tomorrow at my house. I think you'll see I need a person like you to smooth bumps in my operation. That's your job description. What I mean is, I think you'll be able to help me correct some faults in my operation. I'll teach you about undercover work and taking photographs."

Lindsay had to get back to the first problem. She was interested in getting her car back to normal.

"Do you want me to call the gas station about the tire?"

Richard says, "No, I'll pick it up. You'll want to see my operation. I can put the tire on your car tomorrow. It's no problem."

Lindsay shook his hand and thanked him for all the help. He got the flat tire from her car and waved as she drove away.

Richard had a very warm feeling in his heart. His day was packed with wonderful energy. He met someone that could help him. This was an ideal opportunity for him. He was convincing himself this was the perfect situation. He could hire a person to work part time. She had her own protection. She will have unemployment compensation to help her make ends meet. On top of all that the operation actually needed someone to answer the phone when he was gone and perhaps she would live and work in his home. She had a college education or some college training. It was something he lacked. His place was mostly setup for her. She could work from his home and the upstairs bedrooms could be converted into an apartment.

He could teach her some Al Qaeda codes he learned on the internet. Shortwave radio, Nordic running track and a HD TV was all ready for her.

For now he had to buy a handgun before the government ruined the firearm industry.

Driving down the road, Lindsay thought about the job. She wouldn't have to give up unemployment. She remembered him saying, 'You'll be working for cash, one or two days a week. You'll be doing like half of America, which is sitting at home or working for cash and living off a government check. It doesn't get any better than that. This is the new America.'

Lindsay's drive down Mentor Avenue was a good time to wonder about the future. She passed the Lake County Fair Grounds and was approaching her apartment in Cambridge's Court. Fairport Harbor wasn't far away. She could move with a little help. Her apartment lease was coming due. She couldn't afford to stay at a seven hundred and fifty dollar a month apartment.

She paused briefly to look in the rear view mirror and moved to the center lane. It was clear to her as she went over the facts.

Lindsay thought by whispering, "My rent and lease are coming due. I don't have a full time job. I'll be out on the street if I pass this up. This guy is setting me up with a cash job and a place to live. This is an easy decision."

She was burned by Uncle Sam. She wasn't trying to cheat the government. She just wanted to even the score.

She says, "I'm going to soak Uncle Sam for some unemployment checks and pick up some cash. My troubles are over."

CHAPTER 6

PERSONAL WEAPONS

F IRST ORDER OF business, Richard had to drop off the tire. Once at Bertone's gas station the attendant said he'd have the tire ready in an hour. This was good news. The next task was to double back to the gun store and buy a pistol or maybe a shotgun.

Richard's fixation on Lindsay and her future role in the organization was becoming the dominant theme. In just a few hours of being with her he was pretty sure she would take the job. Plus he felt they could work well together even if she was a Democrat. A main concern was for her safety. Based on his past performance he had a tendency to invite trouble. It wouldn't be a surprise for him if unfriendly visitors made an unannounced visit.

Luck was one of Stern's best lifesavers. Cub Scout and Boy Scout training taught him about preparation. Preparedness, that was his motto, although he didn't always live up to the term. Because the day might come when FBI Agent Monica Micovich might not be around in time to rescue him, he had other defenses installed so as to be prepared for any eventuality.

Experience told him to prepare for the enemy. The life of an informer and bounty hunter had created some enemies. Not all the bad guys were in jail, some vanished to parts unknown. Others did get locked up. If the jailbirds got out, they might want to stop over.

Stern's past encounters with mobsters were enough warning. He wanted a safe working environment for himself, so he installed some safety devices to warn and impede the progress of intruders. He didn't want to portray his house as a fortress; however, if Lindsay decided to take the job, he wanted her to know he had taken multiple steps to forewarn or stop a hostile person.

Multiple cameras were installed along with window and door alarms. Other measures in place were particularly unique. He devised multiple contraptions using his knowledge of electricity. House wiring was hooked up to an adjustable rheostat and connected to the fence surrounding the perimeter of the house. Once armed it could serve a number of circumstances. It could signal the presence of an intruder or with the flick of two switches provide an electrical shock that would subdue a foe. Another master switch would fully energize the fence with enough high voltage to make it a first class defense.

The warning system and hostile eliminator, as Stern would call it, was also hooked up to metallic welcome mats inside the house that could be energized by the flick of a switch. Outside door handles and entry doors were also armed to trigger cameras and record the presence of anyone. Opening the door or stepping on the mats would immediately take a snap shot of the person. Cameras were hooked up to a base computer and monitors. They were fashioned to observe 24 hours a day, both inside and outside the house.

Richard Stern had a string of potential enemies. Any one of them might show up one day to even the score. This he knew from experience. Terrorists don't give up easily. With all of this in mind and just in case the enemy did showed up, he wanted Lindsay to have necessary and last resort fire power not just her own personal protection.

With that thought in his mind he pulled his car into the parking lot near the county jail. He was in luck. Best Firearms was still open. When Richard opened the gun shop's door, he saw two men overseeing a beautiful selection of pistols and shotguns.

Clark, the gun store owner and his friend, Jonathan Cassidy, were in a conversation as Richard looked over the pistol showcase.

"Welcome," said Clark.

Without looking up Richard says, "Hello, you guys are probably pretty busy these days."

Clark was quick with a telling response that fit the times.

He said, "Better get your guns and ammo now. The political hacks in Washington are about to pull another knee jerk reaction just like the health care bill. They're going to pass a law without knowing what's in it."

Jonathan adds, "Time after time they make screwy laws to harass the legal gun owners and the laws do little to the criminals."

Richard says, "You guys got that right. Political hacks don't care a lick."

Richard could tell these guys were on his side.

"I'm here to buy a semi-automatic pistol. I want more fire power because I think the next civil war isn't far away."

Clark says, "As you can see I have a decent selection of firearms here, just let us know what you're looking for. Most likely it's here."

Richard says, "I'm a small business owner from Fairport Harbor and it's getting harder and harder to stay above water. What I mean is, we're in a depression, that's what I think."

Clark says, "Not as far as the gun buyers are concerned, they're buying everything."

Richard says, "I can understand that. What's even worse? I see the middle class worker as the big loser because of the economy. The president and his merry men are stealing from the working man and raising his taxes. They're the criminals. It's bad. They're taxing everything. Food, fuel, everything is going up."

Clark says, "Here's my opinion and it's simple. Buy your gun now. But I agree, anyone with a decent job is getting hit. It's bad on the street and it's going to get worse."

Richard says, "I'm not here to cry the blues. I'm definitely in the market to buy a pistol."

Clark says, "If you're looking for a semi-automatic we have some nice used guns. How about a WWII Luger? We got one. Do you want something a little newer, a Glock or a Beretta.

Richard says, "Yeah, I'm interested in the Beretta."

Stern had one more comment to make before getting serious.

Richard says, "I call the group running the country, pirates. The president is turning into Captain Hook and he's got the Republicans walking the plank.

Jonathan says, "Now he wants the gun owners to walk the plank"

Richard wanted to add a better pistol to what he already had, which wasn't much. He had a Magnum 22 and his .32 caliber magnum, a police undercover revolver, was basically lost because of his forgetfulness. He took it in to be repaired and forgot about it.

He was thinking ahead when he explained an issue confronting him.

"I'm in the process of hiring a new employee to watch over my store. I know she totes a handgun because she has a concealed weapon permit. But the more I think about gun, I'd like her to have a shotgun at her side. The way the country is heading every business and homeowner should own at least one shotgun. Congress can't ban hunting rifles."

Clark says, "We're NRA members. They're doing their part to keep America safe."

Richard says, "Yeah, I'm thinking about joining up again."

After looking over the display of handguns, he looks at the shotguns on the wall. He asks to see a single shot .12 gauge shotgun. The owner hands him the weapon.

Richard says, "If nothing else, the blast from this baby would scare the pants off an intruder. Hey, that double-barrel shotgun looks good. Let me see that."

"It's a Savage," said the owner.

Clark exchanges the guns with Stern.

Stern says, "Fox Model B, wow, she'll have twice the fire power with this baby."

"You got that right."

Stern says, "I don't need a street sweeper yet, but I probably should get one. I'm somewhat torn between the shotguns and a semi-automatic pistol."

"You better buy both," says Clark.

Stern shook his head up and down. He pulled out his wallet to see how many hundred dollar bills he had. The Fox double-barrel shotgun was a lot more money than the single shot.

"Buy both you say. Well, it looks like I'm going to blow nine hundred bucks, but do I really want to do that?"

Jonathan says, "You get the best of both worlds right here. You better buy both."

Stern thought for a moment.

"Well, with the way the economy is going, gun control issues, and my budget, I better get both. I'll buy the double-barrel shotgun and the Beretta M9 I see in your display. I mean I know hard times are coming. The nine millimeter pistol is for me and the shotgun is for my helper. I really hope she joins my team."

Clark says, "Let's see your driver's license and you'll need to fill out some paperwork. I've got to run a background check, so it's going to take a little while. We always check. You're not a felon are you?"

Stern says, "Me, oh no, I'm a straight shooter."

They all got a little chuckle out of the comment.

The report was clean. Stern handed the man hundred dollar bills. He picked up the shotgun and expressed his gratitude.

Richard says, "I really like this Beretta. Now this will work."

"You're doing the right thing, buddy. The Beretta M9 is a fine piece."

Stern said he had two small hand guns. His .22 magnum was always loaded, but he wasn't really a gun fanatic. He was only into self-protection.

"I've got a few old shotguns that are collector pieces. I don't hunt anymore. My .32 caliber pistol was being fixed, but I never picked it up."

Stern said he forgot about it and never checked back to see if it was repaired.

Stern says, "I probably lost the receipt and they moved somewhere or went out of business. That's why I didn't check back. I don't know where they went. The place was near the Great Lakes Mall. It's been years ago. I forgot about it.

Clark says, "Veith's Firearms. Yep, they moved. Veith, here's their phone number. Give them a call."

After a half hour discussion about guns, Stern thanked the owner for his help. Back to Bertone's he went. Stern had his guns and the tire. It was time to head home.

After putting things away, the next thing he did was call Veith's Gun Shop. He described the .32 caliber pistol.

Skip Veith asked, "When did you drop it off?"

"Oh, it's been a long time ago, maybe five, six, maybe seven years ago. I know it's a long shot. You guys moved and I forgot about it. I'm sure it's gone."

Mr. Veith said he needed a receipt to confirm the real owner.

Stern ended the conversation by saying the gun was going to be used to train dogs. He certainly couldn't ask a gun shop to hold something for years.

"Years ago I was into hunting. My original plan was to use this gun to train hunting dogs. Now, I'm a high school track and field referee. I have a plugged .32 caliber pistol for running races. This gun would be a backup if I ever had to use it. It's going to get abused. I'll be firing corrosive black powder blanks. I sure hope you have it."

Mr. Veith says, "I might still have the pistol. Look for your receipt."

After hanging up, the phone rang. It was Skip Veith.

"We might have your pistol. See if you can find the receipt."

Richard says, "OK, this will be a long shot."

Stern hung up the phone and searched his files. As a last resort, he looked in the gun cabinet. There it was. The receipt was taped on the cabinet wall.

"Wow, I have it."

Stern phoned Veith's Gun Shop. After reading the serial numbers off the receipt, he couldn't believe the owner still had his gun.

"God is on my side on this one. I found the receipt. I can't believe you still have my pistol. You guys are the best," said Stern.

He was amazed. They still had the gun. Richard was totally happy to talk with an honest dealer. He asks if he was going to be open for another hour. With the confirmation he took off to fetch his long lost pistol.

When he returned from the gun shop, he placed the pistol in the gun cabinet. As he looked at the pistol, a scary feeling inside of him erupted. It sort of hit him in the gut. He wondered if he'd ever have to use it to defend himself or Lindsay.

The day had turned out to be a winner. He got down on his knees to thank God.

"Dear God, please help me. You know, I could really use Lindsay. She'll help us. I know nothing gets done unless you're with me, so please allow this to happen."

CHAPTER 7

LINDSAY'S JOB

L INDSAY CALLED THE next morning. Richard looked at the phone. It was Lindsay. Nervously, but with much anxiousness, he picked up the phone. His heart rate was elevated. Women in general, always caused him to tense up. It was a great moment. He could almost feel the blood pumping through his body.

"Richard, this is Lindsay. Is it OK to come over?"

"Hi! Yes, and I have good news. Your tire, it's fixed. Do you remember how to get here? I'm on East Street. I've got a sign on my house. You can't miss it."

She was excited, but held her emotions in check. The directions to Richard's house were pretty simple, turn right off Richmond Street, go over the Grand River Bridge, right turn at the Y in the road, and head north. She remembered him saying the directions; 'You take East Street, cross the railroad tracks and go by the cemetery.'

The house was easy to find. She remembered the little cemetery and the funeral parlor that he described.

They met in Stern's driveway. They exchanged greetings with a handshake. The mood was warm and happy.

Richard wasted no time with idle chit chat. He wanted to assure her that her car was the first priority and the job would come next.

"Let's get the tire changed and that'll be out of the way."

"OK, but, how much do I owe you for the tire?"

"I took care of that. You don't owe me anything. Let's get the hard work out of the way. You watch me change the tire and then we'll go inside to scope out the job."

"Gee, thanks again."

As he changed the tire, Richard told her he had an alarm system and cameras hooked up to keep an eye on the outside and inside of the house.

Once the tire was changed, he invited Lindsay into the family room, where there were plenty of things to see. It was a combination photography studio, office, and study. A computer table and monitor were neatly tucked in one corner. The walls in the office had pictures on the walls of Lake Erie Lighthouses, Civil War maps, his high school class picture, and a picture of his old navy ship, the USS Enterprise.

Richard watched her scrutinize the photos.

"Lindsay, I was stationed on that ship for a couple Viet Nam tours. I sailed half way around the world and crossed the Equator on that ship. I still stay in touch with a couple buddies from Kansas and Arizona."

Lindsay says, "My high school class was huge. It looks like your class was pretty small."

Richard says, "Fairport Harbor will always be small unless they think big. I tried to lure a casino owner into Fairport, but we ran into some trouble. It's a long story."

Richard didn't want to start the conversation off with the casino disaster. That episode was put to rest. If he was going to make a good impression, he had to concentrate on the history of Fairport Harbor.

"We have a couple nice museums in town. The Finnish Museum and the Lighthouse Marine Museum If you go up in the lighthouse you'll understand why they call Fairport Harbor the Tree City. Actually, I think many towns say that."

Lindsay says, "Southern California is so different. I kind of miss San Diego. It's entirely different, but it's so expensive."

Richard says, "You mentioned my small high school class. We're the Skippers. There's one thing about Fairport Harbor that stands out; we have a close knit community. It's loaded with blabber mouths. That's good in a way. Everybody knows everybody. I can pretty much tell you this community is safe. When a stranger comes to town the police are pretty good about keeping tabs on newcomers."

Richard continued the small talk while observing her demeanor. He wanted her to feel safe and at home. The perfect condition he thought was for her to be in control. The talk about San Diego was a little perplexing to him. He'd be hard pressed to make a comparison between life in the big city where the weather is always nice and Fairport Harbor in the winter.

"I still joke with my old classmates. I mean friends and girlfriends. In fact I started dating. I fell in love with a high school majorette, but it didn't work out. She was a classy person. Anyway, I can't look back. Seems like I'm always finding decent women, but I screw up. I guess I need to try to be a better partner.

Lindsay found the office to be friendly. It had a different atmosphere, kind of inspiring, not scary like she had envisioned.

Lindsay says, "I brought my pistol with me. I wanted to show you this, because I told you I carry a concealed weapon."

"I'm glad you brought it. I hope you never have to use it, Lindsay. I mean at least not here. You're perfectly welcome to carry."

At this point in the conversation Richard grows a Pinocchio with his next statement. He didn't want to get into a discussion of his difficult times.

"I'm not a person that invites trouble."

He had to stay on point and gloss over the facts. He had been in plenty of trouble. Although his work turned out to be a money maker, the sheer danger of dealing with terrorists, mobsters, and hoodlums did invite trouble.

"You'll see how we can find troublemakers. I'll track them. In a few cases they sort of find me. I mean finding the enemy is part of this job. You'll be far from that aspect. If you want this job, we have to find these losers and let the authorities handle the rest. We are strictly informers. I'll show you what I mean."

Lindsay asks, "What about Abdul Madhi? How does he fit in this business?"

Richard says, "Let's take a look on the computer."

Two desktop computers were running. On the double screen was an FBI most wanted list.

"I have insider information that is supplied by various sources. They call and leave messages. Agent Lopez in San Diego told me to check on Abdul Madhi."

Lindsay could see the other computer as it jockeyed from one picture to another picture. It was a random scan of the perimeter of the house. It surveyed the inside entry doors and outside doors. The focus on the doors and outside along the fence line was sharp. The entry doors came into view most often.

"Take a seat at the computer, Lindsay. What you see on the screen is an FBI list. This list is a starting point. You'll do research into the where-a-bouts of certain people. Type Madhi and hit search, the computer will list all these guys. We'll refine the search engine. We're not really looking for each Madhi, so you can refine your search by typing Detroit, Michigan. You know things about Abdul that I don't know. This is how we find out who he knows. We want to know his relatives. Find out who has the money. That's all we need is one good lead."

Lindsay felt like she was in college again. The computer chair was large and comfortable. There were a couple empty water bottles by the keyboard.

"You'll use the computer to track the Madhi background. Using the computer data gets us off and running. I'll go on the hunt when we have a good lead."

Lindsay asks, "How do I know? What's a good lead?"

"You'll know, Lindsay. Trust me, you'll know. The road as the onsite inspector can be boring. You'll supply me with names and addresses of people connected to Abdul Madhi. I take off and visit the places. I'll go to local libraries and use their computers to find out local news on these people."

Lindsay asks, "When am I on the clock. How do you record my time?"

"You're always on the clock. This job is part time. Most of the work is done by Email or the answering service. Like I said, all we need is one good lead. You do research based on the Emails I receive or the phone calls. You're not tied down by the computer or the phone."

Richard could see Lindsay was excited about searching for leads. She was hitting the keys on the computer like a pro. Using her knowledge of computers and the relationship with Abdul Madhi, it was a ticket to a new job.

Lindsay looked up at Richard and says, "I'm digging this job. I know that guy had relatives in Detroit. Look, he's got an Uncle Madhi. He's a banker."

Richard says, "See, follow the money and it will lead us to parts unknown."

Lindsay says, "I'm thrilled about this. How did you ever get into this work?"

Richard told her a few stories about the World Trade Center during the Clinton era. He said some Middle Eastern guys came to Fairport Harbor by boat. That was the beginning of a long journey.

"The FBI got involved. You'll read about all that. This job isn't just about finding the bad guys. You'll answer the phone, take messages, and schedule jobs. Really, it's easy work. You'll see. I've got my hands in many things."

Richard pointed to the opposite wall where he had an exercise machine.

"Look, I don't want you just sitting at the computer. We've got the internet on a HDTV. The treadmill is there with a remote control. If you care to run for fun, the treadmill has a bunch of features. As seen on TV, it's a NordicTrack. You can program it to run races all over the world."

Richard could see she was impressed by the surroundings. He knew this was just the beginning of another adventure. The other side of Stern's world could present a challenge for Lindsay.

"Richard, I want this job."

"OK, you got it. I think you're the right person to help me. I told you; you can live here if you need a place to stay."

Richard could see she was captivated by the surroundings. It wasn't a bad place. That scene vanished. There were no pictures of criminals on the walls, no skull and bones pictures, and he wasn't pushy. Now she wanted him to know. She'll be his helper.

Lindsay says, "I can do some things that could really brighten up this place."

Richard says, "My ex-girlfriend tried to do that. She was right. I'll let you make changes. My cats will keep an eye on you."

She says, "I saw them watching from under the couch. They're really cute."

Richard says an ominous statement at this point.

"They're twins, Boots and Shorts. They're a little gun shy. They know a new person is wandering in their territory."

Richard took her to the kitchen and then to the living room. The place was fixed up to a degree, but it was messy. He called it a bachelor's pad.

"I'll show you the upstairs. This can be your apartment. It'll be completely walled off from the downstairs and you'll have the only lock and key. I'm sure your place will look better than mine. There is an emergency exit. You wouldn't need it. The surveillance computer isn't set up to monitor the upstairs, but I can point it at the entry door."

They walked through the upstairs rooms which were huge. The master bedroom was bigger than the living room. It even had an extra room that could be turned into a study.

Lindsay says, "I could fix this place up. I mean the place wasn't used much. It's messy. You need a woman to straighten thing out. So when do I start."

This statement was music to Richard's ear.

There was plenty to do if she was moving into the apartment. The upstairs bathroom needed a cabinet installed and the stairwell needed a dividing doorway to separate the upstairs from the downstairs.

Lindsay says, "I have to be out of my apartment in six weeks."

"That's perfect. I'll have to make changes to the upstairs if you're moving in. I was going to do it myself, but I better call Harbor Construction. I'm going to add a door at the top of the steps. Maybe I'll add a wall to separate the upstairs and downstairs. I guess I have to do this. If I don't we're basically sharing the entire house."

Lindsay says, "I want some security. And the apartment bathroom is a little outdated."

"That's ok. You tell me if you want a separate walled off area. Like I said, I'll call Harbor Construction. I know the owner, Terry Vale and I went through high school with his brother in law, Steve Babb. They're the construction experts. They'll send in carpenters that will make this place into a two family structure."

Lindsay says, "I don't think you need to put in a wall. Just put in a door."

He says, "That sounds good. I can do that, but that's your call."

She says, "It's ok; you can just put in a separate door to the upstairs. That'll be fine."

Richard starts to get into the things that make her most valuable.

"Lindsay, I think you know things that will help us nail down some serious money."

Lindsay says, "I don't know about that. This is an interesting job. I hope I can help. I'm sure now. I'll move in after my lease ends."

Richard says, "This might absolutely help you make a final decision. Here are the rules. Rule one, there are no rules. There is no lease here. You are my business guest, if you leave in one month or one year, that is your choice. It's ok."

Lindsay was all for those rules.

She says, "I'm ready to start working."

He says, "That's the spirit. Here is the key to the front door. Come over around ten tomorrow morning and we'll get going. Let me finish today by showing you some secret detectors. Some things you need to know are the home security systems."

CHAPTER 8

WILD JOB

LINDSAY DROVE OVER the next day to start her new job. Once inside the foyer Richard greeted her.

They went right to work on the computer. She tried to open a top secret file called <u>The Base, Al Qaeda.</u> Richard told her that it was a special file locked by a password.

"Type Al Qaeda just as you see it. Capital A and lower case l. Space and capital Q. the others are lower case and add a space with number 1 at the end. In case you don't know, it spells out the number one enemy of America. That is the password for all of my terrorist files. You'll see how the files are aligned by date and name. Al Qaeda is trying to take control of America.

Lindsay could see the titles of two organizations. Al Qaeda and the Muslim Brotherhood had close ties to each other. She could hardly believe her eyes as she peered over all the dates of violent attacks associated with the organizations. The two organizations were related. Stern's portfolio on the two groups was extensive.

Lindsay says, "This stuff goes way back to Egypt's president, Anwar Sadat. I was just a little girl back then. The bombing of the World Trade Center was during President Clinton's term in office."

Richard says, "Yes, that was Al Qaeda. They were after the World Trade Center in 1993. They used a truck bomb to explode under the North Tower. The idea was to topple the North Tower into the South Tower. You can tell one thing about these crazy asses. They don't quit."

Richard explained other attacks, like Fort Hood and car bombers in New York.

"The underwear bomber was almost successful and they almost got me."

She had a fearful look. "You're still after them, why?"

"We have to save America. Don't worry about that. We're going to hit the big one. I'm not taking chances anymore, at least not like I used to. They have a Detroit connection. That's why I think you may know something else about Abdul Madhi. You worked with him, so I'm going to Detroit to do a little probing. Toledo is my first stop and then to Michigan. I'll bring you back a Michigan sweatshirt."

Lindsay asks, "When are you leaving?"

"Soon, I've been watching some of these people. FBI reports track many suspected terrorists. We can't control our borders. Lindsay, it's a simple fact. Terrorists and people looking for work are coming into the country in many ways, just like our grandparents. They came into America looking for work. On the other hand the terrorists are coming here to cause mayhem. I think the Great Lakes and our northern border are very vulnerable."

Lindsay asks, "How do we stop that? What do we do? I mean you and me."

"If we're going to make any serious money, we have to find these bastards. You already have clues locked in your brain. You are going to help us make a few bucks. We need to unlock your mind."

She asks, "How?"

"If you let me, I want to hypnotize you."

This idea staggered her, she says, "Whoa! Ah, I'm not up for that."

He says, "That's ok, I'm kind of new at it. It probably wouldn't work. You'll see me studying the techniques from time to time. Let's get back to business. After we study the clues, you might remember more things on your own. Maybe you've already seen or heard things, but didn't think much about it. The enemy does make mistakes, so watch for signs and take thorough notes."

Lindsay was a little paranoid with Richard's hypnotic suggestion. She didn't hesitate to make it game changer. She was a secretary.

"Hypnotize me, we didn't talk about that."

Richard says, "Forget about it. I couldn't hypnotize you if you're unwilling. I'm saying you know much more than you already told me. I'm hoping you don't miss the keys. One of the big keys is money. It's all about the money. Terrorists need money to operate. They buy small businesses like stores, motels, and used car lots. Little businesses are their favorite hideouts. Mosques are another place where they hide. I sometimes think their Islamic religion is just a front, although that might be part of it, but the money trail will lead us to the bad guys. Mark my words. It is all about the money. We have to find out how they make their money."

Lindsay finally calmed down. She was up for secretary duty, but she wasn't going to be some hypnotic subject. With all the things Richard had told her so far, it was quite apparent. He was into a lot of things and he had a good deal of knowledge about terrorists.

He walked over to a stand up file cabinet and showed her stacks of notes, newspaper clippings and magazine articles.

Richard says, "Jot down notes, if you see something unusual. All these papers, they aren't just notes. They can give us a tip. Right now we're concentrating on the Great Lakes. They've tried to get in here before from Canada via Lake Erie. That being said, I'm betting they're out there and will try again."

She was on the ground floor as the researcher. Richard was into explaining the main reason for working the Great Lakes. He had a list of suspected terrorists killed or captured in and around Ohio, West Virginia, and New York.

"You have a library of information here and at all public libraries. Don't limit yourself. "Make used of the Perry Public Library. I know most of the library directors or they know me. At Perry there's an information lady there. Her name is Mary Liz Lateulere. I think that's right. Go there and the Morley Library. They have a quiet room on the third floor. There both mostly quiet. For that matter you can use Fairport's Public Library. I know Carol, the director, and most of the staff. The nice thing about public libraries is the speed of the computers. Their computers are much faster than mine."

Lindsay says, "I can't answer the phone if I'm at the library."

"Not to worry, most of my business is by Email and the phone has an answering system. My cell phone will get messages too."

Lindsay was beginning to worry about the order of business. Richard had his hands in so many businesses. She was worried about confusing secretarial work from detective work.

"I'm so new at this. How should I answer the phone?"

"Just say Richard Stern Enterprises. You'll get the hang of it."

"OK, if you say so. I was a restaurant hostess, so I did a similar job. Well, sort of similar. This job is a little more scrambled. I should help you arrange the loose notes and articles."

He' says, "I'll go to a few libraries with you. All you got to do is get the newest information that you can. Look up FBI stuff. That is the best. Check out the magazines, newspapers, like the WSJ, NY Times, all that stuff on a weekly basis. You check for dates, times, places, photos, all that. You might turn up something."

Lindsay says, "I'm going to need a gas card if I'm running around to all these libraries. Gas isn't cheap anymore."

Richard had a comeback statement for her. He paused to think if he should say something negative about the president.

"Lindsay, I know what's going on. I'm a Tea Party member. The pirates in the White House could take the shackles off the oil producers and we'd be back to two dollars a gallon gas, but I'll pay for your gas. That isn't a problem."

Lindsay smiled and agreed.

"OK, that's fair.

Richard says, "I'm thinking, maybe you've encountered terrorists in San Diego just like you said. I know they're all over the country. In the past I learned plenty from FBI Agent Monica Micovich and

Paula Gavalia. Paula was involved in an auto accident. She's gone to heaven. There were other FBI agents that gave me tips. You keep reading the stuff here. I'll bet one day you'll meet Agent Ron Roman and Bill Wright."

Lindsay groans, "FBI agents, good grief, what did I get myself into?"

Lindsay was speed reading. Absorbing the material came naturally for her. Some of the stories were sketchy. Information about his bodyguards had some frightening moments. She saw the names of people he was involved with. She saw four Cleveland FBI agents, namely, Monica Micovich, Paula Gavalia, Ron Roman, and Bill Wright.

"Those agents, were they really your bodyguards?" She asked.

Richard had a flashback. He could envision the good and bad. The truck stop shooting and the near death encounter at Mack Crenel's Bar. The drunken sex with Monica was one of his big boo boos. He wanted to stifle the subject.

"There were a few hairy moments. I had a bodyguard, Lindsay. I guess I was in love with her, maybe both of them. They were both beautiful women. One thing led to another and I, well, we got boozed up and we got carried away. I'm a romantic and adventurer. That's probably enough said about that. At least you know I'm not a homo."

With a slight chuckle, Lindsay says, "I think my ex-husband was a cross-dresser. Maybe he liked guys more than me. I don't know. He was always getting in trouble with the law. I divorced the drunken ass."

Richard had crammed the newspaper clipping of some of his exploits in one folder.

"I've got a lot of stuff that you can look over."

He showed her a volume of tapes and CDs. He recorded TV accounts of terrorist acts over the past twelve years. It was for good reason. He knew a bad day would return. America would again come under assault from secret cells. He called them the imbedded enemy. His accounts proved they had many operational plans. All with the goal of taking control. His worst fear was an assault on Washington, DC. The enemy was always planning. If they could knock down the World Trade Center, he wouldn't be surprised to see them seize control of a Washington Monument of even the White House.

Richard says, "This may sound crazy, but right now, the way things stand, I suspect the enemy is inside the White House."

For a while Stern thought he might be wasting his money by hiring Lindsay. She was trying to find new leads and doing a good job straightening out his files, but he forgot about the other Emails that he should have showed her. These were little used accounts he used in the past. Another mistake was forgetting about the trash bin. That was the reason she wasn't getting the tips. Then it all started to click.

Much to his surprise, Lindsay found an interesting article in the Oregonian newspaper.

A research vessel was discovered near the mouth of the Columbia River. Near the vessel were men swimming and diving. They were wearing wet suits. The Middle Eastern men were diving in an area that was restricted. They ignored the off limits signs. It was thought that they were poaching sturgeon. Oregon Fish and Game officials conducted an investigation. Evidence of urea nitrate was discovered on the vessel. This fertilizer was known to be used in improvised explosive devices.

There wasn't enough evidence to charge the college agriculturalist. The men were released because of diplomatic concerns.

This convinced him to make a trip to Portland, Oregon. Before Richard left, Lindsay told him she was finally moving into the upstairs apartment. She had done some good and figured life in the small town along with free rent was a good deal. Naturally, Richard gave her the green light to move in.

The upstairs was ready. Harbor Construction had finished the job. Lindsay was quite happy with the living conditions.

Richard wasted no time. He was off to Portland, Oregon.

CHAPTER 9

FIRST HINT

T HE DEPARTURE TO Oregon stumbled out of the gate. When Richard Stern presented his ID to a TSA security agent, a book Stern was carrying caught the eye of the agent. A loose paper, like a book page marker had the words, <u>terrorist hunter, in view</u>.

"Where are yah heading Mr. Stern?"

"This time I'm going to Portland, Oregon," said Stern. "You can see the itinerary. It includes a stop at Midway Airport in Chicago. The airport security agent allowed him to pass to the X-ray station where he passed through the radiation test. Another agent stopped him to examine his book and briefcase. Inside the case were a few photos of Middle Eastern men and documents about terrorists and their activities. This raised a red flag for the agent.

The questioning began with 'where are you going?' Stern could easily answer that question as he did before. He had an airline ticket.

Stern was pulled from the line and a new officer came to ask a few more questions. Stern told them he was a writer and amateur bounty hunter. He wrote articles about terrorism. Additionally, he said he was working on a story about their whereabouts.

The Cleveland TSA agent was clear headed enough to understand Mr. Stern was cooperating. He actually added some points for Stern to digest.

The agent said, "The Great Lakes can hide ships.

Stern said, "What do mean by that?"

"Remember the song about Lake Superior—it never gives up her dead. Homeland security is working with the Canadian Coast Guard to find a missing ship. US Coast Guard is working the investigation on our side. The ship vanished."

Stern asked, "What was the name of the missing cruise ships?"

The officer said, "Green Lake, Green, oh, I forgot."

The TSA interrogator allowed Stern to pass.

Stern finished by telling the agent he had read about some incidents on Lake Erie that involved acts of terror. He didn't want to get into a discussion of his direct involvement with the FBI. The episode with party boats and terrorists was still an indelible picture in his mind. They allowed him to pass.

Richard called Lindsay. He says, "Look up Great Lakes missing ships and see what you find. I think something happened and it's interesting. A ship called Green or Green Lakes is missing."

Lindsay checked on the internet. She couldn't find anything and sent a text message back to him. I didn't find anything missing. No Green or Green Lakes, it's a dead end.

When Stern reached Portland, Oregon he traveled to Astoria where the century's old Lewis and Clark expedition ended. He was lucky enough to be stopped by a Fish and Game officer when he drove off the beaten path with his rental car. She offered some candid information. She told him he could drive his car right onto the beach along the Pacific Ocean.

Stern said, "I'm on a fishing expedition of my own. I'm really not as interested in the fish as I am the illegal fishing in Oregon. I read where your department had intercepted illegal fishermen. She wouldn't say a whole lot but offered some sketchy details about a tourist boat. Stern finished the conversation by saying he heard a mini-submarine was being used for research on the Columbia River.

Judging from her eyes, the middle-aged woman seemed to know exactly what Stern was referencing. She decided to comment on the subject.

"There was a couple vessels involved. They were released after being checked.

"I saw an article in the newspaper about a research vessel being stopped by your officers. Was it connected to the strange sighting of a mini-submarine.?"

She said, "That's an ongoing investigation. I don't have very much to add."

Oregon Department of Fish and Wildlife Wild officers had conducted an investigation of a so called 'research vessel.' If the vessel was somehow connected with the unproven submarine no one knew for sure. All folk would say to newspaper reporters was that partiers had seen periscopes pop out of the water. It remained a mystery.

The agent replied that she thought it was a Canadian research vessel, but left the door open to another answer.

"Rich college kids were going into places they shouldn't," she said. "That's it."

She ended the conversation by telling Stern to drive straight ahead to the shore of the Pacific Ocean.

"You won't get stuck. The sand is hard."

"Thanks, officer."

Stern drove to the beach and watched the waves roll. Off to the right was a rock formation that rose hundreds of feet. The beauty of the beach was so impressive.

He wrote an email to Lindsay saying the trip started off a little shaky, but he was on to something. There's a mystery going on around here, Lindsay. I'm not done. The Pacific beach is just magnificent.

They communicated often. Every evening he would call her. Lindsay was starting to get a handle on the job. She checked his several other secret Emails that he would use. People she didn't know left tips. It was like Richard had a treasure trove of hidden people sending him information about felons or suspicious activity. Tips seemed to come in randomly. Some were from Kansas. Most tips came in from El Paso, Texas and a person named Indian Tracker sent Emails from Detroit, Michigan and El Paso. Lindsay thought it was the same person.

One of Richard's military friends, John Campbell, called with news about a bus being hijacked in California. When Richard was running around with his ex-girlfriend he met John. They would meet from time to time at the Great Lakes Mall to discuss terrorist tactics, homegrown terrorists, and politics. They admitted the potential targets were in every state. Mr. Campbell was one to say, 'Malls, theaters, schools, and buses were becoming homegrown targets.' Richard agreed with Mr. Campbell. That type of terrorism was happening more often.

They agreed on the new type of enemy. The insane guy who had revenge on his mind was on the radar screen.

John would say, 'They always catch them after the fact. A terrorist might drive up in an explosive loaded bus. It happened in Oklahoma City. School buses were easy targets.'

The men had discussed the crazy theories of the homegrown terrorist. A crazy would steal a bus and drive it into a packed theater. They both agreed. If it can happen in Iraq or Israel, it could happen in America.

Bad things were happening in Iraq and Israel and it was migrating to America. Terrorists had conducted cruel attacks in Israel and India. In Israel they had commandeered school buses and threw hand grenade into tourist buses. In India they attacked a hotel filled with tourists.

John Campbell once said, 'There might come a day when we have to put an armed guard on school buses. We have to protect the children.'

Child molesters were always in the news. A child or children could become hostages. An attack like that was all meant to create fear, which was the enemy's favorite modus operandi.

As Lindsay searched through emails she saw one from Miss M and several from other unknown people.

Miss M left a message about border security in El Paso and the Arizona southern border with Mexico. <u>We suspect guns are moving across the Rio Grande River and moving north</u>. Another person wrote about headlines in the Detroit News. The job of researcher for Richard Stern Enterprises was becoming very exciting. She relayed the data to Richard who was still investigating in Oregon.

Richard called her cell phone.

"Lindsay, it's me."

"Hi me, Richard, I'm really into this job." she said.

He says, "I've got a new tip out here. There's something happening on the Columbia River. I'll keep you posted. Keep your ears and eye wide open and good bye."

Lindsay wanted the last word.

"Wait, Miss M said guns are moving across the Rio Grande and moving north. She says in El Paso guns are moving across the border with Mexico, I presume."

Richard says, "This is big. Keep saving the emails. Bye dear, I mean Lindsay."

Lindsay really felt good after he said that. It was like she was part of the team.

With a smile on her face she replies, "Bye, Richard and be careful, dear."

CHAPTER 10

GUN RUNNING

A YEAR AND a half before all the upheaval at the Cleveland FBI headquarters and before the loss of her partner, Monica allowed Stern to visit their son. She was turning to God and believed that dad had a right to be with his son, but her cardinal rule wasn't to be broken. There would be no visits if he was drinking.

The visits worked in their favor for a number of reasons. One, he could play with his son. Michael was growing like a weed. Second, it gave her a break and she didn't have to take him to day care. The visits eased the guilt of his thoughtless act. Stern was struggling to relax the feeling of guilt. He believed in a moment of weakness he took advantage of Monica. To tamp down the feeling of guilt, his twisted thought was—maybe there was consensual sex and it was just normal. Maybe the sex act was best for all three of them. Stern regretted his distasteful act and failed to see the whole scope of how devastating their affair affected Monica.

Another reason his visits were beneficial for him was most interesting. Stern could listen in on Monica's phone chatter about criminal cases from time to time. As he watched TV, mostly on the Fox News channel and entertained his boy, he made mental notes of her conversations. What he was seeing on TV sometimes had a tie to Monica's conversation. She was indirectly feeding him clues.

At times her chat was about a murder of a border patrol agent. A year had passed by in which he collected mental notes of things. He kept his eyes open for Monica's notebook which she sometimes conveniently left on the kitchen table. In the notebook was a reference to arms smuggling happening on the Great Lakes. Richard took advantage of Monica's notebook and copied the information.

When Monica would return from work or was done running errands, Richard went home to unload a bevy of information that few ordinary citizens would know. He often wondered if she was doing this on purpose to help him earn reward money.

Her calendar was another place that would give him tidbits of information. A few times she would call him to watch Michael. She'd write down pasty notes about where she was going, when she was in a hurry.

Stern could see Monica was doing an investigation on someone in Detroit, Michigan. There was gun-running going on from El Paso to Cleveland and Detroit. This was a major concern because of the major arms smuggling case called 'Fast and Furious.' The FBI knew arms shipments were underway, but the mode of transport wasn't known.

The Federal Bureau of Alcohol, Tobacco, and Firearms (ATF) investigation was centered on Arizona. The arms dealers there had already sold two thousand weapons to Mexican gangs. After that they were passed on to the Mexican drug cartel. Some of the guns were coming back by way of Texas and Arizona. They were moving across the border and going further north.

The Washington FBI was considering an operation to stop the movement across state lines. The operation was held back for some odd reason.

There was no question in Stern's mind. Pirates in the White House were involved. They were trying to cover up this scandal. The arms trafficking with Mexican drug lords would be a major embarrassment, since a federal agent was killed by one of the illegal guns.

A congressional investigation was bringing in FBI agents. The attorney general and the Department of Justice's low level attorneys were doing their best to withhold information and stall for time. They were using this delay tactic time and again. White House officials believed this was the best method to quell public sentiment. Most citizens would simply forget about the agent's murder in Arizona by guns that were offered to Mexican gang members.

Essentially, Monica was on the go. When Stern was home and not traveling she would ask him to watch his son as a matter of convenience. Richard was excited to have the opportunity to visit Michael.

To watch Michael at Monica's house was a strange feeling for Richard. The beauty of the situation came when she had to leave and it happened from time to time. Richard took the liberty to nose around the house when she was gone.

He could shop for information and see Monica was working on the Cleveland connection to the gun-running case. How deep she was involved wasn't known to him, but he could tell by her trips to Sandusky, Toledo, and Detroit that something was happening.

Monica's phone had a log of calls she placed to Detroit. He wrote down phone numbers and checked on them. The places linked to the phone numbers were mostly marinas. This made him think that weapons were being moved by boat.

Towards the end of all the visits, he heard a phone conversation that was a little disturbing. He suspected that Monica was using him to her advantage, so she could see her lover. He suspected it was Bill Wright, because he heard her say 'hi Agent Bill, where are we going tonight.' Whether this was intentionally done was something Stern didn't bother to bring up, but it certainly dashed his hopes of being with her. He was foolishly thinking Monica and him might start dating. It wasn't that farfetched, although Agent Wright had her wrapped around his devious finger.

CHAPTER 11

FBI INFORMER

L INDSAY WAS READING the medical files associated with Richard's dreams. The doctors' evaluations were giving her insight into Richard's background. She couldn't believe what she was reading. The dreams and hallucinations he was having were stimulated by alcohol. He used the booze as an enhancement drug to boost his mental capacity.

There were theories abound. Deep in his memory bank, his subconscious drew pictures of the enemy. The information stored in his brain could assemble a plausible computation of the enemies' future plans. His memory may have played tricks on him. Pictures of the enemy, their hideout, and plans were super-imposed on the temporal cortex. It was thought that he read so much about Al Qaeda that he associated the actions of the enemy with newspaper articles. A subconscious paranoia was influencing his dreams. No solid proof was established but by some accounts he was deemed a psychic. The reasons weren't unfounded.

Lindsay was spellbound by some of the files. She read page after page. Then she came to the FBI report. It was an old file.

Stern had made personal appearances at the Cleveland FBI office which led to terrorist arrests. Agent Ron Roman had the first discussion with Mr. Stern. The off the cuff predictions to Roman put the FBI on notice. Mr. Stern was someone they could use as an informer. He had a weird sixth sense. It was dubbed a paranormal reaction.

Lindsay thought about Richard's idea to hypnotize her. He said it was because she harbored some inner fact that he could extract. This information if taken from her about Abdul Madhi might lead to a reward. It was all becoming clear to her. He wasn't a kook. The FBI took extra measures to protect him.

She kept reading. The FBI's medical report was also wild. He had a special medical condition. It could easily be explained by simply saying he was addicted to alcohol, but the informer was possessed by the super natural. Doctors deemed this a mystery of medicine. The FBI file had no clear understanding of his 'talent.' It defied rational logic.

Lindsay was putting it all together. She was more intrigued than ever. If he could see faces of the enemy through her, surely she would lead him to the information that would give them a shot at making reward money.

She exclaims aloud, "That was the reason he wanted to hypnotize me."

Richard had told her 'every piece of information is important.' You may hold a bounty of information for Homeland Security and we will surly win.

She was definitely on board now. For whatever the reason, if the booze brought out revelations, she would watch him to see how he does it. Maybe she could help him figure it out.

Lindsay did see the down side. In the FBI report was an underlined statement: <u>Dealing with Richard Stern was like playing Russian roulette.</u> He was prone to getting into close calls.

The FBI supervisor considered putting new agents around him, but squashed the idea. It was too risky. His report countered that idea by saying it could be a problem for the bureau. He didn't want their agents stepping into harm's way.

Lindsay's thoughts were swirling in her head. At one time Richard had a well-conceived plan with backing from the FBI. He was getting reward money. The amounts varied. Some of the checks he received were in the ten to over a hundred thousand dollars. This wasn't chump change. He had a string of decent months over a few years.

She didn't see any problem with helping him. After all she had protection. She felt the pistol she carried and wondered. Would she end up having to use it to protect Richard?

The file had many references to Agent Monica Micovich, the bodyguard.

There was a second time Agent Micovich came to the rescue.

"Wow, good for Agent Monica Micovich, she saved his life again."

Lindsay kept on reading the FBI stories.

She said out loud again, "This guy is one of a kind."

She opened up the file on Michael Micovich. As she read on she discovered Michael was Richard's son. The more she read the greater her interest became. Agent Monica Micovich was allowing Richard to visit from time to time.

She saw a haphazard timeline of visits and the information he was collecting from her. It seemed to her as she read along that they weren't exactly close, however, Richard noted how easy it was to collect sensitive FBI information. Lindsay wondered if she was setting him up. Monica had a boyfriend named Agent Bill Wright, which made her feel good. Now her thoughts turned ugly. Could she be the black widow? Lindsay's thoughts were running deep. The consensus of the heart was Miss Monica Micovich was kind of playing both sides of the fence. She might still be after Richard and Bill Wright.

Lindsay reconciled in a whisper, "Good, she's seeing Agent Wright."

After reading the file on Michael Micovich, Lindsay found out Richard didn't know he had a son. Monica obviously had full custody and didn't want Richard to know this fact. She felt a sense of relief. Monica and Michael eventually landed in Fairport Harbor. Richard found out he was a father by accident while at Larry and Woody's Redi Go Convenience store in Fairport Harbor. There he saw his son with babysitters, although he didn't know at first. The babysitters gave him the miracle tip he needed. They were babysitting for Monica Micovich. Richard told her he was a bachelor. This information proved this to be true.

Lindsay was reading old news. She didn't know the resent events. There was a plethora of news about Agent Monica Micovich. A shakeup was going on at the FBI Headquarters in Cleveland. Monica was under siege because of her renewed interest in Agent Bill Wright.

Chapter 12

New Agents and One Creep

Supervisor Moses was glad to receive new help in the name of Agent Nicole Swider and Agent Kayla Jacobson. Moses told the new agents to work alongside of Agent Micovich, so he could free up his two man team of Agents Wright and Roman.

Micovich worked with Swider and Jacobson for a few months, so they could get adjusted to life in Cleveland. Swider had extensive training in the medical field and Moses thought she'd be an asset because of an ongoing departmental problem. Agent Jacobson had high tech training along with business and criminal law degrees. He was hoping both agents would help Monica with her personal life. He wanted them to learn from her and be wary of her mental state.

Supervisor Moses had an informal talk with his new recruits. He went right to the point.

Moses says, "Agent Micovich had lost her partner and friend. It was very traumatic. She needed time off, but I'm afraid she still suffers from post-traumatic stress."

Moses' intention was good. He went over the details with the agents.

Monica had to swallow a bitter pill with the death of her friend and partner. Add to the complex she was dealing with a revived romance.

After Monica's partner, Agent Paula Gavalia, was killed in a car crash, Miss Micovich experienced psychological stress from the loss of her best friend and confidant. They were very close. The Micovich and Gavalia partnership was an effective team.

Supervisor Moses saw the dejection and change in Agent Micovich's personality. One strong indicator she wasn't thinking right was her renewed interest in her ex-lover. She started dating Agent Bill Wright again.

He said, "Keep an eye on her. I'm afraid she is on the wrong track. She's a good detective. Go and learn from her and don't be afraid to come back to me with a report."

The new recruits did as instructed. Time passed quickly.

The new agents saw a partial transformation in Monica's personality when she turned to Agent Bill Wright for comfort and companionship. She had a bounce in her step. There was reason for this heavenly feeling.

Monica thought a night out with Bill was going to ease the pain of loss. She hired a sitter to watch Michael. Then she started to use Richard when he was available. She was feeling his love. A few more dates and a couple sleepovers with Bill worked for her. She was starting to feel his full-bodied passion. He could drive a woman out of her mind by robust composition, but it was only temporary. She didn't learn from her previous romance with Bill.

Bill's personality had earned him a reputation around the office as a skilled womanizer. Although he thought he was helping Monica regroup, he couldn't shake his mischievous side. His manhood always got in the way of devotion. Half the office girls had labeled Bill. They said he had a hormonal imbalance, too much testosterone. Some girls nicknamed him woody long pecker, after giving him permission to explore their bodies.

Bill was an excellent federal agent. Nobody thought different. Agent Wright and Agent Ron Roman had a reputation of taking out the bad guys. They worked with Monica for a while until two new agents came aboard. The new hires worked into Supervisor Moses' plan. He wanted to put some distance between Monica and Bill.

Monica thought she had tamed her man. Beauty and handsome set sail on the right course and they were the talk of the department.

Everyone was cheering for them except Supervisor Moses. He knew better. The two agents were trying to recoup the lost love, but as before the trust turned hollow. The love boat only had one oar in the water. Monica was rowing in circles.

Moses thought the emotional love affair between the agents was outshining the bureau's cohesiveness. The investigative work done by Agent Micovich seemed to suffer. She saw Bill advancing on Agent Swider and then Jacobson. This act lit a fuse. Monica had verbal confrontations in the office with her ex-fiancé.

Bill told her to relax. Again they seemed to patch things up and they got back together for a time, but the relationship suffered from a lack of commitment, the same as before. Bill attempted to sway the new treasures to his house. They had been forewarned and told Monica to be careful. Perhaps it was because of the new agents arrival, Bill's affection for Monica suffered.

Tranquility in the office was dropping because of outbursts between Wright and Micovich. They were becoming a major issue for Supervisor Moses. Besides the office quakes, Agent Micovich received a poor performance review.

Agent Micovich wasn't one for holding her tongue.

"You're a cheating womanizer. I saw you looking at Kayla. Did you sleep with her?" Agent Micovich asked. The firebrand woman was desperately jealous.

Bill says, "No, we were just talking criminal law."

"You are a horny piece of crap. You need your nuts cut off." she shouted.

Agent Wright says, "Cool off, Monica. You're making a scene."

Moses was looking over the final overall evaluation on Agent Micovich. It was less than flattering, when measured against her past records. The timing was bad for Micovich as Moses could hear the bickering.

These were signs of trouble for Moses, who was one for dealing with matters without hesitation. He did his best to hold his fury.

Everyone in the office was watching the confrontation between the two agents. They looked to see if Supervisor Moses was watching.

He was. He opened his office door when he heard the outburst. Moses summarily ordered the two lovers to cease and move to opposite ends of the office.

Change would be needed to clear up the issue, because it wasn't going away. It was a sad day when Agent Monica Micovich learned the news. She was being transferred and assigned to El Paso, Texas.

Most thought that Monica still wanted Bill in spite of his shenanigans, but she couldn't accept a philanderer. Even though he made overtures to repair the damage, she was heartbroken over his constant flirtations with the new hires. Moses knew he had to make a move and Monica seemed to take it in stride. Even she was tired of fighting with him.

Moses had to agree with her, but his role was supervisor, not marriage counselor. The explosiveness of their discussions made other detectives uncomfortable. They would have made a fine pair, if only Wright would have stopped being a playboy. Bill Wright had his own career to protect and it was being tarnished.

Agent Ron Roman knew the office girls thought Wright was godly handsome. All Roman cared about was one thing—his partner was a sure shot, handgun expert and their exploits were second to none. Agent Ron Roman and Bill Wright were renown throughout the bureau.

Bill shed thinly veiled tears when he heard Monica was being transferred. He tried to repair the damage done by his wandering eyes, but it didn't work.

The problem for Monica was her own fault. Her loose behavior with Mr. Stern upstaged a stellar career. She made it known to Moses that it was her feeling for her son, Michael that caused her to go after Wright again. Michael needed a father figure like Agent Wright. He was growing up too fast and she was starting to see gray hair. Although she was still very attractive, finding Mr. Right to marry seemed elusive for her.

Monica barged into Moses' office in a fit. She explained her position. "Cliff, I know Agent Wright loves me."

Moses had an answer for that. He wasn't going to be sympathetic. Her emotions were overgrown and running wild. He wasn't going to be swallowed up by emotions. She got away with that when he learned of her pregnancy, but it wasn't going to change his position this time.

"You know Wright's personality and I do too. I don't need to say anything more. Nothing has changed; you're going to El Paso. I've got to fix this discombobulated disruption. You have a career with the FBI and I'm not going to let you ruin it by chasing Bill Wright."

One thing for sure she didn't want to hear the truth. What's more she didn't want to hear any more straight talk from Moses. She had a woman's scorn, although in the back of her mind was something other women experienced. She loved her sex with Bill Wright, which was one reason to stay with him. It was a driving desire commanding her to keep seeing him. He was a passionate bedmate and her son needed a dad.

The office tumult was most unfortunate. Wright was just a victim of his own outlandish style. His actions were so blatant He just couldn't control his devilish desire.

Sure, he was grieving for a short time. It wasn't too bad. His heart was made of marble. One lost love wasn't such a big deal. He knew another friendship would be around the corner. The opposite sex was a game for him since high school and college. Wright's weakness and a cure for his over active manhood were to find another beautiful lady to romance.

He met so many people on the job it wasn't difficult to find a new friend. In this case he would take the next step which was to personally explain his latest investigative nuances to Agents Nicole and Kayla.

Agents Swider and Jacobson were quite attractive and Bill wasted no time trying to make time with them.

Ron Roman looked up to see his partner, Bill, in action. He just shook his head in disbelief over the fabricated lines he used to open a conversation with the agents. The female agents didn't take the bait. They didn't get trapped by his coerciveness.

"Bill, I heard what you told them. 'Come over and see my collection of pistols.' You got the harpoon ready?"

Bill recoils, "What's that supposed to mean? We're not going out. Nicole flat out turned me down. Anyhow, maybe Kayla will go for an afternoon lunch. She didn't exactly say no."

Ron started to question his buddy's modus operandi. Knowing Bill's charades, he quickly surmises the next move.

"Come on, Bill. I know what you're after. I remember when you asked the girl cleaning the offices to come over to your house. I know you took advantage of her. You started fooling around with Monica and now you're on another fishing expedition with one thing on your mind. I can tell when you're trolling for women."

Bill says, "That girl did a nice job cleaning my house. She really did clean and went out of her way to satisfy me. She earned a reward and we both enjoyed it."

Remember fishing in Parkersburg, West Virginia. You're out fishing again, not with the John West lure. You're using your tongue. You're fishing all right, except there's no water, only women and a line of bull.

Wright says, "Oh, give me a break. My line is in the water just like any other guy. Trolling for women comes natural for me."

Roman returns fire. "What I'm saying, buddy, you're trying to hook up with two new agents and it's going to get you in trouble. Monica has already got her marching orders because of you. Don't give her another reason to attack. And, if Moses could see what you're doing, he'd hit the roof."

Wright wasn't buying the advice.

Agent Wright says, "I'm just a Romeo. I can actually see us. Is there anything wrong with a threesome?"

"Oh, my God, a threesome, that's what you're thinking."

"You'll see. They'll be eating out of my hand."

Agent Roman replies, "One of these days you're going to run into the Black Widow."

One thing Ron never told his partner. Deep down he really wanted to marry a girl like Monica and he didn't want her to leave. Seeing her get slammed by Bill was hurtful.

Ron paused and finished with a self-induced proverb.

"You're always after fresh meat. I got a new name for you, buddy. It's Billy the Stiff Pole. The man is always looking for a new hole to fill. That's you, Billy"

Bill says, "Well, you and I know fresh line catches trophies and those girls are trophies. I'll just have to come up with a fresh line to reel them in."

Ron was now targeting his own feelings. He honestly wanted Monica to be his girlfriend.

"You want it all, my friend. I would be a faithful companion."

Slightly agitated and knowing full well his partner was right; Wright replies.

"I haven't done anything wrong. Besides, both of them sort of rejected my offers. Miss Swider is a trained health clinician and I admire that. I may need to get some healthy advice from her. You know, we have some mutual interests. I know first aid. I'm very good at mouth to mouth resuscitation, but it only works on women. You know her partner is a brain. Maybe I can convince her to come over and see my gun collection."

"Good God, Billy, you're a real piece of work."

The new agents were well aware of Bill Wright's temperance.

Weeks passed without incident. It was Friday. Supervisor Moses called Agent Swider and Jacobson into his office. He wanted to refresh their mind with good advice. They were advised to stay professional. He had enough trouble with Agent Wright and Micovich. Moses said he respects everyone's rights to work in an atmosphere of peace and respect.

"It's where we can all work together in harmony."

Moses pointedly says, "Wright has earned a reputation around the department."

The two women quickly tamed the supervisor.

Agent Swider went first. She said she has a boyfriend. She told Moses she isn't interested in Wright.

Agent Jacobson says, "We're not buying his line, Cliff."

Nicole says, "Wright will never get to first base with me."

Moses announces, "You're right about that, Agent Swider. You two are going to meet up with Agent Micovich in about six weeks. Get ready to travel to El Paso. It's a temporary assignment."

Nicole Swider and Kayla Jacobson looked at each other in disbelief.

Moses says, "Monica is getting her personal affairs together. She'll meet up with you in due time. Soon we'll need more agents in El Paso according to the bureau. There is a small war going on along the border. The Mexican drug cartels are moving guns from Mexico to Texas. It may be the guns are moving to the Great Lakes region. We're working with ATF agents to stop the flow of illegal weapons. This is becoming a big underground business.

"The president wants to change the meaning of the Second Amendment and that is creating more work for us. It has a lot of people buy guns. Plus, I'm not going to let Monica go on a special case alone. She's vulnerable right now and needs your help."

One month passed. Monica had found a place to rent in El Paso. It all worked out for her. The government promised to buy her house. They moved her belongings and she was back on her feet. This time El Paso, Texas was her home.

Supervisor Moses told Nicole and Kayla to get ready to move. He meant pack your bags.

Agent Swider was excited, "We're going to El Paso. I've never been there."

He says, "You'll join up with Agent Micovich. I'll brief you tomorrow."

Moses had made the right moves. He wasn't going to deal with a contentious situation, bordering on turmoil. He couldn't absolve either Monica or Agent Wright for the ruckus they were causing.

With all of that out of the way Agent Bill Wright and Agent Ron Roman were totally back on message. They had a new assignment to find the shipment and landing zone of arms heading north.

Moses earned his stripes by being levelheaded. If the apples were getting spoiled, it was time to separate the good and the bad. He took control. If he had to he wouldn't hesitate to make another correction. In this situation Moses had to be fair to all. Monica was the most at fault. It was a correct decision and the organization in Cleveland returned to normal. Bill Wright felt a ting of guilt. He didn't suffer. Roman was the man who had a heart of gold and he let Monica know by personal mail that he would miss her.

Agent Micovich was Moses' favorite investigator. He was grooming her for his job, but it didn't work out as he had planned.

He signed the papers that helped Monica sell her house. As he signed the papers, he hated the experience of losing a veteran agent. She was almost a daughter to him. It was crushing. He lost two wonderful agents in a span of three years.

Moses didn't see what was coming his way. Agent Micovich was inspired by the move. She wasted no time putting her career back on the front burner.

CHAPTER 13

WEEKS LATER

A GENT MONICA MICOVICH was pretty much relieved to get out of the Cleveland office. She had her fill of excitement with Billy. He always seemed to hit the right spot, but that was over now.

El Paso, Texas was new and exciting. She found a nice place to live. It was in a block of newly built apartments. Finally, after a couple weeks of moving furniture she was settled in El Paso. She had a beautiful place where she could play with Michael. She even found a nice grandmother that had lived in Perry, Ohio to use as the child sitter. Carol Meyer said she could care for Michael while she was working.

She received news from Cliff Moses. Soon she would be joined by agents, Kayla Jacobson and Nicole Swider. She had worked with them for a short time in Cleveland. It would be a little reunion for them. They still had a lot to learn and Agent Micovich was ready to lead the team.

Jacobson and Swider would need to do surveillance in a whole new area of America. This was going to be on the fly on the job training from veteran Micovich. The three agents had to learn cohesion as a team just like a football team. Together they had to watch for the gun-running operation being conducted by Mexican war lords.

When they first met in El Paso, Agent Micovich showed off her apartment which was nicely decorated. Little Michael had his own room. She was so proud of her work. Micovich was happy to move out of Ohio and make new friends in El Paso. She could start a new beginning. She didn't see the opportunity at first, but it turned out to be a perfect move, although her tenacious reputation as a crime fighter was to be trouble for executives in Washington DC.

She was also glad to be joined by female agents a little younger than her. It gave her the encouragement to be a team leader. In Cleveland the three agents didn't have much time to get familiar with each other, but that would quickly change. Drama was coming their way.

During their first few meetings in El Paso, they exchanged background information again. Jacobson was a business major with criminal law experience. Swider was medically qualified as an EMT and a martial arts instructor as was Monica. That was a common bond. The blend of talent was perfectly suited for the upcoming mission. It was a matter of getting to know each other. Nicole and Kayla were given their own rooms in Monica's spacious apartment.

Agent Micovich talked about her demotion to El Paso as a 'get even' checkmate by her former fiancé and lover, Agent Bill Wright. She explained the whole story to her partners.

Nicole says, "We were supposed to keep an eye on you. Supervisor Moses was worried about you. He kind of filled us in on all the things going on in the department. Bill has quite a reputation doesn't he?"

Monica says, "He's a handsome son of a bitch."

Kayla says, "We met Bill and quickly assumed he had one thing on his mind."

Monica replies, "Yeah, to get in your pants."

Monica went on to say the bureau demoted her with this assignment, but it wasn't a bad job. She didn't treat the assignment as a demotion. The move was a bit of a pain. She just had to relocate and that was a strain on her son, Michael.

The subject of her son came to light and Monica explained.

"Listen, you two, if you ever have to guard an informer named Richard Stern, you'll need to be on your toes and keep the work purely professional. He can get into trouble and I don't want to hear any bad news about him."

She went over the facts with the agents. Mr. Stern was a heavy drinker. He caught her in a moment of sorrow.

"Mr. Stern is a smooth talker. He thinks he's an amateur bounty hunter. He's interesting, clever, and I had a baby with him. It was a one night stand. It really hurt my career, but it's something I don't regret now. Michael is so special. Now don't get me wrong, I almost gave him up at an abortion clinic, because I was totally defeated. I thank the Catholic priest, Father Pete, for being a guiding light. My son is very special. My mistake was an error in judgment. The error still haunts me a little bit.

Nicole says, "That's in the past, Monica. We're here to tackle the enemy."

Kayla tried to comfort Monica with reassuring words. It helped, but Monica still felt a sense of defeat.

Kayla says, "We're going to blend. Don't worry, Monica.

Monica says, "You know how Supervisor Cliff operates. He approved this move to El Paso and I think it's all because I slept with Mr. Stern and got pregnant. I was Mr. Stern's bodyguard. I let him take advantage of me. You understand what I mean. I felt like he was going to marry me, because he and I were drinking on the job. I was smashed. He took me to a hotel and we continued to drink. He got a room for us and the rest is history."

Kayla says, "You don't have to tell us. We've all made mistakes with men."

Monica continued. "Then I compounded my mistake by falling in love with Wright. He was going to be a great father for Michael. I'm sorry; I just can't win with men."

Tears welled up in Monica's eyes. She was ready to crack. Agent Swider saw the remorse and changed the subject. Nicole said she wanted to play with Michael once in a while.

Nicole says, "Let's have dinner at some Mexican restaurant and discuss our project. That's why we're together. Monica, you need to forget about Bill Wright, he's a wolf. He'll never change. You're the boss and we have to make the best of this investigation.

The agents hit it off quite well as they discussed a plan of operation. Details were worked out and over-lapping shifts would begin the next day.

Even though Monica thought the move to El Paso was a 'get even' checkmate by her former fiancé and lover, Bill Wright, she made the most of the move. It was good for her career. She was back in the saddle like a thrown horseback rider.

Two weeks had passed without much trouble. The team was getting a feel for the area. From time to time Monica slid back into sorrow and the agents would help her. She made a point of being honest with Nicole and Kayla.

"I feel bad again. I had fun with Bill. See what I mean. I compounded my mistake by falling in love with Wright. Maybe I'm still in love with him. He was going to be a great father for Michael."

Nicole says, "At some point, Monica, you have to put the tear away. You have to say it. Just admit the love affair is over."

Agent Swider saw the remorse bubble up again. Monica's eyes were watery red.

She says, "We're doing well, Monica.

The operation was working out. They had a good stakeout and a plan of action if trouble came their way. The mission started in the evening and lasted till the morning.

Nicole says, "Let's have a late lunch tomorrow and discuss an exit plan if we have to follow the gun-runners.

Monica says, "Yes, I'd say we better go over security if one of us needs help."

They had lunch the next day and beefed up their action plan. Towards the end of the conversation Nicole slipped in a pep talk. For the betterment of the team she wanted to drive home a point even if it brought back sour memories.

She says, "This is my last tip, Monica, forget about Bill Wright. From now on we have to focus on the Rio Grande. It's where they're moving the guns back and forth. You told us to be ready for late night trouble and we agree."

Monica says, "Yak, he tends to pop into my mind from time to time. It's OK, agents; it's time to investigate and nail these bastards."

The next night the agents worked in silence. No cell phone talk was allowed. They kept repeating the job just as they discussed it. After a week the plan of operation didn't produce any results. They kept moving to new locations. Then they tried something different. Details were worked out and over-lapping shifts would begin the following night covering a greater area.

MONICA'S SECRET

Agent Micovich never told the other agents about her secret relationship with Mr. Stern. After Micovich left for El Paso, Texas, she mailed Richard Stern a stack of old files. She was really on his side, mostly because of Michael. She was acting on her own, maybe using him to finish an investigation. She could always tell her son that his dad was a real unusual man of many talents. He was a true vigilante, a real crime fighter for America. He didn't need a badge.

She was confident that Richard would look into how money moves around in Detroit. She knew the Detroit government was corrupt.

Agent Paula Gavalia and her spied on a Detroit bank. It was likely to be the source of Al Qaeda's money supply and she believed Richard could use the information to find the real criminals. The money was flowing to Cleveland and Detroit. Somehow Toledo and Sandusky were linked with the big cities. Although she was off the case, it still bugged her. She was hoping Richard would look at the people running the money between the bank and a

Detroit mosque. She wasn't able to tie the people to the money supply. She didn't get far enough in the investigation to know how it all worked, although she did bust some government officials for corruption. There were more criminals involved. Unfortunately, she was being transferred.

Even though she was afraid for Richard, she wanted him to follow up and work as an informer for the FBI on the case. She wasn't about to tell Supervisor Moses that she supplied Stern with special information. He was her undercover vigilante.

She was certain he would travel to Detroit and do his own investigation. She knew he wanted to be a serious bounty hunter, but he was reckless and careless about his own security and that scared her. He was a freelance informer. Her experience with him put her in jeopardy many times. Still, she found him to be a good guy.

Protecting him was a real chore. Richard could get into trouble with the drop of a hat. The nice thing about his job, he was free to roam. He wasn't subjected to the same rules regular police had to follow. Her greatest fear was the way he operated. He was prone to do things his own way and get into hairy situations.

Agent Monica prayed to God the night she decided to send the files to him. In a way she was being told to connect with Father Pete again and she called him the next day.

She told Father Pete she was in El Paso, Texas working on a new assignment.

He told her to follow her conscience and do God's work along with her job. The advice she received was just what she needed. She asked Father Pete for a prayer. He prayed with her. He told her God is with her at every turn. He will help her and make her a success, but she will have to make the best of every opportunity.

He says, "He provides what you need and you have faith in Him."

It was true. She had a renewed sense of vitality. She felt her team of agents was going to score a big win.

She wanted to get one more thing off her shoulders so she called Father Pete again.

"Father, you know me. I'm so mad at Richard, but I want him to do well and be safe. He's so prone to get into trouble. You know how he drinks. I'm afraid he'll do something stupid and I won't be there."

Father Pete says, "God will show him the way out of his misery. This is one of those mysteries that you may not understand. Richard has to take the right road. It's all about choices. Don't worry about him. Take charge of your life and Mr. Stern will find life is better when he finds the right road. He has a path to God. We have to let him take it."

That was enough spunk for Monica. She was ready to take down the enemy. It all happened within a few days after her call to Father Pete. It was as if God had a hand in the operation. They spotted an arms dealer loading a small boat.

A dragnet was set up to capture the arms dealers that they spotted on the Mexican side of the border. She reported the news to her supervisor. To her surprise she was told to hold her position. He would follow up with new orders. If he moved to the US side of the border, she was to let him pass.

Within the next hour she was ordered to back off. The State Department was taking over. They would provide a special agent to work on the Mexican side.

Agent Micovich was puzzled by this sudden change in direction. She was called back by a low-level operative and supplied with sketchy details, which made her all the more suspicious. This same pattern of events happened to her in Ohio.

The details said a special agent would be helping with the apprehension, but he would work on the Mexican side of the border. She had to let him handle all of the interrogation going forward. Weapons would still cross the border and her job was to follow the trail as details became known.

Agent Micovich had a suspicion she was being set up. She could sense the investigation was being manipulated. Her sixth sense was true. It was because of her overly zealous investigation. She was hindering other activity. Washington DC leaders had to rectify her fervor.

The special agent, an Indian tracker, had experience in Mexican affairs. He would extract information and supply her with the gun-runners plan. Micovich explained the news to Nicole and Kayla. They all wondered about the sudden change of plans.

Agent Micovich told them flat out. "We're into something big. Washington DC operatives don't usually interfere with an operation."

The Indian tracker was a bit mysterious. He had a way of showing up in times of peril.

Monica told a story to the agents about Richard Stern, when he was in Oregon.

She said, "Richard Stern told me an Indian saved his life in Oregon. She didn't believe him, because Richard was intoxicated. He said the Indian came out of nowhere and cut down a terrorist that was about to kill him."

Agent Nicole says, "This job can be spooky."

Kayla agreed with that. The agents had to just watch and monitor the conditions until they heard other orders.

The tracker made a phone call to Agent Micovich and mentioned meeting a Mexican gun runner. He told her that he was going back to buy a few automatics from the man and the man was going to introduce him to a sailor that works on a ship in Sandusky, Ohio.

He says, "Hold your position until I get back with you. I'll be shooting some arrows into their plans. I believe some guns are already in El Paso."

Monica asked, "Who are you?"

The phone went dead. Agent Monica looked at the other two agents. She was totally bewildered by the short narrative.

With all the sketchy news and it was somewhat baffling to the female agents. They waited for the Indian tracker to call or return from Mexico.

After phoning Agent Micovich the Indian tracker made his way across the Rio Grande. His stealthy style was the mark of a man that was cloaked in mystery.

In a private meeting in Le Masita, Mexico, the special agent took charge and worked his magic. He was dressed like a Comanche warrior. A bandana held back black, flowing hair. His worn buckskin shorts covering his waist and groin area gave him a surreal look of an Indian fighter. His muscular body had a quiver of arrows draped over his back. Even his speech was broken, as if he came from an Indian reservation.

The Indian tracker liked to use arrows and knives for self-defense. His reason was understandable. 'They don't make noise.'

Extracting information was just one of numerous tricks he had at his disposal. As he talked with the Mexican he pulled a bottle of Tequila out of his nap sack. They engaged in small talk for a while. The tracker served the Mexican national plenty of Tequila to help him flap his tongue. The gun runner spilled the beans and talked like a parrot. He told the tracker about the guns that were moving to Toledo and Sandusky.

"We have a used car lot in El Paso on Pershing Drive. Leave half the money with us today. You can pick up your guns there, when you pay the second half. This is where we unload our items. Our van moves the equipment north during the day.

He told the Indian to meet his sailor friend in Sandusky, Ohio at Shoreline Park in a couple days. His friend would explain the routine. How and where to board the sailor's ship would be told to him when he reached Sandusky, Ohio. His friend would introduce him to Brother M.

"He's a crew member of a tourist ship. If all went according to plans, the tracker would receive a special pass to have some ladies take care of him. If he gambled at the high stakes table, he could have fun with any of the girls on the ship.

"Now we have to sell you some nice guns. You won't need a bow and arrows any more. We have plenty of guns to buy at the right price. We have them locked up on the American side. Tell me right now do you have the cash."

The tracker pulled out two wades of hundred dollar bills from his waist band. The gun runner was impressed.

"I've got four thousand dollars for today. I want to see the guns. Tomorrow, I'll pay another four grand for fifteen Automatics, AR-15s. He put the money back in his waist band.

"No money until tomorrow, after I see the guns," said the tracker.

The gun runner says, "No, half the money today. Tomorrow you get the guns. This is how we do business hombre."

They were bickering about the arrangements.

The tracker asked him, "Where did you get all of these guns?"

He laughed, "Haven't you heard of 'Fast and Furious? We buy them in balk. Oh, we get so much from Zebra. He lets us get away with so much merchandise. He has a fine home in Washington DC.

The tracker asks, "Zebra, what's his real name?"

Although the tracker acted drunk, he had poured most of his drinks on the dirt floor.

The gun runner explains, "Give me another shot of Tequila. I'm just starting to negotiate with you, but you ask too many questions. I don't give away guns, money, or secrets."

The conversation between the tracker and the intoxicated man centered on his weapons experiences. The tracker said he fought the Russians in Afghanistan. The gun runner said he could build bombs and set IED's. His jihadist belief left him no choice but to fight for his religion.

The Mexican gun runner replied, "We're recruiting new members in America. We are finding a new supply of anti-American fighters. They can move our guns much easier."

The gun runner admitted hating Jews. He said 'maybe more than Americans.' Now he was starting to blab. The booze was causing him to wag his tongue.

He divulged key information. His men were carrying two cargos to defeat American imperialism, although he didn't specify exactly what they were carrying. It seemed one cargo was from the Middle East. The other was of his making.

The Indian tracker says, "I too learned how to make bombs."

The tracker quizzed him further believing he held a greater secret. At some point the tracker became disgruntled in the gun runner's attitude toward Jews and Americans. The inner mechanism set off the Indian. He could sense he was going to break the man's neck. What he wants to do using terrorism was quite maddening. The gun runner wouldn't say exactly what the other cargo was. However he said Zebra would help the Muslims defeat the Jews just like we took care of the American outpost in Benghazi, Libya. The tracker did his best to hold out for more information.

They were using john boats and pirogues to carry the arms across the Rio Grande.

"We sneak across the border at night. During the day we load the merchandise."

They kept the mission simple to avoid detection. Most of the time weapons were moved across the Rio Grande, but they did have an airplane to move heavy weapons.

"Now you talk to my arms dealer, Carlos. He might let you see some nice weapons. I think, maybe, fifteen is too high. I drank too much Tequila. I'm so drunk. I can't stand up."

Carlos told the tracker their method of moving guns north. It was the same story. The Indian tracker had enough information and was close to ending the conversation. Carlos said they transfer the guns across the Rio Grande to a truck which moves the weapons to a used car lot on Pershing Drive. The guns are then loaded into a van.

"We do it all under their noses at the Five Points used car lot. Now give me your money Indian. I want to see some green."

The Indian tracker had heard enough. He didn't waste any time when Carlos made a reckless move. Carlos started to pull a pistol out of his pants pocket. The tracker could tell by the tone of his voice that negotiations had been broken. It was time to react. He watched him for an instant and the shit hit the fan.

"You'll both see stars and Mars, said the tracker."

The Indian was lightning fast. He punched Carlos in the throat and knocked the drunk off his chair with one kick to the chest. Swooping back to Carlo, he grabbed him by the throat and held his thumb against the carotid artery. At the same time he placed him in a head lock until he went limp and dropped him to the floor. The drunken gun runner tried to reach for his weapon and the tracker snapped his neck with one sharp kick to the side of the face. His head turn violently to the right. He poured Tequila over them and lit a match. If they were still alive the fire would cover his brutality. The fire spread quickly and burned them to death.

He had a bounty of information. The Indian made his way back across the Rio Grande in a short span of time. He then called Agent Micovich to tell her what was coming her way.

"The guns are at the used car lot on Pershing Drive. It's called Five Points. They move them in a van. I'd say follow them and see where they're going."

He filled her in with an exact location to watch. He said it might be tomorrow. He wanted her to score a victory, because the people he met were connected to jihadists. She asked him if she could meet with the main weapons people he met. He had an answer for her.

"The way they acted toward America, you don't want to see them. They drink too much. I'm sure they're soaked in Tequila. You wouldn't want to meet them now, just trust me. I must say; they got burned by the Indian. Good bye, Agent Micovich."

The tracker was in a hurry to leave El Paso, so he couldn't be any longer on detail. He really didn't have anything more to add. This was his style. He told Agent Micovich he had another assignment to do up north. He was heading to Sandusky, Ohio.

Agent Micovich said, "Wait, I want to meet you."

The phone clicked and that was the end of the conversation.

Agent Micovich was disappointed. She really wanted to meet this mystery man. She told the other two agents what transpired.

She says, "Wow, agents, this guy comes across like a fireball. He makes his point and the phone goes dead."

The Indian tracker left the job to Agent Micovich to finish. She had the Five Points used car location pin pointed on her phone. She set up a plan to divide their roles in the action. This would be around the clock surveillance. Monica split the shift so she would work with both Kayla and Nicole. It would be twelve hours each.

Agent Nicole Swider and Jacobson would be alone for six hours each. Monica would relieve them so they could sleep. They looked for a location that would be ideal for keeping track of the used car lot. They had to watch for the van.

The time passed fast. The next day, sure enough, Agent Swider spotted the van. It pulled up and was being loaded with trunks. She reported the progress to Agent Micovich. Most likely the shipment of guns, if they were in the trunks, would travel north using the van just like the tracker said.

Agent Micovich and Jacobson followed the van from a distance when it left the used car lot. It passed through a number of states. From Texas it went through Oklahoma, Arkansas, Tennessee, and caught Interstate 64 in Kentucky.

Kayla called Nicole to inform her of their progress.

"Nicole, this is turning into a full day of travel. We called ATF when we crossed into Oklahoma. They're bringing in people to help. We'll keep you posted, bye."

From that point the agents linked with Interstate 77 heading north. It was tedious work. They had to find out where the trunks were going.

Monica and Kayla made bets with each other.

"Five bucks he's dropping the weapons in Sandusky," said Monica.

"That's what I was going to say. That's not fair. I'm not betting," said Kayla.

So far they had no proof he was carrying guns. State police were notified in each state to let the van continue. A helicopter and plane joined in to help follow the van. Agent Jacobson called in ATF officers to let them know they were following the van as far as it goes. They weren't going to hand off the main van.

After traveling from Texas to Ohio, they considered this mission their job. They were going to follow this guy to the end of the line.

The driver fueled his van a few times and made a long four hour pit stop in Kentucky. The agents were able to trade duties a few times and each was able to rest. They stayed back from the van and request a change in cars. Other FBI agents obliged as the chase moved along.

Before he entered Ohio he stopped at a rest area for another hour. He made it to Canton, Ohio. At that point he surprised the agents by turning east to Salem, Ohio. It was six o'clock in the morning.

It was hard to believe Salem, Ohio was the destination. They had traveled over 1700 miles. The sun was coming up when the driver opened the van doors to unload a trunk. The agents looked at their GPS and computer monitor to see exactly where they were.

A landmark, which had something to do with an underground railroad during the Civil War, marked the area. There was an old house off Elsworth Street where the driver met another man in a van.

Agent Kayla Jacobson asked the ATF officers to follow the new van and they would continue following the first van.

ATF officers followed the second van until he pulled in his driveway. They pulled in behind him with guns drawn. He surrendered after the officers revealed their identity. The trunk was loaded with weapons. An ATF officer called Jacobson and told her the news.

Monica and Kayla breathed a sigh of relief knowing that the mission was going as planned. They continued the journey. It took them north on Ohio Route 11 all the way to Route 84. He turned east again and drove to Kingsville, Ohio, where he stopped at a small public library parking lot. The Kingsville library was just opening.

    Kayla pulled their car into the Kingsville post office parking lot. It was well away from the library and afforded them a good field of vision to watch the action.

    A green van pulled in and the gun runner worked to unfasten the trunks. He opened the back van doors and the men unloaded first one and then a second trunk.

Kayla joked with Monica when she said, "Oh, They're book worms.

Monica says, "Look, his friend can't stay and read. I'll bet he's disappointed.

At that point a second and third unmarked ATF car drove by.

Monica and Kayla knew they were following. One ATF car followed the green van as it departed the library parking lot.

After the green van left, the other ATF auto pulled up next to the agents. She rolled down her window and identified herself as ATF Agent Dana Marie Bohatch. Both cars were side by side the US Post Office building. This was a perfect place to exchange greetings.

Agent Dana Bohatch said, "Here you go agents, I bought you girls coffee and breakfast sandwiches. We've been following and knew you two must be famished and exhausted. You two are setting a record for tailing a criminal."

Kayla replied, "Yep, we're going to nail them. Monica and I will stay with the lead van.

Monica and Kayla were most appreciative for her kindness.

Monica says, "Thanks, Dana. That was really nice. We're going to kick some ass."

Agent Bohatch said, "We'll be hanging with you. The state police are in the area also. We want you to know that he or they aren't going to get away."

Agent Micovich and Jacobson were grateful. They definitely were hungry and tired. Hours had passed since they grabbed some mediocre sandwiches and coffer along the way. They did get some sleep and exchanged driving duties; still it was a long journey. They wondered how long this trek could go on. They had been on the road for over a day with only a couple two hour breaks and several gas station stops. Agent Micovich told Kayla to call Agent Swider.

"Tell her to book a flight to Erie, Pennsylvania. Let her know where we are."

They followed the van north to Route 531. It went east to a Conneaut Township Park. At that point the driver unloaded the last trunk into an awaiting van. This was the end of the line.

ATF Agent Dana Bohatch ordered the drivers to stop and raise their hands. They were under arrest. Ohio State police cuffed both drivers.

Agent Micovich and Jacobson watched as the mission came to an end. It was a long day plus ten hours before the journey ended for the agents.

The operation was a huge success. ATF and Ohio Highway Patrol police nabbed the drivers in the act of transporting and transferring stolen weapons.

The fact that Northeast Ohio was becoming a hotbed of gun-running dealers was troubling. The people involved were a mixture of mafia, Al Qaeda, and homegrown radical jihadists that needed the weapons. They were working together.

ATF and FBI interrogators worked tirelessly looking for more clues. The enemy wasn't giving much information as to the reason so many arms were being moved north. It was assumed that money was one reason for the mafia to be involved. There was a divide between good and bad. No honest gun shops were involved with the deals. The interrogators learned valuable reasons to be wary. Al Qaeda had something planned for the Great Lakes region. Instructions with bomb making materials were found in the last trunk.

The criminal drivers, that were nabbed, were all connected for one reason. It was money. On the other hand Al Qaeda terrorists were suspected of buying and selling weapons for future attacks. The guns were coming from Mexico and passing through home grown outlaws. The underground syndicate was involved, but no leaders were found. Something diabolical was being developed.

Agent Micovich called Cliff Moses to tell him what had happened. She ended the discussion with a key statement.

"Cliff, somehow, I just know Richard Stern is going to be involved, if he isn't already."

Supervisor Moses replies, "Monica, that wouldn't surprise me one bit."

CHAPTER 14

A WEEK LATER

THERE WAS A buzz in the Cleveland FBI office when word spread that Agent Monica Micovich and her team of agents tracked the gun-runners from Texas to Ohio. The band of criminals rounded up broke cases that had been under investigation for years. Even Justice Department officials in Washington DC noted the extraordinary work the team of agents performed.

All this good news made Supervisor Moses' decision to transfer his top agent to El Paso a mistake in judgment. He should have untangled the personnel problem without transferring a superior agent. Although Moses' decision was done with good reason, he could have resorted to a less radical degree of punishment.

Heaven knows he tried to reconcile her crazy behavior. Agent Micovich forced his hand.

He was having second thoughts and trying hard to be objective about his hasty decision. With Agent Monica Micovich cracking rings of gun-runners and shining light on Al Qaeda intentions in Northeast Ohio, he believed she should be returned to Northeast Ohio.

Moses actually imprisoned himself in sorrow by sending her to El Paso. It was a harsh punishment for a top agent. He lamented and sulked as employees came to him with statements that highlighted Agent Micovich's exploits in El Paso.

El Paso, Texas seemed like the right move to make at the time. Agent Roman didn't help matters by added his own words.

He says, "Hey, boss, I bet you want Monica back."

Moses received a reprieve from FBI Headquarters in Washington DC. The DOJ was behind an alternative plan. They suggested Agent Monica Micovich had completed her work in El Paso, Texas. The message was clear. Her career would be enhanced by returning to Cleveland. An Email sent to Supervisor Moses' computer read like a hint more than a command.

<u>Wouldn't it make sense for the FBI bureau to send Agent Micovich and her team back to the Great Lakes Region? Cleveland was more conducive for a special agent.</u>

Agent Swider and Jacobson performed admiralbly. The team members came through their tour of duty with flying colors. They would be ordered to pack up and come back to Cleveland. Since the three agents had done exceptional investigative work by busting the gun runners and taking hundreds of guns off the street their work was essentially finished. The operation shifted to Ohio and opened up new doors to the enemies intensions up north.

After talking with Agent Monica the week before, Moses was feeling remorse. He realized his own miscalculation. A permanent transfer was like banishing Monica. It only made him feel woeful.

Fate changed the picture for Supervisor Moses. He received a message from heaven. His face lit up. Moses started reading the miracle message. It came from Department of Justice, Washington DC. The Washington FBI Bureau working in conjunction with DOJ believed a recall would be necessary for Agent Monica Micovich. JOD people had a political problem with Mexican authorities over the FBI's high handed intervention in Mexico. Obviously, they were referring to the Indian tracker's high handed tactics, but the rap was being pinned on Micovich. The Mexican drug lords that controlled areas in Juarez near El Paso applied political pressure.

The hierarchy in the White House and DOJ found their hands bound with Mexico's turmoil. The Micovich team was creating political noise and the music was off key. Something had to be done to address this political conundrum.

Her duty was to investigate the movement of arms across the border and across state lines. Intervention in Mexico was a problem. She went beyond the boundary.

During the Mexican investigation a serious breach happened. An agent attacked two Mexican citizens. This was beyond the intent of FBI involvement. It was assumed that a new FBI agent(s) had overreached and when beyond the limit of the mission.

Mexican territory had been compromised. The DOJ pinned the trouble on newly arrived Agent Monica Micovich, even though they were behind the Indian trackers involvement. The murder of two Mexican citizens, even though they were cartel members, was over the diplomatic line. This caused cross border agitation. Hostilities between the countries could easily escalate.

The message from Washington DC to Supervisor Moses said FBI agent(s) and (Monica Micovich) caused a political backlash with Mexico. Moses should submit a 'request for recall.'

Wasting no time Moses wrote down his reasons for requesting a recall authorization. He wanted to bring Agent Monica Micovich back to Cleveland, Ohio to resurrect cases she had handled in the past. Even if it was only a temporary return, she was a key component in his department. If that wasn't possible, maybe she could be moved to Erie, PA, Toledo, or Columbus.

Supervisor Moses believed there was more to the story. The Department of Justice was mishandling a number of cases. Their trustworthiness was dubious. They opened the door to release Agent Micovich. He wasn't going to cause any ripples on a lake of new found promise.

He wrote the words, <u>Fast and Furious</u>. This was the lynch pin that troubled the DOJ. Agent Micovich was tackling some of the ringleaders involved with gun running. During the investigation she was stepping on political toes.

Other departments knew the same. An ATF memo reported a job well done by assisting the FBI. ATF officials had high regard for their teamwork, but a dispute was still festering between DOJ and ATF officials. ATF Agent Dana Bohatch emailed Agent Micovich with her words of congratulation and expressed the same theory surrounding Fast and Furious.

Agent Dana was acting like a friend to Monica even though they barely knew each other. In her email Agent Bohatch cautioned Agent Micovich about the political upheaval in Mexico, especially around El Paso.

Moses made an assumption. He knew the Department of Justice in Washington DC was involved in 'Fast and Furious.' All the facts didn't bear out the truth about 'Fast and Furious.' A reward was offered for the arrest of men associated with a border agent's death. Maybe Agent Micovich was closing in on the men responsible for his death. The people receiving Fast and Furious guns came in contact with Agent Micovich and that was likely the reason for recalling his top agent. Agent Micovich was likely doing very well on the case and JOB officials were worried. That was his suspicion.

DOJ agents were moving guns to the Mexican war lords. For good or bad, he didn't care. He was bringing Agent Swider and Agent Jacobson back to Cleveland immediately.

Moses sent an Email with the recall request to the Washington DC Headquarters and it was approved the next day. Like the words 'Fast and Furious' DOJ officials wanted Agent Micovich off the investigation. She was being sent back to Cleveland for the good of the bureau.

Moses read the approved order to Agent Ron Roman. They were both elated by the news.

He told Agent Roman to relay this commandment to Agent Wright.

"Tell your partner to stick to women outside this department. Under no circumstances is he to involve himself with female agents in this department."

Agent Roman answered, "Yes sir!"

After Roman left his office, Moses was in deep thought about FBI rewards. It triggered a day dream. The first thing that popped into his head was Richard Stern. He was one guy who could mess up a sweet dream.

He mumbled, "How could Monica allow Stern to screw her?"

Moses was still distraught over the affair. His thoughts traveled to the money that Stern received. He was more trouble than a barrel of monkeys, if that's possible. Although he helped the FBI, he screwed the best agent he had, got her pregnant. On top of that the FBI paid him a huge reward.

His mind traveled to the great work Monica had done. She faced danger time and again. Paula and Monica took down the Washington DC terrorists. Monica was Stern's angel. She had to save Stern's ass end time after time.

Moses kept day dreaming. The walking time bomb was Stern. Always drinking and ending in the hospital, he wasn't normal. He hurt everyone around him. Stern was an albatross on Monica's career. He had to separate the two. Stern and Agent Micovich were too close to each other. His relentless problems with alcohol made him a liability. He had to find a way to keep her from tying up with him. It was Monica's child that would unite them again. That was sure to be a problem. She'll end up sleeping with him again.

He woke up from the daydream. He had to get Stern out of his head. Stern did get some treatment from time to time, but he wondered if it did any good.

Moses whispered, "That's why I sent Monica to Texas. I wanted her to get away from Agent Wright, but it was really Stern that bothered me."

Moses started thinking like a grandfather. Moses' thoughts turned to trying to reconcile things that happened between Wright and Micovich. Somehow Stern was involved. Moses knew Stern and Monica had lived in the same town and Stern was watching Monica's son, Michael. Well it was Stern's son too, it all added up to trouble. With Stern alone at Monica's house, that was trouble. Moses knew how Monica felt about her son. The boy meant everything to her and he was growing up with an unmarried mother.

Moses believed God had something to do with Monica's return. He called Monica to tell her the news; she was returning to Cleveland. They chatted for an hour. All the uproar was over between them. They didn't even bring up the subject of her relationship with Agent Wright.

Monica called Father Pete to let him know she was returning, a least for a while. Father Pete encouraged her to stay focused on Michael and herself.

He wisely repeated two things. She was blessed by God; He gave her a son. She should work to raise her child as a Christian. Though the two messages didn't need repeating, he had other words of wisdom. Her life's work was important and an inspiration to all.

"You have to follow the rules, Monica. God gave us the Ten Commandments. It's easy. We have to follow the rules."

She admitted her own lack of disciple at times, especially getting pregnant.

"Mr. Stern has to do the same. I know you pray for him. There is love in your heart. He can recover. He'll benefit from our prayers."

She wanted to believe her life was on track. All the turmoil was behind her. His words were music to her ears; however, her future tune would clang rather than ring and it would be tragic.

Chapter 15

Home and Water

RICHARD TOLD LINDSAY the good news, "I just landed in Cleveland. I'll be home in an hour or two."

Lindsay knew the approximate departure time of his flight from Portland, Oregon to Cleveland, which included a stop at Midway Airport in Chicago.

With all she had learned, she went out of her way to have something special made for her boss. She had spent some time and her money buying the right ingredients to make lasagna. The various selections of Italian spices were right, because it filled the air with an Italian aroma.

When he arrived, she was dressed in a well fitted tee shirt and jeans. She opened the door as he pulled into the driveway. The smile on her face was quite telling. She was happy to see him. The minute he hit the doorway, he could smell the aroma of Italian cooking.

"What's going on," he asked?

"Oh, I figured you'd like to have a home cooked meal after being on the road."

"You got that right, Lindsay. Well I thought I would ask you out for dinner."

They were overly polite to each other at first. Stern dragged his luggage into the house and told her he had a couple of beers on the plane to settle his nervousness.

She had bought red wine for herself, but decided to bring out two glasses, since she knew he was drinking. A toast was made to honor her and their first dinner together. This was a warm welcome and Stern loved it. In short order he was ready for another glass of wine.

Soon after the timid exchange of words, they were both relaxed and feeling at home. The first dinner together was going as planned. It wasn't exactly a date, but the occasion was somewhat of a transition from boss meeting employee to man meeting woman.

Their understanding of the situation was handled pretty well. As they ate dinner, Richard talked about all the events going on in Portland. He met a wildlife officer while driving along the Pacific Ocean. She expelled some information that he thought was quite useful. Learning some clues was the reason for the trip. The cost was a bit high. He spent a thousand bucks to travel.

In their short time together it was like they became close friends. Mostly, it was because of their emails and phone calls. What started out to be a friendly business meeting and a cautious social dinner turned into a bonding of man and woman. The flicker of a love light turned from caution to green. As the evening wore on a cozy friendship developed. As one teenage song put it, 'all intensions were good.'

They talked about the communications, emails from El Paso, Kansas, and Michigan. Richard could tell Lindsay was all aboard with the job. Even her perfume was making him notice her anticipation. After two more well filled glasses of wine, he was relaxed.

Like a professional secretary, Lindsay had notes and calendar dates in order.

"Mr. Heyer called, but I told him you were out of town. He hung up right away. All he said was OK."

Richard says, "He was looking for a referee."

Lindsay says, "I saw his Email to you."

Lindsay said she even emailed him back letting him know that <u>Mr. Stern wouldn't be returning until the end of the month.</u> The calls and email she was receiving covered many sports, so he told her to let him know when he was returning just as she had done.

"Butch Lauderback called. He left a message on your answering service. He said he got your letter. Then he called again. He asked me to tell you to call him when you get back."

Richard says, "Butch is the guru of softball. He assigns baseball and fast-pitch softball games to over a hundred umpires. He's a busy guy."

Stern wasn't used to having a person intercept his phone calls. He couldn't get over the fact that she was so perfect for the job. Miss Wagner was working out even better than he expected. She seemed to have the secretary job nailed down and her surprises kept coming.

Lindsay says, "Some woman called. She said she was a Painesville Commissioner's executive secretary. I think she said her name was Brenda Clark. I'm not sure what she wanted. She asked me who I was. I told her I was your secretary and she hung up without saying anything more. It was kind of strange. Actually, she was kind of rude."

Richard slightly dodged. He told Lindsay that he worked with Brenda Clark on a few government jobs and thing didn't go well. He said they were almost getting close in a relationship, but it fell apart when he was drinking.

"She had a thing for younger men. That was a problem for us too."

Lindsay says, "Monica Micovich emailed and said she might be coming back to the Cleveland FBI office."

Lindsay didn't like that email one bit. She didn't say anything more. Her thought was a little possessive. She knew that Richard and Monica had a son. She didn't want Monica making a move on Richard.

After dinner they chatted about shifting the office furniture and sprucing up the bachelor pad. He was feeling good, almost in the party mood. His temptation was to go out. Instead, Lindsay suggested they have another glass of wine.

One of the most interesting topics to come out of the Oregon trip was the newspaper clipping of a submarine sighted in the Columbia River. People in Portland expressed surprise at seeing a periscope pop up in the river. The newspaper article suggested that the partygoers were full of alcohol and were creating a suspenseful story. This was something of a revelation for Stern, since he knew of the Middle Eastern men diving around the same area.

Richard didn't want her to over react to the submarine and Middle Eastern men as he had done the same thing many times. False hopes had ended up wasting money in the past.

"Lindsay, that dinner was supreme. Would you like to go for a stroll around town?"

She was all for that. Her mood was changing in many ways. Free rent, an interesting job, and an older guy that seemed to like adventure, he was awfully contagious. She was willing to take a step forward and see where the chips would fall.

"I'm sure you read some of my files. I'll say this. As you already know, I can get into some serious trouble. You know how guys can be. We screw up here and there. The Fairport police kind of know that."

Lindsay abruptly kings his statement.

"You get into trouble everywhere you go. I can see that. I'm surprised you're still alive. I'll have to be your guiding light. One thing you have to know, I'm not a big drinker."

This was the person. She wasn't a big drinker. Stern was looking for a girlfriend that didn't drink. Here she was, Lindsay. His mind was whirling. The two friends were on a mutual understanding, but that would change in a dramatic way.

Lindsay says, "You really do need a secretary, because we're on to something big. You can be famous. At least I think we're on to something big"

She didn't stop. It was almost like she could see some of the things on his mind.

"If you want to be an umpire, a photographer, a writer, that's ok by me. I have this strange feeling. You're going to make serious money and I'm your secretary, so that means I will be getting a piece of the pie."

Lindsay had read plenty of Stern's exploits. She was already trained to ignore the foolishness of a drunken man, though she wouldn't put up with an abusive man.

Richard asks, "Let's go for a walk, I mean will you go for a walk with me?"

"Sure."

Before they left the house, Richard had a shot of blackberry brandy to mellow out the dinner. She watched him down the drink.

The fresh air was needed. They headed north toward Lake Erie.

She says, "I know I can help us make some serious money. You don't have to hide your problem. You drink too much. I read all about the hospitals. You have to control yourself."

Richard says, "I tried all the programs. Met with the shrinks, went to AA meetings, hospitals, recovery plans, you name it, I've probably done it. This may sound strange, but I can honestly tell you what does work."

"Tell me."

"Water and God!"

Lindsay asks, Water?"

"Yep, anyone that asks God to help them, He will. You're blessed by water when you're baptized. When we're at a low point, we have a drink, but God will intervene if we let him. He says, 'drink water.' You don't have to drink coffee or high energy drinks, but you do have to drink plenty of water every day. It is a simple formula. If you're drinking alcohol, drink water."

Stern was preaching and became more scientific. The doctors always gave him liquids to replenish his depleted water content. Water was essential. His personal physician told him to take a vitamin every day and drink plenty of water if he continued to drink.

"I'm sorry if I'm starting to talk stupid."

"No, you aren't"

"Lindsay, why do alcoholics do the same thing over and over?

Lindsay says, "I know them. I married one. I've been to AA meetings. I've seen their actions. Doing the same thing over and over is insanity. Isn't that an Einstein theory?"

Richard says, "Could be. Actually, we all do the same thing over and over. Like war for example. We have a cause to fight for and we fight. It seems good at the time. I'm a veteran of the Viet Nam War.

People have called it a conflict. At the time we thought it was right, because the president says, 'it's a military action; we're stopping the spread of communism.' People get tired of war. They turn negative and that runs the political machine. I remember how bad it was. If you were a returning Viet Nam veteran, it wasn't that nice. I don't want to say anything more. Oh, I'll finish this way. At the time it seemed like most citizens were against war and took it out on our military."

Stern was implying the facts to a woman that didn't live in the same era. As with many veterans of foreign war, there was a cultural change. Each war had different types of veterans.

The scary thing about defending America's freedom was the realization that America didn't have the money to be everywhere. War was expensive. Fighting and defending so many nations was putting a huge burden on the worker. America was running out of money.

"One of these days I'll say, 'let's go to the vets club.' I want you to meet some of my friends. Ever since I started going to the VFW Post in Painesville I started saying this sentence. 'Let me tell you a true story.' It's funny. You'll understand when it happens."

He had a small flask in his pocket and downed more shots of Blackberry Brandy. He started talking away. With those shots under his belt he related a few true stories. He started to talk about his own experiences. He was a navy guy. Lindsay listened like a wife with an ear for her husband.

"One of these days I'm going to take you to Gettysburg. You'll see some historic sites. Something else I have to tell you. At one time I thought they were going to build a casino in Painesville Township at the old Diamond Shamrock property. It's next to Fairport Harbor. I shouldn't bring that up, because Brenda Clark and I were working on that deal. I'll say it this way. She and I ran into some bad people and some decent people who wanted to do the right thing. Well, I've been with some very nice girls over the years."

Lindsay says, "You're with one now."

"Yep, I know that."

Richard had taken his previous girlfriend to Dayton on a weekend get a way. He had such a good time; he didn't want to return. He wanted to stay with her in Dayton.

"Come to think about a good time, maybe we should go to Wright Patterson Air Force Base in Dayton, Ohio. That's where they have the Martians. Did you know they have the outer space people there?"

"They do?"

"Lindsay, let me tell you a true story."

Richard explained the story to her.

He says, "I get a rush out of the past. Every time I travel; I pick up a little piece of history. Did you ever hear about the aliens crashing in Roswell, New Mexico?

She didn't know the story. Richard explained it to her. There may have been a cover up. The incident was studied by numerous groups. Things were gathered and flown to Wright Patterson Air Force Base. It's not really in Dayton. It's in Fairborn, Ohio near Dayton.

Richard says, 'Stories just seem to mushroom. In the case of the Viet Nam conflict I say that was one huge blunder. Let me really change the subject and go in the opposite direction, like making love. We're obviously not insane if we do it over and over."

Stern was feeling pretty good from the brandy. He was overly talkative, but making sense most of the time. Lindsay went along with the subject and threw out a message that really turned Richard's head.

"No, we haven't.

She slowed down and finished her thought.

"I mean we haven't done it yet."

Richard caught the gist of her words. It was clearly a future reference.

He says, "This walk is really doing some good."

Lindsay says, "I think you're right."

CHAPTER 16

GOOD INTENSIONS

THE NEXT DAY Lindsay made an Irish lunch. Corn beef with a side of cabbage, because she was part Irish, so it fit the mood. It was a late lunch and they went for a walk to the beach with a belly full of food. Interesting, they left the house with good intensions, but the end of the walk developed into quite a mystery. The route they took was east and west for a spell. They passed around the park and then through the park to Second Street. On Vine Street they passed by his mother and father's old homestead. By the time they got near the beach it was six o'clock in the evening. The sun was setting over the US Coast Guard station.

"I know you may have read this, the enemy was here."

Lindsay asks, "Is this a true story."

"Lindsay, we're going to find out something one of these days and I'll say we hit the jackpot."

Richard was in the mood to stop for a frosty. He meant for a brew at the lake side pub, which was insight.

"Let's stop at the Sunset Harbor for a brewski."

"You have a brewski and I'll have water."

"One of these days I'll get you to spit a beer with me."

"Maybe! Wine is fine, but I wouldn't hold your breath on the brewski. You know; I'm not a big drinker.

Richard pointed back to the old street as they reached the beach road.

"We were on Prospect Street. Most of Fairport's early citizens settled toward this end of town. They must have been big time fishermen back then. Do you see why they built the lighthouse?"

Lindsay says, "No, but I just know you're going to tell me a true story."

"Lake Erie can kick up fast. It isn't always a calm lake. One day you'll read about some boater making a mistake by being out on the lake when high winds are posted."

He asked her to look back.

"Think about this, Lindsay. The lighthouse on the hill was being used as a real lighthouse back in the late eighteen hundreds and they built a new lighthouse in the nineteen hundreds."

They stopped for a time to watch the waves roll across the shore.

He told her story after story about fishing on the US pier where Grand River meets Lake Erie. He went on with ice fishing and then reverted to his childhood days.

"We had to play on the ice."

Richard went on to explain one episode after another.

"When the ice broke up on Lake Erie we had a ball. I mean this was when I was a kid. My friends and I would sail on large floats of ice. They were ice pads twenty feet long and ten feet wide. It was cool to jump on these ice flows. They were all along the shoreline. We'd crash into each other by pushing our icebergs using long pieces of driftwood. To stand on these huge mounds of ice and push along was like you owned a boat. Sometimes, when we rammed the other guy, the ice boat, it would break apart and then he would have to scramble or swim. There was a race to get back to the beach. It never failed. Someone always fell in the water and we'd hustle to my mom and dad's home to dry off."

For Richard it was becoming increasingly clear; he had a new girlfriend rather than just a secretary. She mostly listened to his stories, but the lake was so captivating. She was more interested in the sailboats and the nuclear power plant blowing off plumes of steam.

She says, "This is really a beautiful beach. I should have come here once in a while."

He says, "We better move on. I can keep telling you true, true, stories. Like when I was gill netting with Captain Raymond Nelson. He fished me out of the Honey Hole Club to be one of his deck hands. What an experience that was."

By the time they made it to the restaurant the place was filling boaters coming off the lake. A big game was on TV. Some of Richard's old friends from high school were seated in the dining area. They joined with two of his friends, Ronnie Curliss and Sherry Curliss Fisher. Richard dated Ron's sister many years ago.

After Richard introduced Lindsay as his girlfriend, they all started sharing small talk. The girls sort of kept a two way conversation as the men gabbed about the past.

The men talked fishing as if they were out on the lake. And the beer was flowing. It was a little boring for Lindsay and Sherry, but they played along.

Ronnie says, "Let's move to the open gazebo for a view of the lake."

They moved to a table with a better view of eastern Lake Erie. They could see Painesville Township Park and the floating red buoy in the water.

The restaurant had the succulent aroma of deep fried fish coming from the kitchen. When the waitress came over with a second beer, Lindsay was all for having an appetizer with her water. Sherry second that plan. She'd have the same.

Then the fun began to happen. Lindsay looked around the gazebo to see if she knew anyone. She remembered that some of the Lake County deputy sheriffs had boats moored at the club. The sweeping scan startled her for a moment. She didn't stare. Instead she turned to Sherry and asked if her hair was messy.

Lindsay picked a mirror from her purse and spied on a couple men seated in the corner of the dining area. She was sort of certain they were at the Oasis Club one time or another. She thought maybe one of them came to see Abdul Madhi, but she didn't want to say anything to Richard until she was absolutely positive. More likely, she wasn't going to say anything, because they looked like they were Middle Eastern men. She was afraid he might say something crass because of his drinking.

The bar talk was getting louder as the two men reminisced days gone by. Sherry and Lindsay were quite content after the waitress brought over the shrimp appetizers and a third round of beers. Ronnie was actually hoisting a fourth cold Bud to his lips when he spotted an unusual object on the lake. Though it was at least a half mile or more away, far to the left of his view, Ronnie exclaimed with excitement.

"Holy crap, it's a dam sub."

Almost in unison, Richard, Lindsay, and Sherry followed his finger pointing to the lake.

Ronnie kept pointing with his finger extended. Out to the east something came up and started to dive. Richard and Lindsay looked at Ronnie and then turned, but their view was blocked by patrons passing by.

The Sunset Harbor restaurant was in a festive mood. The size of the crowd kept everyone close together. Some people were at the bar, some were watching the college football game and others were out on the deck.

Ronnie jumped from his chair. In his exhilaration he jostled the table and almost knocked over the empty beer bottles. Like an NFL linebacker, as he tried to race for a better view. He weaved through a party of young adults.

"Watch it, man," said the agitated patron, who was obviously a Michigan State fan.

Typical of his manner, Ronnie retorts, "That's what I'm trying to do, bub."

Ronnie bobbed his head and moved sideways for a better view. A sign temporarily blocked his sight. He was still too far away from the open area to see. The restaurant crowd didn't help as he worked around them to see the submarine. By the time he made it to the row of large cement blocks the object was gone.

He held his position for a few minutes thinking the sub would come back up. The two men in the corner were watching him, which made the entire event more interesting.

Lindsay had a bead on them and Ronnie. She was starting to connect the dots. The one man was the person holding the wet suit outside the Oasis Club, but he shaved his beard. Positively identifying the person would be a big help to Richard. Again she was fearful to say anything.

It dawned on her to check her purse. Inside her purse were her sunglasses. They'd probably be enough of a disguise and she could walk over to the area near them.

The idea was a good one. It might have worked, but Ronnie turned and walked back to join his friends. His eyes were glassy and Sherry commented.

"You almost pushed that guy's girlfriend over. What was so important?"

"Sis, you have to visualize this. I think I saw a submarine," said Ronnie.

Richard looked at Ronnie with inquisitive eyes.

He could recall something FBI Agent Monica Micovich said while talking on the phone. She mentioned that an Al Qaeda internet transmission from Nigeria was intercepted. 'Some terrorist group, maybe the Egyptian Islamic Brotherhood, was planning a water mission. They were using john boat and pirogues along the Rio Grande.' At the time Stern wrote the name pirogues on the inside of his wrist. Richard remembered Monica turning to see if he was listening. He was listening, but acted like he was drawing pictures with Michael.

Stern thought for a moment and said a mouth full. Normally tight lipped about things like this, he was openly excited and slightly drunk.

"You never know, Ron. I was in Oregon just a little while ago."

Lindsay cut him off.

"Richard, look at the time, we have to go."

Lindsay had one thing on her mind. Get Richard out of the restaurant and tell him about the guys sitting in the corner.

At this point there were lots of things to talk about in private.

CHAPTER 17

NEW CLUES

A NOTHER WEEK PASSED by and a timeout from a busy day was on tap for the bounty hunter and his girlfriend. They were assembling notes to draw a crude picture of the Lake Erie submarine. Although they never saw the sub, they were relying on Ronnie's visual.

"Let's take a walk and unwind."

Lindsay said she would have to freshen up. It didn't take her long. Out the door they go, following a similar pattern taken days ago. Working their way northwest, they crossed in front of the Marine Museum. The towering lighthouse had a few visitors walking around the upper level.

Down the steep High Street hill, Lindsay assumed the eventual destination would be the restaurant.

Sunset Harbor Bar and Grill was filling up with afternoon diners. Fairport Harbor's shoreline restaurant was becoming the hotspot. High above the eatery heading due south was the remains of the old Diamond Shamrock headquarters building. A steep bank surrounded and contained the calm Lake Erie waters.

Restaurant owners, Tony, Tom, and Toni Novak looked like they were about to leave, but Toni came back to help Fran at the bar.

Happy-go-lucky patron, Bob Boyle, couldn't resist cueing up a bet with Stern on the football game. A few more wagers were made with Stern after hearing his outlandish prediction. Ten more minutes passed and Stern was joined by his old friend, Sean Joseph. Joseph was a security guard for a local hospital. He had a catch-all eye for strangers. He could pick out a con man in a second.

Mr. Joseph says, "Hey, Richard, I'm watching out for you.

Stern knew the reference. He had ended up at the hospital over the years for trying to douse his nervous condition with alcohol. Richard down played the comment.

"You're not going to see me in there. I'm done going too far.

Lindsay couldn't help, but add her own two cents.

She whispers to Richard, "No you're not. You can go too far, just don't do it with booze."

Obviously, she wasn't talking about excessive drinking.

She had hinted more than once that a loving time was approaching. He held steady. Anticipation was building a fire. The fruit on the vine was ripe and he could feel the heat of being inside of her.

A couple walked in and sat close to them. They were Bob Beardslee and Charlotte Schuttpelz, who were waving to Richard to get his attention.

Richard and Lindsay sat near the lakeside window hoping to see a periscope or the sub. They finished ordering dinner and were having a great time just being together. Richard pointed to a poster on the wall. Singer Jimmy Brymer was the evening entertainment.

"I know him," said Richard.

In walked talkative Bob Boyle, who was a tall stocky man. Richard ran into him at the Morley Library where they spoke about the local government. Mr. Boyle had some differences with the Fairport Harbor bureaucrats over a dilapidated restaurant that was next to his house.

Boyle voiced his position to Stern, "They had to do something with Good Eyes. The old tavern was an eyesore and it was infested with skunks, mice, rats, and only God knew what was in there. He didn't hold his fire when attending village council meetings. Tony Scheiber and his demolition crew finally knocked it down, after the persistent urging of Boyle.

Mr. Boyle wasn't a man of few words. He had stories to tell and vetted them with a strong emphasis on physical punishment, if people didn't heed his warning. His hard-hitting description of local events pointed to an interesting subject, which Richard and Lindsay found fascinating. Boyle ran into Middle Eastern characters one day.

Bob said he was fishing on the bank off Painesville Township Park when he was challenged for his fishing area by two swimmers with olive colored wet suits.

"I told them, 'No swimming here, boys. He referred to them as 'boys' even though they were men in their twenties. Bob was the elder and he demanded respect.

"They were rag heads, excuse my French. I mean I think they were Arabs. They didn't listen. I said it again, 'no swimming here, boys. The one guy got on his cell phone and started quacking away in Arabian. I don't know why he was upset. I could tell his bullshit talk was about me. What he was saying; it didn't bother me. Piss on them, I was there first. The one dressed in the wet suit started wading into the water. It looked like they were going to challenge me. They didn't get it."

It appeared to Mr. Boyle he would have to reinforce his statement.

He says, "Anyhow, my fuse was lit. Normally, I'd give ground to friendly folks, but you know I was there first."

Lindsay says, "Maybe they didn't understand you."

Mr. Beardslee and Charlotte Schuttoelz were listening. Bob's story had a connection to his Blackmore Road nursery.

Mr. Beardslee broke into the conversation and said "I'm seeing foreigners driving down my road. They'd stop at the end of the road and scan the lake. They looked like Middle Eastern guys and I know most of the Mexican nursery workers. These guys weren't nursery workers."

Mr. Beardslee continued to listen after apologizing for butting in.

Bob says, "Hey, no problem."

Bob says he wasn't going to put up with them moving in on his territory. He proceeded to put his fishing pole down and walk over to the guy with the cell phone.

"Let's just say, I got my point across, when I shoved the cell phone in his mouth. I bloodied his lip. The swimmer and his friend left."

Bob was satisfied with his point and went up to the bar for a beer.

Richard comments in a soft voice, "You know, Lindsay? The more we look for clues, the clues end up right in front of us. Something tells me those two guys Mr. Boyle confronted are."

Stern paused and then stops before saying more.

Lindsay asks, "Maybe terrorists?"

Richard tamps the question, "I told you—don't jump to conclusions. I'm not going that far, yet, but I'm thinking something else. Maybe they're arms smugglers, you know, like Mafia."

Lindsay asks, "Is it time to contact the FBI?"

"No, I don't want to pull the trigger yet. We still have to gather more clues. It wasn't that long ago, some kids found dynamite washed up on the store in this area."

The very idea that terrorists or arms smugglers could be infiltrating the area sort of fit the emails from Monica. For all reasons the unsolicited news seemed to fit a bizarre sequence.

"Nothing is out of the question at this point."

Miss Schuttoelz asked, "Hey, mister, weren't you the one who bought some things from my garage sale?"

"Yes, Charlotte, I thought I recognized you. You were at Mr. Beardslee's place. I've got a million dollar memory. See, I even remembered your first name."

She says, "I remember something you said. Aren't you a bounty hunter?"

Stern was dumfounded by her remark. He must have been intoxicated when he was touring the garage sale circuit. He could have been boasting about hunting down terrorist.

At this point Lindsay jumped in, "He goes overboard. He talks about becoming a bounty hunter. It's like a childhood dream of his."

Charlotte was positive he said that.

"What do you do for a living, Richard?"

"If I said bounty hunter, I was just joking, I'm a referee and umpire."

Then Richard had to add a little more history.

"I do photography and write for magazines on occasion. The amateur bounty hunting story always comes up in my articles."

The question Schuttoelz had asked started Stern thinking. She was certain he said bounty hunting was part of his secret life. Stern needed to close the discussion.

"Little money-makers I call them."

Lindsay also wanted to turn off the facets of Stern's life and she pitched in.

"He made a bundle writing for a magazine. He pretends his life is that of an informer for the government. I catch him once in a while living the dream. Watch what you say around this guy. He'll turn you into a magazine character."

Charlotte says, "Well, I'd like that. I had a dream of going to France with my friend, Jennifer. You should write about the Garden of Elyse."

The chatter was getting out of hand. Lindsay and Richard, almost in unison, agreed to finish dinner and make tracks.

Once in the parking lot, they walked up the hill to Prospect Street and down East Street to his home.

"Richard, we're doing pretty well, wouldn't you say?"

"My dear, we are doing well."

CHAPTER 18

HEART GROWS FONDER

W AS THE COUNTRY falling apart? Was the country being invaded? Bad signs had been appearing each year as the nation's debt problem continued to soar. The past two presidents were running up a debt far beyond all past presidents. The industrial exodus to China wasn't helping the situation. China was supplying the credit and stealing the jobs.

Richard says, "I'm shock at the way this country is going. Look, the computer ad is advertising for gay marriage."

The family structure in America had taken on a different meaning. Marriage was reduced to Adam marrying Adam and Eve marrying Eve. The latter was a fatherless marriage. For Richard Stern it was stupid. Marriage between a man and man or woman and woman was merely a partnership for tax and medical insurance. Maybe it wasn't a big deal, but Richard Stern thought the whole Homo-Lesbo union was goofy. He pondered these questions with Lindsay.

"Lindsay, I want you to answer these questions. Why do men attract men and women attract women? I mean how could civilization survive?"

"Don't worry, honey, I'm not that way.

Richard says, "Neither union can have children," said Stern.

Lindsay replies, "I'm not that way."

Richard says, "I know that."

Lindsay says, "How do you know, I'm not a lesbian?"

"You're too pretty and you were married."

She wanted to have a baby. After going through a rotten marriage, she was happy she didn't get pregnant. Now she was growing older, although she wasn't really old at all. To be childless she thought, wasn't normal. She moved close to Richard. Her perfume radiated the area around the computer.

As she moved very close to him, she massaged his neck and shoulders. He spun around and eased out of the chair. Once on his feet they were face to face. The momentum was building. He was melting like a candle. His attraction to her at this point was riveted on her eyes. Love making was a spontaneous incident. It had been on his mind and they had hinted at tearing down the barriers. Now it was happening.

He looked at her, inviting her to pull them together. The moment seemed to mesh as they faced each other. Closer and closer they slowly moved almost nose to nose. Desire swept over him. She was ready to release hesitation. Slowly their lips met. The timing was explosive. He was headed for the moon as her breasts hit. He felt her tongue snake into his mouth.

They engaged in a strong kiss. She was no longer an employee. The pair worked at each other for about a minute maybe two. Finally, they broke free.

"I'm sorry," said Richard, "You're so beautiful."

She put a finger on his lips.

"It's OK. The timing is right."

Smiling, Richard says, "I can tell we're starting to get along."

"Yeah, I guess so," said Lindsay. Her heart was pounding.

Richard says, "You're a winning combination, Lindsay. You have the smarts, beauty and inner strength. "We're definitely becoming a serious team.

Lindsay says, "Let's move to the couch and work on the team approach."

She let him go farther and farther as he had her tee-shirt off. He was fully at attention and she could feel the readiness on her leg. His hands wondered to the hooks holding the mounds in place. Although a little clumsy, he managed to free her suppleness. They were smooth, ample as he had imagined.

Lindsay found his manhood. The first experience was moving like lightning. Positive and negative charges attracted as they worked on each other. His tongue found each nipple and a sweep bought out a moan. The tempo was fast moving to her belt. He was desperate to unfasten the next surprise.

She asked him to stop.

"Richard, we can't go that far. We have to stop."

Disappointment slapped his face and he obeyed to protect her. He wasn't going to do anything without her consent. He made that mistake once and it ended up being a terrible experience for the mother.

She says, "Don't be mad, I'm not ready, please understand.

CHAPTER 19

CODE NAME ZEBRA

S LEEPLESSNESS WAS A constant problem for Mr. Stern. He tried many types of sleeping aids, but they didn't always work. He turned to old faithful, which were several beers and a couple shots of blackberry brandy. In the aftermath of watching a news cast he fell asleep.

During the sleep cycle a dream produced a mysterious quandary in his mind. *Who was responsible for the downward spiral in America? The finger pointing was aimed at each party.* There were guilty parties on both sides of the aisle.

When he awoke, his last dream was about the Tea Party. He was at a convention as guest speaker. Consumed by the government ineffectiveness, why hasn't the president brought both parties together?

He fell asleep again and returned to the same dream.

At the podium he cried out the words 'hope and change.'

'It's been years now and I see only losers, I mean pirates in the White House. They're robbing us. They're robbing our children and grandchildren. The pirates had set sail with the new president. So who is the guy sitting in the White House? Is he like the pirate Blackbeard?

'His script, 'hopes and change,' was supposed to repair a broken economy. Instead he fired empty promises. He is continuing to campaign and living large on the taxpayer's dime.'

He woke with the dream became imbedded in his memory bank.

The next night he was going through the same drill. Finally dosing off, he could visualize another Tea Party speaker.

'His speeches were like cannonballs fired from a tall ship. They hit the mark, which is the Republican Party. The Tea Party must come together like we did in 2010.'

Stern woke up thinking about the health of the country. There was no stopping his plunder. He is spending the treasures of America. Trillions were being robbed as far as the Tea Party was concerned. Over and over again, when would it end? The American worker is being pushed into the sea.

Lindsay woke to noise. Downstairs, she could hear Richard. It was so early in the morning. She could hear him rattling pans in the kitchen sink. She dosed off for a moment. It was morning when she came down in her bathrobe.

"I heard you washing the dishes."

"Sorry about that. I had a crazy dream. Lindsay, remember hope and change; that was an old campaign slogan."

Lindsay says, "Yeah, I remember. We can translate that to hopeless and disdain."

"Listen, I had a dream last night and a lot of things stuck in my mind this morning."

He went on telling her some of the things he remembered.

"Maybe I was the speaker at a Tea Party rally. The country was suffering from a plague of bad ideas. I saw the pirates in the White House."

He continued his desperate attempt at remembering the entire dream. He saw change. Stern saw a glimmer of hope in the 2010 election. Hope was with the TEA PARTY. The Tea Party had risen like Jesus from the tomb. The grass-roots organization was putting a scare into both parties. The Tea Party hook was slowly being cast into Congress. The election hook pulled out the dead wood politicians. The replacements had conviction. This was only a start. In order to heal America's problems a new leader had to be called into action.

As he recalled two nights of dreams other parts came into view.

"Events were being planned by enemies far from our town. I think it was El Paso, Texas and Oregon. These foreign forces were invisible like a submarine. The depth of a hostile invasion was coming unnoticed to the Great Lakes. I'm serious."

Lindsay says, "I'm going to take a shower. You can fill me in after I get dressed."

Richard was racking his brain, because he knew there was a piece of the dream that would help them earn a reward.

Nothing became of the nightmarish dream. His sub conscience was working overtime, but not producing an answer.

A few days later they sat next to each other in the office and he told her of another dream.

"Last night a dream of fishing on Lake Erie danced in my head."

Lindsay says, "That shouldn't be anything new."

His fascination with trolling for walleyes and bottom fishing for perch was the start of a dream. A hazy dream erupted.

Stern couldn't remember the entire dream, except for a tiny bit. He spoke like he was in a trance. His sub conscience was playing tricks, but it revealed two words—Zebra and Submarine. It was almost painful for him to recall more information.

"I'm not sure of the dream. I'm asking you. What does it mean? Zebra and Submarine, I think it's a code."

Lindsay says, "You need to relax. Let's go to the couch again and I'll massage your body. I'll force you to remember."

He asked, "How?

"I'm going to kiss you on the lips and force my body on you."

"She was trying to start his engine and she did. Richard enjoyed the magic of the moment. She was passionate. It was quite a stir. He wasn't ready, but savored her move.

"Did it work?" She asked.

"No, but let's try again." He said.

The romance in the office was light-hearted without going overboard. On occasion the touching and grabbing pulled them off the job. They got back to business, but the relationship of boss and secretary was taking on a new meaning.

The next day as they were working together in close proximity to each other he asked her the magic question.

"Will you help me remember my dream again?"

She did it again. This time the kiss was longer. She was thrusting her mounds forward.

Richard says, "I'm really happy we're working together, Lindsay. You've extended my thinking and picked up the business plan. I can tell you: I'm growing."

She could take that comment in a couple ways. He went on to tell her more.

He says, "You're the best person one could have for this job."

She says, "I can detect something alright. You're definitely growing."

Lindsay told him to be prepared for a girlfriend who liked having rich, hot fun, order, and cleanliness. She got to the point of her style and it was frank.

"I've got to teach you some things. We're not two bachelors. First, we're going to tidy up this place. You're stacking papers and notes on the desk without any order. And the bookkeeping is outdated, no ledger listings for March. Don't worry. I'm really glad I took this job. This stuff can be fixed. I have to have some control over you."

This was the first hint she was taking control. She was leading him along.

He says, "We're building trust. I can feel your body move me. It's a male thing."

"Yeah, I know, you're horny."

Richard kind of knew she would take control. She had that take charge mentality. Take the bull by the horns, muscle it to the ground. She was going to be on top. He knew that could happen at any time.

Richard says, "I'm on the go, maybe too much."

"Yes, you need to slow down. You don't sleep well. I said you don't keep good books and you need a woman's touch to help you see how excellence is rewarded."

Richard says, "I've never had a woman as an employee. I guess I'd never had known how wonderful the operation could be until you arrived. Now it looks like the facts are coming at me all the time. Without you I never would have known."

Lindsay stood up and looked at him.

She says, "I'm going to find a way to make you relax."

The clock on the wall was at eleven. The morning sunshine hit the melon colored drapes she had bought to spruce up the office. The warm glow seemed to predict a tender moment. If not natural, it was surreal. They faced each other as equals. The partnership was transitioning into heavenly friendship. It was time to move to greater heights. She pressed the go button. The opportunity to expand a romantic horizon was now at half throttle.

Almost in unison they moved close. The gentle hug was greatly appreciated.

"I want you, Lindsay."

Another look and she closed her eyes as if inviting a firmer reaction. The kiss led to a trance. A French kiss on the neck was inviting ecstasy. She welcomed his fire. Summoned was the male upshot as he grew. She felt his reaction as they held each other. She wanted it and dropped her guard. They didn't stop. Continuing to kiss was turning up the heat. Hearts were racing at full throttle. He adjusted his position to feel her left breast. The clothes were in the way.

Quickly the temptation to explore and dig deeper was inviting. There was a fantastic bond brewing. Pressing closer she moved his hand to the cotton line holding her jogging pants. The sign to go beyond was eminent. He pulled on the string and the cotton pants fell to the floor. As he reached down, he could tell she shaved. His hands moved above to lift the tank top over the breasts. She had no problem helping him. She grabbed his head to move him over the mounds.

She was equally busy. Removing his shirt, undershirt and unfastening his belt. She searched with two hands for the hook and zipper. Wandering hands were met with a panting sound and soft murmur. The sound of passion was soft. The heat was on.

They locked in a tight hold. Their own desires were approaching a boiling point. She worked at his shorts as he carefully massaged perfection. His lips released each nipple one by one. The suppleness of warm jutting mounds excited him. She helped him kick the clothes out of the way. He was holding the two rockets. Her lower boy part was ready to be massaged. She moved her feet apart and pushed him down to his knees.

The office floor was hardly a place to continue the frolic, but it didn't matter. The carpet was thick and soft. It wouldn't have mattered if it was concrete in this case. All the stars were aligned. Loneliness and anticipation was over. The passion stoked fire. He worked her to a boiling point. The red warning flag was dropped in favor of green as if it was a road race. Stopping wasn't in the equation at the moment. Excitement enveloped the two grappling adults as she pushed him to continue. The loving couple had reached a mutual agreement to go farther. The tempo escalated as his fingers brought her to fulfillment for the first time. He was rising to find lips as she exploded. The next play was to fully inject the next temptation. Now they were off the chart. Like young teenagers groping for the right spots, desire was dictating the moment.

It was tantalizing for Richard. She was overly excited and happy. He wanted to take control. The time had come to plunge into her nest.

As he tried to find the mark, Lindsay was having second thoughts. She wasn't ready to go so far so fast. With concern in the back of her mind she could feel him pulling her around to be on top. He was successful. Her warm body parts were exposed. She wasn't prepared for total consummation. His continuous attempts didn't find the inner flesh. He stopped as she shifted him off of her. Moving quickly, she moved to work on him to lower his pent up fervor. His threshold was being pumped away. The release couldn't be stopped and he knew it. She succeeded. Once the desire was unloaded, she was relieved as he finished on her rather than in her.

Lindsay said, "I had to do that. We couldn't go that far right now." She enjoyed the passion and hoped he felt the release was satisfying.

She says, "I mean it's not the time, honey. I'm sorry we can't go all the way. You don't' have protection. We went over the edge. So please, let's rest for the moment. Hey, I'm sure you feel pretty good right now."

Richard says, "Yeah, I feel very relaxed."

She says, "Seriously we really went too far. I can't believe you took me out. I had a powerful wave sweep over me. Look at us, we're like young lovers. You better get dressed while I clean up. You put a little mess on me."

"Lindsay, you were so good."

"Well, that might be lover boy, but nine months from now a whole lot can change. I wasn't ready for that. We're not teenagers. That's why I had to take care of you. I need to take a shower; then let's have lunch, ok"

"I'm all for that."

Richard was pulling himself together. His body was heated, almost feeling like a warm bath towel just coming out of the dryer. Gathering his clothes he watched Lindsay leave. She was a real fix for a lonely heart. He knew they would continue to explore. This was round one.

Being much older, he understood the ramifications of her concern. He wasn't a perfect match. Under the circumstances that didn't matter when the love light is beaming. Love weaves and grows in so many ways. The consequences of unbridled peccadillo had to have a safe outcome. Because of her quick thinking and experience in love making, she saved the best for another day. She knew they could have plenty of fun down the road.

The contact had escalated so rapidly as if they were married and had known each other for years. It was experience that taught her lessons to rely on. His tempo had to be controlled and she knew how to do it. It was a good save at least this time.

As Lindsay showered, she examined her body. Once out of the shower she looked in the mirror to make sure no marks were on her neck.

She thought this man was out of control in such a short time, but she was proud to have regained control. It paid off. She was confident she kept him from dropping the male part of life into the sweet spot. By her measure the tantalizing romp was quite pleasurable. This was a step up. She knew her relationship with Richard was going to expand. New heights had been reached.

She hurried to get dressed. It didn't take long. Richard was equally fast in getting himself together. His concern was natural. Did he go too far and too fast with her? That was quickly answered by Lindsay.

She says, "I'm ready. We're going to be ok, because I prevented you from going to . . . well you know. I kind a think we're real good partners now."

He says, "You're right about that, Lindsay. We're partners alright. OK, let's go!"

They came back from lunch and started working in harmony.

He gave her a few instructions on working with his camera equipment. Lake Erie and the beach were a perfect place to learn about snapping landscape pictures.

"Sometime this week go down to the lake on your own and snap a few pictures."

The computer had a file set up for pictures. He wanted her to download her best shots. They could review them together when time permitted.

"I have to drive up to Detroit this week and see if I can find Abdul Madhi, so you hold down the fort, while I'm away.

Jokingly she says, "Ok, Mr. Stern."

The atmosphere between the two took a sharp turn. It was more than a budding, high grade friendship. The roll of employee was completely removed and replaced with business partner and girlfriend. There was satisfaction established and she wanted a return engagement. Lindsay was no longer even thinking of finding a better job. Her gain with Richard was security. He could provide for her even if she became pregnant.

She saw the records. He wasn't a poor man just getting by. Richard Stern Enterprises wasn't in the tank. What he needed was better record keeping. In fact she could see a maturing business. Her business expertise would be a plus for him.

The control she had over everyday operations would help him be more productive. He had some good qualities. What's more, his ability to assemble facts pointed to a smart investigator. Maybe it was just luck, but he seemed to fall into good fortune in spite of his haphazardness. All she had to do is keep him under control. Her formula for that was just proven. If she could stay close to him, they had a change to go places. She had to control his drinking habit and she had a plan to help him.

That night he had trouble sleeping again, so he started to over use his usual medicine. This time he stopped and turned to water instead. Through the night his dream of being with her was like they were married. As he woke, he was a little groggy. A shower helped to revive him. It was nine thirty in the morning. By the time Richard walked into the office, Lindsay was at work. Sitting at the computer, she spun around and watched him take a seat next to her.

Lindsay says, "It looks like you didn't sleep well. Your eyes are red."

Richard says, "Dreaming again, I have to ask you again, "What do these words mean? Zebra and Submarine, these words are still on my mind. I want to know what they mean."

She kissed him and said with a smile on her face.

"Do we have to start so early?"

Richard responds, "At this point with you, uh, we can start early, midmorning, night, whatever. I can see all the good you have to offer. Your kiss is exactly how to start off a day. I'm in the mood to explore every inch of your body."

"Down, boy. You're going to get us in trouble."

"OK, Lindsay, I better go or we'll never get anything done. I'm leaving for Detroit in a day or two. You know: When I stare into your blue eyes, I have this feeling, we're going to have a rush of fun way beyond normal."

"You better cool down, buster."

Lindsay knew she really turned him on. He had a schedule to follow. She wasn't going to let him break her down.

Lindsay says, "Maybe we'll have some fun later. You have a track meet at the Wickliffe Middle School. It's on your calendar."

"Oh, that's right. Can we resume our adventure later?"

"Maybe, if you behave."

"OK, the meet is at the high school. You know, after I'm done, I might stop at the Wickliffe Public Library and do some research before I head to Michigan."

She knew sex was the key to helping him. She had to help him overcome the poor sleeping habit. It was one reason he was drinking so much.

CHAPTER 20

FACE TO FACE

REFEREE RICHARD STERN says, "This wind is way beyond normal. Let's call this meet before someone gets hurt."

The track meet had to be cancelled because of high winds. The athletic director agreed with Stern when the finish line tent blew over. Stern had another place to visit, so cancelling the track meet was no big deal and besides, they had to pay him anyhow.

When he pulled into the Wickliffe Public Library, Stern saw young and old people walking to and from the library. There was a group of Middle Eastern people huddled in the parking lot. Because of his inquisitiveness, he pulled a few car spaces away from them. Then a black BMW automobile pulled up next to him.

The ringleader looked up and around like he had something to hide. The irony or the fate of the situation built a volume of suspicion in Stern's head. Perhaps these guys weren't friendly.

Stern pulled away and parked his car in a more strategic place. His first impulse was to call Lindsay. Although he had no reason to think he would stumble upon the enemy, a bit of caution was being summoned. The way Richard and Lindsay were stumbling on clues, he figured it was time to be careful. Here it was another circumstance just happened out of the clear blue sky. Maybe it was nothing, but seeing a black BMW could be a terrorist calling card.

For the past two weeks the soft facts were falling like dominos right in front of Richard and Lindsay. They both acknowledged a possible enemy plot was brewing in Lake County, Ohio.

Richard weighted up the facts. Lindsay knows Abdul Madhi. He's driving a black BMW. The Oregon trip produced some evidence. Mr. Boyle sees a man in a military wet suit. Rag heads are watching over Lake Erie on Blackmore Road. Two Middle Eastern men appear at the Sunset Bar and Grill and Lindsay says she might know one of them. These were not coincidences; they were links.

Richard wondered if the enemy had sleeper cells all over Lake County. It would be impossible for the government to oversee the entire borders, North, South, East or West. Crossing Lake Erie from Canada by boat was easy. Terrorists had done it before. Quite possibly, they may be trying again.

The government never installs a complete southern border fence. The intrusions were still happening. Agent Lopez told him that. Agent Monica Micovich was getting a personal bird's eye view of the border along the Rio Grande. The enemy was still infiltrating into America.

Stern's thinking cap was still pondering about these Middle Eastern folks in the parking lot of the Wickliffe Library. Could they be silently meeting in a parking lot, yet in a public place? There were too many pieces of unsubstantiated facts for him to jump to conclusions. However, the evidence was mounting.

He called Lindsay.

"Lindsay, I'm at the Wickliffe Library parking lot. The track meet has been cancelled because of high winds. I'm giving you a heads up. I see a half dozen young Middle Eastern men congregating in the parking lot. They look like Arabs. I think we saw one of these guys. Maybe you know them. Now don't get me wrong. Maybe nothing is going down. One of the men looks like he was in the Sunset Harbor Bar and Grill.

Lindsay says with a ping of alarm in her voice, "No, please don't say that."

"This is really getting bigger than I could have imagined. You drive here now. I mean now. I'm going in the library and then I'm leaving. I won't be far away. You check these guys out after I'm gone. See if you recognize any of them. Use some makeup and put sunglasses on, I don't want you to raise suspicion. Call me when you get close to the library."

Richard wasn't taking any chances. He saw the symbol of a winged lion on the windshield of the BMW. The neighboring car had an identical symbol. This was a symbol he saw years ago at an enemy landing strip in Oregon.

At one time Stern thought the enemy would leave America after Bin Laden was eliminated. That wasn't the case. The pirates in the White House wanted citizens to think that. It wasn't the case. The Boston Marathon attack dashed that lie.

Stern acted nonchalant as he walked from his car to the library steps. He looked one last time to see if the meeting was still going on. Once inside the library, he slowly started assembling something of a sequence of events on a piece of paper.

What he had on his mind was something for the FBI, but it wasn't enough. He needed rock solid proof to cash in. Even he was a bit shy of actual facts there was reason to be concerned. It appeared the enemy was formulating another attack along the shore of Lake Erie. Was all of this circumstantial activity a wake up call?

Stern didn't have enough evidence. He'd never get a reward at this point. The next attempt to breach Perry Nuclear Power Plant's defenses had to be understood. There were too many unknown questions that had to be answered. The first question would be easy to answer. Why are they here, if they're really terrorists? To cause mayhem, that's the answer.

He walked from the library and copied down license plate numbers as best as he could without drawing suspicion. The last thing he wanted was for one of the Arabs to see him taking notes on their activity.

It was becoming apparent that Stern was steadily moving closer to the enemy. He was being driven by dreams and fate. It happened to him all too often. Was this meeting at the library by Middle Eastern men an audacious pregame conference or was it just nothing. Was it a repeat of his past confrontation with the enemy? What was coming into focus? Stern believed an answer was forming in his mind. There were too many implausible things to ignore.

He had been bombarded by Satan in the past. Somebody tried to poison him, because he was getting closer to the enemy. It had to be the evil angel descending to discourage his meddling. Ex-girlfriend Sharon would say that. Was it going to happen again?

Richard searched the magazine rack while waiting for a call from Lindsay. It was 5:50PM when Lindsay called back.

"Richard, I'm crossing the tracks on Lloyd Road."

"OK, girl, I'm leaving the library and I'm going south. I won't be far away, like at the end of the road. Pull into the parking lot and check on these guys. Maybe you'll recognize one of them. It's probably a long shot. Give it a try.

This was a case for Agent Roman and Stern knew it; except, he didn't want to disclose all the facts at this time.

If Agent Roman was around, he would use his listening device to hear the conversation of the Middle Eastern men.

Richard left the library parking lot with license plate number copied to his note pad. He was kind of sure they would amount to nothing.

A few minutes later Lindsay pulled in the library parking lot. Her palm were moist, the anticipation was growing as she could see the men. She had Richard on the phone.

He says, "I'm parked down the street. Go on in if they aren't in the parking lot."

Lindsay says, "I'm already in the parking lot. I can't see very well wearing these prescription sunglasses. They're for reading. I'll have to take them off."

Richard says, "Don't let them see you spying on them.

Lindsay excitedly exclaims, "They're here and I see him. It's him. Richard. Oh, Lord, it's him. He saw me."

Confusion clamped a hold on her wits. She knew he recognized her. It was written on his face. With the tension building, she talks fast as she opens the glove box for magnum shells.

She repeats, "I forgot to load my pistol, Christ, it's him. It's the same guy who I saw in San Diego. He was at the Sunset Harbor restaurant. It's him, Richard."

Richard says, "You get out of there right now. Don't stop, go. Turn left as you're leaving the parking lot. Punch it. Get out of there."

Lindsay did a button hook around the parking lot. Her tires screech a bit as if she was in a hurry. She tried not to let her face be known or give away the fear on her face. Cars were passing in front of her, so she couldn't exit the parking lot. Regaining her composure she loaded the pistol as fast as she could. The shells spilled, but she got six bullets loaded in the chamber.

"He's getting in his car. They're coming after me, Richard."

"Do you have your gun?"

"Yes, I'm done loading it now."

Richard says, "Listen to me. OK, go left and drive south to Route 84 and turn left. You'll see me. Just keep driving Lindsay. I mean drive fast; I'm going to stop these guys."

Lindsay drove a few blocks to Route 84 where she saw Richard. He was out of his car standing at the corner. He motioned for her to go left as the traffic light turned green and she turned left as he said. The black BMW was speeding to catch up to her. Richard walked slowly onto the street as if he had a leg injury to prevent the BMW from going any farther unless he drove over him. The driver had to slow down or risk hitting Richard. The stop light turned red which also halted the BMW. This gave Lindsay a sizeable lead and more breathing space.

She turned north heading back to Route 20. Her heart was beating fast in a way she never thought imaginable. She held the Colt Blue Python .357 magnum pistol in her right hand all the while watching in the rear view mirror for the BMW.

Stern had dropped his cell phone in the street as another stalling tactic. He put up his hand asking for the driver to wait for him. The driver was bowing his horn in disgust. Other drivers behind the BMW were equally aggravated. The delay paid off for Lindsay.

Richard walked back to his car which was parked off the side of the road with the emergency flashers blinking. He hopped in his car as if nothing happened. The entire episode lasted five or six minutes, but for Lindsay, it seemed like an eternity. A shiver rushed through her body as she realized the coast was clear. She was heading back to Fairport Harbor.

Richard called her to make sure she was heading East on Route 2. "Lindsay, are you ok?"

The answer was yes, she was frazzled and heading home. The suspenseful day was crazy for both of them. The good that came from this hair-raising chase was twofold. Lindsay was introduced to Stern's dangerous world and he had license plate numbers of the enemy. They also affirmed another key point. These guys were probably terrorists, although they lacked substantial proof. No one broke the law.

When Lindsay pulled into Richard's drive, she ran to the door. She went inside and poured herself a full glass of red wine. She had to hold the glass with both hands. The terror of the chase had her trembling. After she downed the first glass of wine, she heard the sound of Richard's car pulling into the driveway. She felt much better knowing he was home.

She hugged him as he came into the house.

"Lock the door, Richard."

Richard tried to calm her down. He could see she was still a bundle of nerves.

"Try to relax, it's over."

Lindsay says, "Yeah, for you. He saw me. I was dropping bullets on the seat of my car as I tried to load the pistol. You don't know how scared I was."

Richard says, "Yes I do, Lindsay. I pissed my pants in Oregon, when confronted by a terrorist that was pointing a gun at me."

In the evening they talked about everything that went down. She was still shaken by the thought of being chased by terrorists.

"Lindsay, I want you to realize something from this experience. We're getting close to people who will butter our bread. We're going to make some serious money if you have the stomach for this."

She says, "I don't want to get shot or killed. Do you realize I had my pistol in my hand? I was ready to defend myself."

Richard says, "I think you need to decide right now. Are you with me?"

She grabbed his hand and pulled him close so as to whisper in his ear.

"This is getting crazy, but I'm with you, Richard. I love you."

CHAPTER 21

MYSTERY OF THE DREAM

S LEEP DID NOT come easy. After a couple beers, Richard dosed off for an hour. The TV was flashing a commercial of an old quarterback explaining the goodness of prostrate pills. Nature called and he relieved himself, downed a sleeping pill and tried successfully to sleep for one more sleep cycle. It was during this time he was languishing in a sea of dreams that were meaningful but choppy.

In the dream an SOS alarm was sounding. *Lindsay and Richard were watching a fair sized ship from shore.*

"Take a picture Lindsay," said Stern. The cruise ship was coming to the rescue of a smaller vessel. Stern could see both the rescue ship and the boat in distress. The heavy fog degraded his visibility. She had the zoom lens, so she could see a naked woman waving her arms.

Someone threw a net over the woman and they fell to the deck.

As he awoke his memory was somewhat disengaged. Stern wanted to write down the vision he had.

"Note paper!"

He fished around for a pen.

"I have to write this down."

The bedroom computer was only steps away where he could type down fresh thoughts about his dreams. Sadly, he didn't have the will to get out of bed. He was partially drunk and had taken the sleeping pill. Together they made him quite drowsy. The substance of the dream was another clue. To sleepy was he as his head plopped back to the soft pillow. The images of his dream floated away like smoke from a cigarette. He raised a hand to the night stand to fetch a pen and notepad.

He mustered up enough energy to hand write a phrase. <u>Caught a net.</u>

He may have been dreaming, but it was more like hallucinating from the beer and the sleeping pill. Through the night he sought to unlock the mystery of the mind. So many dreams were coming in view.

The next dream was friendly. It took him back thirty years.

He could see the old Honey Hole Club. One by one middle class guys stopped after work to wet their whistle. This was a normal routine to meet and chit-chat at the club. Each man used a special key card to get in the building. The code was on the card as if each male member needed a top secret clearance to get in. There were wives and girlfriends in the parking lot who met their guys at the back of the club. They didn't have the top secret card.

When Richard Stern arrived, the parking lot was starting to fill. A dozen cars and trucks were parked in the lot. He had news to share. Not big new, but he didn't need a reason to stop and drink some favorite spirits.

In the morning newspaper Stern had read where a dead lake sturgeon had washed up on the beach in Euclid, Ohio. Now that was big news. Lake Erie, once thought half dead from pollution, was bouncing back. Stern cut out two pictures from the newspaper which showed a four foot fish lying on the shore. An accompanying old photo, taken in 1915, was of William Stange, carrying a 57 pound lake sturgeon. Stern's cousin Edward Stange had once said his great uncle was pictured in a book holding up a monster sturgeon. This fish was at least five foot long.

That was reality, but really wasn't a reason to start drinking.

Behind the club's parking lot and over the embankment was the Grand River. A Great Lakes freighter was in port unloading its stone.

Could it be the Edmund Fitzgerald? He couldn't see the ship's name.

A group of men formed at the bar. It was after 4PM and the barstools were nearly all occupied. This was the first shift crowd and each man was sharing his story of the day. They all knew each other.

Tom, Dick, and Nellie, they had stories to share. Stern was quick to grab an open seat next to Nellie, who owned a good size commercial fish boat.

Stern pulled out the newspaper clippings of the sturgeon. The fish stories caused a stir. This was the topic of the day.

As time passed by and several more rounds of beer were drunk the topic turned to netting fish. Ray needed volunteers to assist his crew with pulling fish nets. Here was a new adventure for Stern. He would help Captain Ray Nellie Nelson and crew pull the nets. Joining this fishing trip was right up Stern's alley. After all he was a US Navy veteran.

Volunteerism chasing dreams and booze was the chief reason Richard Stern got in so many jams. He had to pursue the mysterious and he loved adventure and good looking women.

The Ray Nelson crew would meet early the next morning, whether drunk, blind, crippled, or crazy. The nets had to be pulled before the next Lake Erie storm came barreling down.

Being an ex-navy man at least he could swim if something went wrong. With Nellie at the helm there would be no fear.

The men continued to discuss the work planned for the next morning.

Captain Nelson says, "I'm still looking for a gill net. It's out there somewhere. The damn lake kicked up and I lost the buoy marker. Some asshole probably took my marker, the net and the fish. It was probably filled with perch, damn poachers."

When Richard finally woke up, he attempted to analyze the dreams. Gill netting had nothing to do with the enemy's movements. He didn't see a connection, but there was one.

During the dream they were traveling east, north of the Diamond Shamrock chemical plant that was on the Lake Erie coast, so something had to be going on in this area. It's where Ronnie Curliss saw the submarine. How did lake sturgeon fit in the picture? He wasn't sure. By deciphering little bits of information he gained from dreaming, an image was being drawn. Now the task was differentiating the connection between reality and the subconscious images. This was a bit perplexing.

Stern didn't realize there was truly a trail of signs leading him to the enemy. This was almost the exact circumstance that happened when Agent Roman and Wright interviewed him in the hospital seven years ago.

The most startling revelation came to him. It had nothing to do with terrorists. As he sat up in bed he put lovers and life together. He understood God's intension. He had to make up his mind about Lindsay. Should he subject her to danger or find out the hard way. He knew the combination of alcohol and women always ended up being his downfall. He didn't want to ruin her life or any other person he met. Every time he hit rock bottom from drinking, so did his relationships suffer.

It may have started with Bonnie Clark, the secretary of the Fairport Harbor Port Authority, but it continued after their brief mingles. Bonnie Clark's sister, Brenda, got involved with him and they uncovered the enemy, but that was different. Brenda Clark led him to the unscrupulous politicians and mobsters. That almost got them both killed. Thank God Agent Monica and Paula Gavalia arrived to shoot it out at Mack Crenels Bar and save them.

Tracing back before Brenda was Agent Micovich. She seemed to enter his life all the time. Maybe she was an angel. Monica helped him uncovered clues about Al Qaeda and that earned him decent reward money. She was such a great person.

The last woman on the scene was Sharon. She may have been leading him to the next step in his life until they broke apart and ended their relationship. Along came Lindsay and she was filling in where Sharon left off.

He had no doubt there had to be a connection to God for all these things to happen. He was always involved with decent, good looking women. He thought, maybe booze had nothing to do with it, but he was only fooling himself. His dangerous lifestyle and doing things his way only ruined relationships, that is, until Lindsay came along. She was changing him for the better. She had control, giving him an outlet through her tantalizing ideas. She could make a mark on his life. In turn they would grow as a team.

Dreams and the recollection process were transporting him closer to an FBI reward. Like a gambler, he could feel it. All he needed was a little bit of luck. Looking at the present events, Lindsay was his lucky charm. He wondered. How would this chapter in his life play out? What type of luck was she? Would she be bad luck or good luck? Time would release that secret.

The day started off on the sunny side. The morning sun came bursting through the window. A trip to the bathroom helped Stern recover from a poor night's sleep. He slapped water in his face to wake up. When he walked back to his bedroom, he saw the note.

<u>Caught a net</u>—Richard remembered parts of the dream. His mind traveled back in time. It took him to commercial fishing on Lake Erie. Captain Raymond Nelson was the skipper of the boat called the Rae Ann. It was so long ago. He snapped out of it.

Richard was running late. He didn't dwell upon the thought. Lindsay was probably waiting for him. It was time to meet up with his partner.

Stern didn't connect all the dots mostly because he wasn't rested. Subconsciously his memory was linking to the enemy; however, he didn't know the enemy was having a problem and the nature of the problem was something that happened many years ago.

CHAPTER 22

MISSING NETS

RICHARD STERN HAD a forecast to make like a weatherman. He had been reading articles scribed on the internet news pages about the president and House Speaker. Congress and the president were locking horns over the fiscal cliff. It was big news for internet bloggers. Democrats and Republicans were crying as they normally do about taxing the rich and the bad economy. Stern had an answer. It was time to sort out the news at the Honey Hole.

Lindsay was out of the office doing some grocery shopping. As the clock struck noon, it was time to listen to Rush and drive around town.

He side stepped the Honey Hole for a brief stop at the bowling alley. There he met a barmaid just coming on duty. They exchanged greetings. Matilda Rittenhouse was mild mannered and Richard Stern thought a new friendship was in the works. Stern found out football referee Dave Rittenhouse was Matilda's uncle. Richard worked with Dave on a few games mostly at Lamuth Middle School.

"Your Uncle Dave taught me a few lessons on the football field. He knows the finer points of being a top notch referee. I went to see him a few years ago. He and his wife have a nice place by Riverside High School."

Matilda was happy to hear this and a true friendship started to mature. Because she was a Tea Party member, they ended up exchanging phone numbers and agreed to meet in the future. Stern told her he had a girlfriend and they stopped from time to time at the Sunset Harbor Bar and Grill.

"Lindsay and I will probably be there Saturday afternoon. I want you to meet her. She doesn't have many friends in Ohio. She's a California girl."

Richard felt pretty good about meeting Matilda. He thought Lindsay would like her. A bit of a flashback crossed his mind after leaving the bowling alley.

Agent Paula Gavalia warned Stern time after time when she was his bodyguard. 'Stop drinking Mr. Stern and you'll find a good woman.' Stern went along with her for a time and would quit for months at a time, but somewhere along the way, he talked himself into having one. Then it was two and more and more.

He couldn't resist stopping at the next social club, he went to the VFW in Painesville and pulled into the parking lot of the Honey Hole to conduct some economic research, although it had more to do with sampling a few brews. As the drinks were flowing, friends of Stern sat down. Husband and wife, Mike and Mary Leininger sat to Stern's right. To the left were Bob and Jan Jones. They were joined by Judy Kakas. Judy's friend was busy playing one of the skill machines.

The conversation quickened when the subject of unions came up. Mike was a union representative when the Perry Nuclear Power Plant was being built. To avoid the pro and cons of union versus non-union activity Stern changed the discussion.

His previous night's dream had something to do with that. A hardy subject turned to fishing on Lake Erie. Richard started talking about harvesting Lake Erie perch, which meant gathering perch using gill nets. It was a controversial method of fishing. Many years had passed since Mike and Richard had gone out with Nellie Nelson on his fish boat to help pull gill nets. It was a time consuming job just to travel out to the nets.

Gill nets often became tangled with debris when the weather turned nasty. It was best to pull the nets early before the lake kicked up. Sometimes, Nellie had to rustle up a crew in a hurry to get the nets out of the water. And sometimes he couldn't muster a crew in time. Buoy markers to indicate where the gill net were set would get blown off course, but Ray Nellie Nelson had the experience and where with all to master the job. He was the captain of the RaeAnn and he loved his boat.

Mike says, "Ray's wife was a saint. Shirley put up with the crew and Ray. Her challenges came in all directions." Stern readily agreed.

Stern says, "You know, Mike, I'm sure one or two gill nets are still out there."

Mrs. Kakas added an ominous recollection.

She makes a noteworthy statement, "I remember seeing the gill net markers off Painesville Township. That's where those boys from Township Park found dynamite. Good thing the Lake County Sheriffs were on the ball."

Richard Stern remembered this too. It was moments like these that triggered subliminal pictures in Stern's mind about terrorists.

Stern says in a worried voice, "I wish you wouldn't have brought that up, Judy. I'll have weird dreams tonight."

Mrs. Kakas says, "You met those Middle Eastern guys at the boat ramp years ago, when you were on the port authority. I bet they were terrorists."

Half smiling, she asks, "Did they make you have bad dreams?"

Stern abruptly says, "Yes! I ended up in a mental hospital and I had to see a shrink over that one."

Mrs. Kakas didn't believe him. She thought he was joking. Stern was laughing and everyone thought he was just playing along. Truth is; he was in the mental hospital.

The conversation was see-sawing from terrorists to fishing and back to the economy. After an hour the group started to leave. Naturally, Stern was the last to go.

When he got home, it was supper time for the cats. The cats were listening to him ramble on like a man with a belly full of beer.

"I may not sleep well tonight. We still have a terrorist problem in this country even if the White House won't admit the same and I see another Middle East war coming. This one could be a real bummer. One reason is our debt and Iran. The president has to get the people thinking about our debt and the economy. That's problem number one and two. So I guess number three is Iran. They're trying to build nukes."

The cats were too busy with supper. They most likely understood Stern's condition. He was under the influence again.

"The Palestinians can't solve their problems so they blame Israel. Pretty soon they'll drag us into the folly. Iran is the agitator."

"Arab leaders in North Africa don't want to find a solution, because America keeps sending them taxpayer's money. We gave Egypt a bunch of money. We're stupid. We get into shooting wars because they have problems. They can't get along with Israel. One thing is for sure, we can't keep bailing everyone out. We keep borrowing and printing money. It isn't going to last. You cats don't give a damn just like the low income voter."

Stern was on a roll. He clicked on the TV for the latest Fox update.

"Iran has dirty hands all over the Middle East. They're selling guns to Syria. Maybe China is doing the same thing. This just causes tension. The price of oil goes up and OPEC wins again. Well cats, I'll tell you. They're all lying. They want to keep oil prices high. It's all a massive plan and I believe the White House is involved or they're getting snookered. Like I just said, they're all lying."

He says, "Sharon said 'the end is coming.' She told me to read Revelations at the end of the bible. That'll really make me dream."

Stern moved away from the TV and sat back in his seat in front of computer number one. On another computer he started playing a game of hearts. He wanted to get his mind off all the turmoil.

"I have to do something good."

He looks up one of his favorite presidents. It was J. F Kennedy. Reading the quote on the computer screen sends another subliminal message to his brain.

"Remember, 'Ask not, what your country can do for you, ask what you can do for your country.' It isn't that way anymore, Mr. President.

We're breeding takers not workers. The president and the Democrats have a new way of life for half the citizens."

A free for all was taking place across the nation. Free stuff (government handouts) for the poor, the unemployed, and the deadheads was becoming a way of life. Free cell phones, free food, and the list of free stuff were growing. The government was expanding just like the people on food stamps.

The wind of change was growing. Hard work or work was becoming a dirty word. It was thought every American deserved a home. Federal regulations forced banks to make risky loans to folks who had no realistic way of making monthly payments. This was a program that nearly bankrupted the banks. It put Washington on the hot seat. On top of all the stupidity, money was dished out like candy on Halloween. The government was printing money willy-nilly.

Stern thought it had to be a plan. The Democrats were building a base of voters who had to depend on the government for help and this would keep them in power.

What Stern didn't see at first was something much larger. Oh, he suspected more was involved and it was all a master plan. It was a scheme to create a one party system. The worker was the fool paying for the lower fifty per cent. That fifty per cent would be the president's voters. The next shoe to drop was coming. It was health care for all. The tax payers would have to pay for all the people who didn't have health insurance. It was another slap in the face of regular workers.

Lindsay opened the door to hear him preaching to the cats.

She says, "Hey President Kennedy, help me with the groceries."

Richard says, "OK, I've got a lot on my mind. I think the terrorists are on the move, Lindsay. They're going to do something real nasty."

Lindsay says, "Speaking of something nasty, I think you have been drinking or should I say; I want to tell you a true story. You've been over served."

CHAPTER 23

MISTAKES AND PRACTICING EVIL IDEAS

T HE DEPARTMENT OF Homeland Security had reasons to send more FBI agents to Cleveland. Something big was coming to Middle America, but they didn't have an exact location. The questions about security on the Great Lakes were as mixed up as the president and congress. Nobody had a clear view. The president was proving one thing. He didn't know how to run a democracy.

The president and his men were befuddled on nearly every issue confronting the country. The president had enough power to order the EPA to allow the building of the oil pipeline from Canada to Louisiana, but he was playing the 'Green Energy Game.' He didn't do it. Immigration, gun control, national debt, North Korea and Iran's nuclear ambitions were confounding an administration that had won another four years. The Benghazi fiasco was still a sore spot on his watch. Someone should have put a sock in his mouth when he started talking about Syria.

So much was going on across America, the president and his pirates were totally confused. The Commander-in-Chief had little trouble finding time to golf, shoot some hoops or vacation. About the only good news was using drones and killing Osama Bin Laden. All of those operations were actually mastered by CIA agents and professional soldiers. The president had little control over the outcome.

The president did have one masterful accomplishment. The master usually found time to campaign. Raising money was no problem for the cagy leader. He was doing well on that account. Rather than work on the economy, it seemed his primary job was to raise money for the next election.

Drawing attention away from mistakes made on the job was the national news media. Most major news outlet worked well for him. They carried his water. If the president's news media were rabbits, the Fox station did hound the rabbits. In this case Fox did more than just hound rabbits. It was after the truth, which hindered the pirates in the White House.

The terrorist leaders could see the powers in Washington were mostly bags of wind. Pulling rabbits out of his hat was becoming increasingly difficult. The pirates were hog tide. Syria was a thorn on his chair. The president's shield wasn't clean and shiny as it had been. He drew a line in the sand over the use of chemical weapons and that was another nail to the proverbial coffin. The president was all set to launch an attack on Syria, but he found himself out in the cold. Great Britain decided to sit out the attack on Syria.

His trump card was played in September 2013. He blamed the UN and congress for drawing a red line. The national media had a hard time swallowing that blunder. They were even turning against him.

Saving Washington DC's skins from scandals was a major problem. Washington's political decisions were based on polls. The polls were stinking because of scandals, lies, and a woeful economy. When it came time to make a serious decision, like solving a crisis in Benghazi, the president and the pirates acted like bears in the winter and hibernated.

Terrorist leaders saw the indecisiveness. They had to have patience. The leadership would decide when to strike. Concocting many of these operations were two terrorist masterminds. Their names were West Coast operative, Farouk Aziz and Great Lakes leader, Akmar Mehsud. He had trained in Pakistan and was hand pick to launch the underwater sneak attack. Mehsud replaced two dead leaders, Captain Awad and Sheik LeBigg.

Farouk Aziz had owned the Oasis Club in Santee, California and moved to Portland, Oregon. His job was to develop and transform the submersible program. When the pilot program was nearly finished, he decided to close the restaurant. He dispatched Abdul Madhi to Astoria, Oregon to help finish work on the pilot program. They had a workable prototype submersible. From there Abdul Madhi traveled east to repair a small rebuilt submarine stored at a Detroit marina. It only took a month to finish work on the submersible, Little Base. The operation was going well. The sub was loaded into the mother ship.

The day had come where a shakedown cruise was needed to test the sub and the crew. The training mission began in July. The mother ship, Green Whale sailed into Lake Erie and began testing for the next terrorist mission. She unloaded the submersible a few times well off the coast of Ashtabula, Ohio. They were in deep water and the exercise when well. The next part of the operation would involve training the attackers in shallower water. Each night they would move a little closer to the target. Very few Perry, Ohio residents had any idea they were being targeted. Bob Beardslee had a suspicion something dirty was going on.

Sometime in August the people of Northeast Ohio planned for an invasion, but that was a prearranged battle by the good folks in Conneaut, Ohio. It was a version of the Normandy invasion. This exercise would come into play in a mysterious way.

Al Qaeda first started experimenting with a submersible off the Pacific Coast near Astoria, Oregon. Her mother ship was called Green Whale, which was a private cruise ship that was decked out for two widely different reasons. She could act as a tourist ship and carry a submersible. Green Whale had more infamous reasons to sail than transporting tourist. It was more important to make her an exclusive terrorist ship. She was far more effective by working exclusively for evil operations and she had a perfect disguise. She looked like a rich man's toy.

Green Whale sailed through the Panama Canal and made her way north and through the St. Lawrence Seaway. The final destination was Cleveland, Ohio. Her activity was just beginning. She acted as a tourist ship for a few months until it was decide to buy a new vessel.

The Brother M was purchased to take over the luxury duties of Green Whale. Brother M was first used in Lake Huron and then sailed to Lake Erie. Once in the shallower lake, her berthing base was changed from Michigan to Sandusky, Ohio.

Brother M was being used by the very rich for gambling and transporting terrorists. Until a new vessel was bought to transport personnel Brother M would have to do dual work. The crew was mostly made up of double agents, who didn't really fit the role as tourist guides. They tended to party with the ladies and guests. Some got carried away with the young ladies.

Detroit banker, Kalid Mehsud, who was the chief financial officer for Eastern America, was the owner of Brother M. He was not impressed with the behavior of a few crew members. He decided to remove the men and purchase another cruise ship. On the new ship the bold and brash pirates could stay until it was time to attack. This third purchase, a smaller cruiser, called the Lock Hearts, was stationed in Toledo and could sail among the Great Lakes to transport weapons to other terrorist cells. It would see action in the future. For the time being it was used exclusively as a transport craft.

Fine tuning the mission was the job of Captain Amjad Walliki. He was the skipper of the Green Whale. She had a special mission on Lake Erie and it was Captain Walliki's job to ready all participants. His ship would give birth to a baby sub to examine targets along the southern coast of Lake Erie from Toledo to Conneaut, Ohio. It was his duty to summarily decide upon a target. From his command ship he would report to Akmar Mehsud for final instructions once he picked out the attack zone.

The rich gamblers on board the Brother M were merely pawns. They helped pay for most of the ship's operation and money was skimmed by the captain to promote jihad. It was a well-constructed scheme. Rich guys liked young women and they liked to gamble. While they were playing games and being entertained by young ladies, the mother ship was working with the submersible. Brother M was strictly a money laundering machine and only to be called into action if there was an emergency.

The Brother M mostly catered to a select group of rich Middle Eastern men, although they would take special people in some cases. These men supported the Muslim struggle. Men that had the money and free time to gamble and play with pretty ladies were sworn to secrecy. They didn't really care about Al Qaeda. Play time was the prime reason to travel on the yacht. The Brother M was the modern day love boat. It was a floating penthouse of ill repute.

Brother M had just completed several tours. Good news spread among the Middle Eastern sheiks and affluent. The tourist trap took off. Brother M was providing a service. It was all set up to provide high class gambling and erotic adult entertainment. These were the main games played on the one hundred twenty foot white and gold yacht. In reality it was a beautiful brain storm of the mastermind, Banker Kalid Mehsud. When money started rolling in, it was obvious the main purpose of the tours was a splendid idea. Extracting money from wealthy patrons was easy.

The top secret part of the mission was to finance arms shipments to the Great Lakes Region, so the sleeper cells would be well armed. When Captain Amjad Walliki finished training the crew along with the submersible's crew, he would attack from land and sea. In this case it was Perry, Ohio's nuclear power plant it was tried before, but this time Captain Walliki had a full proof plan. The watery underbelly of Lake Erie would give them the advantage. The captain enjoyed spying on the target from afar. The billowing steam from the power plant was a dead give a way.

He trained his crew to be obedient. The only way to satisfy the brazen captain was to snap to his orders. The crew feared him. That's the way he wanted it. Always training and waiting for the right time to attack was the key for him.

An underwater craft, a submersible, would be the vital to the operation. Captain Amjad Walliki told Abdul Madhi the time was approaching.

"Is the sub ready for the attack?" He asked.

Madhi responded, "We still need to test shoreline activity, captain."

The captain snapped, "I ordered you to be ready and trace the shoreline. You have three weeks. Will you be ready?"

"I will be ready, captain.

The captain radioed a coded message to Akmar Mehsud. He had selected a target and was practicing for the main event. Mehsud gave the captain complete control to launch an attack as he saw fit.

Brother M had just off loaded rich tourists in Sandusky, Ohio. The marina was a safe weather protected harbor. As luck would have it, the captain was told of an emergency. A coded message came from Detroit, Michigan. The captain was ordered to get underway without delay. The unloaded yacht was to proceed east.

The mosque Imam, Mehsud's deputy, reported a serious problem. She was directed to sail from Sandusky to an area east of Fairport Harbor and help, if needed, with a rescue mission.

Brother M didn't displace as much water as the bigger Green Whale. She may have to tow the submersible out of a snag.

This was highly unusual. The captain of the Brother M knew they were scheduled to receive more arms. Zebra was coming and she was loaded with guns.

Zebra was a black and white transport van with a huge shipment of rapid fire weapons. The code word 'Zebra' was used to indicate a new delivery using the van. Shipments of automatic weapon will be coming.

Richard and Lindsay had plenty of information, but no concrete money-making data. Richard wasn't about to spring the news yet. He figured time was dwindling down. The FBI knew of the gun-running scheme. If the enemy was going to strike, it would have to be soon.

The terrorist's submersible worked mostly in deep water. They had to go into shallower water. Very few times they tested the periscope or bring Little Base to the surface. Using the periscope during the day was limited. The terrorists worked to hone their skill. The crew had to see if they could recognize certain landing zones near the nuclear power plant at night.

Not everything went as planned. They had to surface and dive fast during the day and that was a miscue by the sub's crew. For sure they didn't want to ever be detected. They almost slipped up when Ronnie Curliss got a peak at Little Base.

Weather was another factor that made retrieving the sub difficult. The terrorists had to learn the conditions on the lake. Lake Erie had some tricks she could play. Then it happened. Nature and human error played a role in an accident. The unknown stopped the sub dead under water. The boatswain man and frogmen couldn't open the hatch to find out what happened. The crew didn't understand the predicament.

A desperate call was made to the mother ship. Little Base was in trouble. Captain Amjad Walliki from his two hundred foot cruise ship radioed back to the submersible to find out why they stopped. Green Whale was a mile and a half from shore and couldn't go into shallow water to help the sub. It was simply too heavy.

The sub had run into a nasty snag. She was tangled in a commercial fishing net. The strength of the net had the little submarine tangled like a fly in a spider's web. Up to this time the submersible was doing well. This exercise was supposed to teach the terrorists how to plant dynamite. Instead they were stuck.

Even though Captain Ray Nelson was in heaven, he had caught one last diabolical fish. Nellie's net caught the sub, Little Base. Unfortunately he wasn't on earth to see it. He was in God's place to enjoy the sight of his best catch.

They didn't want to empty the ballasts to raise the craft to the surface for fear of being detected. It wasn't far from shore and the water was deep enough to keep the sub out of sight.

Little Base was well west of the nuclear power plant, off Painesville Township Park.

Captain Walliki summoned his shore based men to swim out to Little Base and free the trapped sub. Two terrorists drove down Hardy Road to Painesville Township Park. They drove by the Metro Park softball fields. Nobody was playing because the fields were muddy from a heavy rain the night before. This made the rescue team feel safer, but trouble was ahead. The rescue team ran into problems. There was a fisherman in the area. They knew he wasn't going to give up his fishing spot. One of the rescuers phoned the captain using his cell phone.

"Captain, he's not a friendly. We've met him before. We can't risk a fight."

The captain was furious. Under the circumstance he told them to back off.

They aborted the rescue for the time being. They knew the swashbuckler wasn't going to allow them to pass. After a strong reprimand from the captain, it was decided to retreat. They drove away and waited in a tavern near a race track. There wasn't anything they could do until the fisherman left.

Time passed where they felt comfortable about returning to see if the fisherman was gone. Thankfully, he was gone and they resumed the rescue mission. One man put on a wet suit and diving equipment and made his way to the stricken sub. The net was full of debris. The job was quite a task for one man. Working with a knife, he was able to free the tangle. It was a half hour of work before the vessel could accelerate in reverse. Slowly the sub managed to break free.

By this time it was getting dark and the craft returned to the mother ship.

This hairy encounter was just a beginning example of Lake Erie's antagonism. She had more tricks to play and man-made creations would play another trick. The shoreline off the coast of Conneaut was the setting for a mysterious conundrum.

More problems were ahead for the sub crew and it was going to be twice as scary.

The captain gave the sub crew a tongue lashing for wasting a day even though they were a victim of Lake Erie's anatomy.

There were unanswered questions. They didn't know if the power plant had underwater detectors and that was a big unknown. The water off Conneaut was much deeper and there was another power plant in the area. Their idea was to test defenses around the coal fired power plant. They weren't ready to test Perry's power plant's defenses. They spent another week off Conneaut and then moved closer to Perry, Ohio.

The submersible's problems seemed to be behind them. However, something quite unusual was coming. The captain was about ready to launch the attack. He decided to forego any more tests. After contemplating an array of ideas, he waited for a nasty storm on the lake. That weather event would likely hide the sub's movements and prevent sonar signals from detecting the submarines presence. Another calculated attack would take place on land. Even if there were underwater detectors, their land attack would subdue the main guard station and disable emergency communications.

CHAPTER 24

BAR HOPPING

HIS EYES WERE a bit bloodshot, but Stern wasn't overly intoxicated. He had just returned from the Honey Hole, Rich's Bowling Alley, and Walt's barber shop. There was one stop in between. Richard maintained he was fine and he told Lindsay he was a little bit drunk. He'd be OK.

She says, "You're definitely under the weather. I can tell your last stop was at the Honey Hole. Let me imagine the other places. I'm thinking; it's Rich's bowling alley."

I know the barmaids there. They won't serve you if they think you're under the weather. Brian and Jerry Rich have a respectable bowling alley. I'm wondering maybe you stopped at some other places, because I smell perfume. Were you with another woman? Tell me the truth."

"Lindsay, my honey, you know I wasn't with another woman."

She says, "Man, I can tell. You're shit faced. I'm not nit picking, but I can tell you stopped somewhere. It's ok. I know you have a medical problem. I can understand the drinking, honey. I just want us to work together. I know how to help you."

Richard says, "I stopped to get a haircut.

Lindsay says, "I can see that."

"When I was talking to Walt Gerino, the barber by the bowling alley, Don Whitaker and his wife, Michele, walked in. Michele probably had perfume on her jacket. Our jackets were next to each other. I'd say it's as simple as that. Then John West came in. We started talking about the Fairport Skippers bowing team and politics. Jerry Rich Jr. coached the bowling team. In only a few years he took the Skippers team to the state semi-finals. They finished third in the state. Now I'd say that's splendid coaching. One of the Skipper's bowlers was second in the state. The Rich bowling alley is really good for the kids. Jerry and Brian Rich have really made that bowling alley into a fun place to bowl."

Lindsay says, "We should join a league."

"Hey, that's a good idea. I'm glad the school board approved Rich's and added bowling to Fairport's sports program. This bowling team put Fairport Harbor on the map again. They're getting ink in the newspaper. We couldn't stop talking. We turned to politics."

Lindsay says, "I know. You slammed the president."

"We talked about the economy and terrorists. Walt knows Fairport Harbor. He gets first class gossip. Don and Michele made some good points about the economy."

She says, "Then you went to Rich's Bowling Alley. From there you went to the Honey Hole. Am I right?"

"Yes!"

Lindsay thought about that answer. That was too easy. It wasn't like him to just finish like that. He was hiding something. She wasn't satisfied by the simple 'yes.' The last stop had to be the Honey Hole.

"Well, at least you got a good haircut. I'm going to change the subject for one good reason. I know you don't sleep very well and I think that's a reason you get intoxicated. Your sleeping habits are terrible. You have to see a sleep specialist. I'm going to make an appointment for you. I have to help you make a change, so you can sleep better."

Richard says, "I'm fine. I don't need to see a sleep specialist."

Lindsay says, "I'd feel a lot better if I know what you were up to today. You're hiding something. I made my point about poor sleep and you say you weren't with another woman."

He says, "You know I wasn't with another woman."

She wasn't satisfied by the answer. The perfume still bothered her.

Lindsay says, "It's the perfume. That bothers me."

He says, "OK, I'll come clean. I went to the Painesville VFW. Kate was the barmaid and the TV was messed up. I offered to help her fix it. You don't know this, but all the barmaids are nice and they're friendly."

Lindsay heard the key words and asked a question in one sentence. "Nice and friendly, what's that supposed to mean? Kate, you know all the girls."

"Don't read anything into that. Kate is married to Fuzz Swiger. I was moving things around, trying to fix the TV. The cable wires and power wires were running all over. One of the barmaids may have had an open perfume bottle behind the bar. I probably got perfume on me without realizing it. That's my perfume answer. It could have been on the back bar and I got into it somehow. Every barmaid that works at the Post probably wears perfume. Anyhow, my friend, Mark came in and found the remote control for the TV. He pushed a few buttons on the remote control and the TV started working. The club gave us a free brew for fixing the TV."

Lindsay says, "Now you can tell me a true story."

"I was talking with Kate and Mark. Then there was a shift change. Anette McKinney took over for Kate. I had to have another cold one. I didn't want Anette thinking I'm running out the door because she's coming on duty.

Lindsay says, "You had to have one more, because Anette McKinney took over."

Richard says, "Yes and somebody, I think Anette's uncle bought Mark and I another beer. So I probably had three or four beers at the Post. It's on Liberty Street, Post 2595. It's a nice club and all the barmaids are good people. They can get busy. They don't complain. It's a safe place to sit down and relax."

Lindsay jokes, "You're relaxed. I can see that."

"From the Painesville Post I went to the Honey Hole. I was talking with some woman at the Honey Hole. She was the barmaid. I forgot her name."

"OK, tell me the other women you talked with today."

"That's it. My last stop was the Honey Hole."

Lindsay says, See, I was right. I just want you to start sleeping without drinking yourself into a coma. That's not normal."

Stern explained, "I know my sleeping habits are terrible. That's the way I am."

"You have to see a sleep specialist."

"Sleep specialist, that's bullshit! Are you going to take charge?"

"Yes, because you're not listening, I'm going to take charge."

Lindsay and Richard were close to making some serious reward money. She had read the FBI report on how he acts. The closer he gets to the enemy, the more he drinks.

Lindsay say, "Come with me to the office. I have to show you something."

She pulled the FBI files. After reading his FBI medical report, she knew he was on the verge of earning a reward. It was in the files. His drinking habit brought out a mental mystery.

She says, "You do this all the time. This is your pattern, Richard. You always do heavy drinking just before a big reward. The FBI knows this. The FBI files say you have a mental anomaly."

Richard says, "I remember the doctors telling me all their ideas. Nothing works."

Lindsay says, "We need to move the subject to a remedy. Right now you're full of beer. I'm not going to let you get away. You have to let me take charge."

Lindsay was plenty concerned. Lack of sleep was going to ruin his health. She didn't want him falling apart.

"I can tell you this. Turning to greater amounts of alcohol as your remedy is not going to work. You'll end up in a hospital and that won't help us. I have to help you and you have to listen to me."

There was more on her mind. It had to do with all the facts they were assembling. They were really close to making some serious money. She could see the facts. The FBI report was right on the money. The closer he gets to the enemy, the more he drinks.

Lindsay says, "I'm not sure the medical team checked on your sleeping habits. I read the FBI medical report six times. How close are we to making some money? I don't want to base our investigation on how drunk you're getting. We need the reward, but not at the expense of drinking yourself to death."

"Lindsay, we're going to hit a nice one."

She says, "I told you this before. This is your pattern, Richard. You can't stop. The heavy drinking is happening to you."

"You know; I think you're right. My drinking was the reason for my visions. I guess maybe it was just drunken luck."

Lindsay says, "You're just trying to be funny."

Richard says, "Yep, I know; it's the booze."

Lindsay says, "You were bar hopping. It looks like you had a few brewskis at a few too many places. I should go with you the next time."

Richard maintained he was fine. He told Lindsay he was OK.

She says, "Mr. Stern, I can tell. You're taking chances. I'm not nit picking."

She nailed all the details. He wasn't ready to face the facts.

Lindsay says, "I'm starting to find out how you operate."

She wasn't going to let him get sick. She'd have to deal with his sleeping habits. She had all the proof she needed. He would continue to drink more and more, unless she put her foot down, but she tried one more time to be reasonable.

"At this point all I can say is at least you got a good haircut today. Tell Walt I approve. I really think you have to see a sleep specialist. You know I want to help you. I have my ways. How about an appointment to see your personal physician?

"No, I had a physical."

"You need to see Dr. Mark. He can prescribe medicine to help you. Work up that Stern courage. You can do it."

"No, I saw Dr. Mark not that long ago. He prescribed Librium, but told me not to take it if I was going to continue drinking. So I quit taking it."

Lindsay says, "I can see; I have to take charge."

Lindsay was afraid and concerned he was already overloaded. He wasn't normal He was turning to greater amounts of alcohol as his remedy. She really wanted to help him get a good night sleep. He said he was dreaming some spectacular visions.

She went over the facts again.

There was more on her mind. She had to keep him together or he'd end up in the hospital. She was still his secretary. The job was to keep him together. The heart of her loyalty, as girlfriend, was to keep him safe. She was going to go as far as needed to get him back to normal.

"Look at you! I want to reach you. You're not well when you're like this. Please listen to me, ok. I have to help you."

Richard says, "OK, I'm listening."

"I'm going to wear you out. We have to walk every day. We have to get the booze out of your system. Now focus on what I say. We have to walk to the beach and after that I'll reward you. That's just a start. After you start to feel better, the reward gets better. I'm going to sleep with you, maybe for the next two weeks and I'll record our experience. If it turns into an X rated video, then we did just fine. I'll bet when we're finished; we'll find out what Zebra means."

Richard caught on to those words. Now he wished he was sober. Her words caused him to think about the Zebra dream. It was right in front of him. There he was on TV, the Zebra. The very idea of having sex with Lindsay caused his memory to ring like a bell. The power of a woman's suggestion was activating his frontal lobe and maybe his lower lobe. Shaking off the booze by closing his eyes, he had a vision. He saw the answer.

"Lindsay, the thought of doing it with you is electrifying. Now I know. I know what it means. He's the Zebra. It's him, it's him. It's not the Detroit banker like I thought."

He was pointing to the TV.

"It's the man or men in the White House. They're supplying weapons to the Mexicans."

She says, "Ok, really, why? That doesn't make any sense."

"Look, everything going on in the country is dictated by the pirates in the White House. I think the code word Zebra is him or them. It's like hot and cold, black and white.

"What are you trying to say?" She asked.

"It's him or guys working for him. He's half black and half white. He didn't do a damn thing for those diplomats in Benghazi. They're killing the working men and women with outrageous taxes. You keep getting laid off. Gas prices are going through the roof. That's because of the pirates in the White House. Zebra, it was right in front of me"

Lindsay says, "I've got a job, because you're a rich guy. You are a Tea Party Republican. I'm not buying into your theory."

Richard says, "My dear, you will see it my way within the next twelve months."

Lindsay says, "You will see it my way in the next two weeks. That's a promise."

CHAPTER 25

SLOW DOWN

L INDSAY WATCHED HIM sit in the recliner and fall asleep
for about forty-five minutes. She hoped some of the booze
would wear off. On TV was the president. He was giving
a speech on automatic weapons. They wanted to control the sale
of automatic firearm and clips that could hold large amounts of
ammunition.

The president wasn't finished. He was crying about sequester
cuts and blaming the Republicans. Some Democrats wanted to
pass a bill that would limit or take control of automatic weapons.
All sorts of ideas were being pondered. This was firing up gun
buying all over the country. There was one powerful lobbyist
organization that wasn't going to let the government mess with
the 2nd Amendment.

She thought about Richard's statements regarding the Zebra.
Maybe it was true. Were the president's men involved with all the
problems in America?

The unfortunate problem with government involvement was a
new group of criminals were taking advantage of the situation. The
Mexican underground syndicate was making money running guns
across the Mexican border. Al Qaeda cells in America were buying
guns and they had their own black market.

Richard woke up in time to see an insurance commercial. He missed the president's speech, which was a good thing for Lindsay. She would've listened to him rant for a while.

She continued to bark. "Look, if I know you had a few brewskis and if the cops would have stopped you, they would arrest you for DUI. That would really hurt us. Come on, we're close to a reward. Don't mess this up."

Richard maintained he was fine. He was in denial. The mistake she made next was a doozy.

She says, "You missed the president's talk about gun law."

Stern was a member of a national gun association. He knew they would do everything possible to block the law.

Richard retorts the same line.

"It's him or the guys under him. I'm telling you; I saw the Zebra. I saw three faces on TV. One of them is the Zebra. They don't speak the truth. Radio talk shows said everything about the president's policies. They said he's a narcissistic person. Nearly everything he says, are fabrications. The pirates are strangling the country. Maybe he can't tell the truth about the economy. Tea Party members know we're in trouble. The truth will bring him down."

"You're a racist. That's why you don't like him."

Richard says, "I'm not going to get into that, but here we go. It's time to pull out the race card. The talk show in the afternoon taught me how to deal with this race card crap. You're blinded by the Democrats. Look what's going on. The Tea Party said this before; he's driving the country into bankruptcy. He's the food stamp president."

She says, "If that's what you think, that's fine, we're making progress. At least you're thinking without drinking."

She was giving ground. The idea he pronounced about the Zebra could be taken a couple ways. Not every spoken word was in black and white. Another thought was the president was born in Hawaii. He had diverse parents. He was close to Muslims when he was growing up. He claimed to be a Christian. Everything wasn't in black and white.

She says, "He's not the Zebra. I think you're wrong."

Lindsay wasn't giving up on the president, although she was concerned about a number of issues. Stern was a Republican and a staunch Tea Party member. She needed to learn more about what he called, 'Pirates in the White House.'

She says, "I'm going to open up to you. You wanted to hypnotize me. I'll let you do it, but I want it to feel good, not scary. We can't do it until you're completely sober."

Richard asks, "What do you mean when you say we can't do it?"

Lindsay was being provocative. She walked over to him and whispered in his ear.

"I want you to doggy me, when you're healthy. Don't you want me?"

"Lindsay, I'm with you, honey."

"Listen to me. Do you think my imagination is running wild? Think of it this way, like I'm stripped naked and standing in front of you. I want you to do some wild things to me. You spin me around and double me over. Here's the best part. We record it."

Richard's jaw dropped. If he could wring the alcohol out of his body, he'd do it in a second. She was offering a perfect deviation from alcohol. She started to unbutton her shirt.

"You want me don't you? Pleasure and physical contact with someone who is enchanting will help you. You have to get better before we go all the way."

Her shirt was completely open as she bent down close to him.

"I'm going to let you play in a couple of days, maybe in a couple hours. We'll see.

Richard says, "Let's go for the couple hours or minutes."

Lindsay was turning him on. She moved the conversation to hypnosis.

"If you can hypnotize me, I'm sure you'll extract a name of the guy in Detroit. I think Abdul Madhi told me about his uncle and their business. I can give you what you want."

He says, "You ain't kidding.

He wanted to feel her at that moment, but she turned away.

"Oh, no! You have to get better first. We'll have the best time and you'll have the best time if you're healthy."

In her eyes it was a long shot to get him straight. Other women had tried. She was going to let him sober up for an hour or two. He needed to have some food while she made suggestive advances. She made soup and a sandwich for him.

As he was eating supper, she showered and put on some perfume. The robe she put on was nicely tied in a bow.

She had an erotic plan. She had to put him over the edge. This wasn't going to be a one way proposition. She wanted to truly enjoy the experience.

After an hour she came down the stairs.

"This is my evening outfit. Do you like it?"

He says, "I love the person that's in it."

"Remember, be good."

She says, "If I say 'I love you,' you'll know I was over the edge."

Richard says, "I think I'm starting to understand your treatment program."

He's almost in a state of shock. He wanted to be in good favor, if they were going all the way. He asked her to hold her positive thinking while he takes a shower and brushes his teeth. It seemed like the best show on earth was in his living room.

Lindsay says, "That's my guy. You go on shower up. I'll be waiting. We'll see how you feel. We might have to hold off or maybe let me experiment.

He made quick work of a shower and was back in the living room.

"Not now, you know the rule. We have to let your body undo the booze. We have to go slow. We can do some wild things and I want you to tell me how good it is to be a lover."

He was caught in a woman's trap. There was nothing flimsy about Lindsay. All he could think was 'teach me your secrets.'

He says, "Lindsay, teach me; show me how to make you feel good. I want to know what excites you."

Lindsay was definitely for that. She wanted to feel it. This man had to push her to the end of the rope.

She says, "You're starting to come around. Maybe, we're going to do this tonight. It's your turn. I'm going to tell you where to go. I want you to satisfy me."

By that answer he was ready to try it immediately.

"Let's do it now." He says.

"We have to bring you down slowly. The more I think about it; I'm going to ease you off the alcohol. I don't want you to go cold turkey.

"You better grab another beer, honey. I'm going to have a glass of red wine before we get involved in something heavy."

Maybe she wasn't prepared. She allowed him to drink. This was breaking her rule. Rather than slow down she was moving to pump him up. The close face to face suggestions were stimulating. She was doing the spicy act.

The tantalizing talk was stoking his engine. This was turning into a late afternoon delight. She needed to slow him down or he'd gush before the first quarter. She thought another beer would help him slow down, even though she wanted it.

"You can have another beer."

Really, she felt sorry for him. She knew his sleeping habits were terrible, so maybe she could convince him to see a therapist. One way to convince him was utilizing a woman's charm. On the top sex in the late afternoon might help him relax.

She says, "I don't want to turn you off by this, Richard, but go ahead and have the beer. I still think you need to see a specialist. The body needs to relax and then we can really get pumped up."

Richard says, "Look below, I'm pumped up right now."

She tried to get serious.

"You might have a post war affliction. I saw the ad on TV. I heard the VA has people that can help."

"You can help me right now, Lindsay. You just have to pin me to the carpet."

She says, "Actually, that's the right idea. I can smother you."

She could see he was ready. Her main concern at this point was to slow him down. She didn't want her man to lose it in seconds.

Even though her main concern was his sleep deprivation, she wanted to have fun too.

All of their work was coming together. She wanted to help him and there was more on her mind. The thought about marriage and a baby. They were close to making some serious money. She had to keep him together.

"I can see you're ready! I want you to relax."

Richard says, "I'm relaxed, trust me on this one."

"OK, here's my idea. You follow me to the couch."

She took his hand and led him to the couch. Brushing against the front of his pants wasn't an accident. She pushed her ample breasts against his hardened area at the same time pulling up his tee shirt over his head. He pulled on the bow of her robe to reveal her breasts. He lifted her higher. Without a bra they landed on his chest. When she felt him push the robe off her shoulders, her arms just slinked out. They cuddled for a moment.

"Not so fast, Lindsay. You're taking advantage of me."

She says, "You got me half unrobed."

"I can't help it."

She says, "I'm going to wear you out."

He says, "I'm ready. We have to slow down or I'll lose it.

Lindsay says, "OK, let me put my robe back on. I know you like them.

"No!" Richard protested.

She needed to talk him down or he would lose control.

Lindsay says, "This is what we have to do. We have to walk every day. We have to work out together. I say we walk or jog to the beach and then I'll reward you at home. After that, we can go to the Sunset Harbor. That's just a start. I'm going to sleep with you like I said. For the next two weeks we experiment. I think you'll start sleeping better. I know heavy duty sex will make you sleep. I'll have to prove it. I said I want to record every position we do."

Stern wasn't that intoxicated at this point. The food and shower gave him the timeout he needed. Although he had been at the VFW, the bowling alley, and the Honey Hole her idea was the best news for a horny man. Almost in shock Richard looked at her to find out if she was serious. He already knew she was an experienced lover. He knew she took him overboard in the office. Now it was his turn to do her.

For a short moment he realized the truth. She was turning into the greatest partner he had ever known. How could he top all the things she offered?

He wasn't dreaming. Stern had a couple beers under his belt that helped him slow down. She made these sumptuous conditions. He saw her as majestic. On his end the time for pleasure was now. The idea of making it happen with Lindsay was certainly like hitting a grand slam homer. She was put together like Eve in the Garden of Eden. Certainly Adam had no chance with a woman like Eve. Richard wouldn't stand a chance keeping up with Lindsay.

He didn't know she wanted to have a baby.

"Holy mackerel, Lindsay, I'll have to buy thirty-six condoms for the month."

Lindsay answered. "No, you'll need more than that."

Richard says, "I'm going to stop drinking."

Lindsay says, "No, you won't. You don't have to lie. You only have to work on me. If you do that, you might slow down your drinking. If this works, I can do so much with you. I know what a man likes. I mean sometimes I like to act like a doe in the woods. I bet you know that means excitement. Do you get the point?"

"Do I get the point? Am I dreaming?" He asked.

"Your drinking will go away." She says. "You have to go slow. You can go down on me. Just take me."

Richard says, "Yes, I got it. Jeez, I got it. It's going to be tough."

She says, "You don't need to drink to do it. I want you to make me feel good."

He was stunned. Here she was, maybe this was his unconditional partner. He was trying to hold his fire. How could he not resist her? Richard looked at her to find out if she was serious. He had the vision in his mind of the office frolic. Was she becoming his wife? For sure he didn't mind her suggestion.

The next beer under his belt had an effect. When she made the vivacious suggestion, he was following her words as if he was listening to his favorite female singer.

She says, "You wanted to hypnotize me. Well, I'm going to do the same thing to you. You know what I mean. There's a condition. You better make me lose it."

He took off his clothes in record time with her help.

She bent over and the invitation was enough for him.

"You want me to do it now."

She says, "No, not yet. I'm teasing you. You need a condom and go get your camera."

The crazy maybe awkward performance was recorded. It was far better than he ever had. Afterwards, he had to have two more beers to bring him down. She had another glass of wine and reminded him about the workout.

"You should be relaxed. I want you to go to sleep tonight and dream about this experience. Let's lay on the floor for a while. We need to cool off."

Later that evening the bedroom setting was in order. The camera and candlelight was in the right place.

She snuggled close to him to get ready for fun. They didn't waste much time. Her nightgown was unfastened to give him a preview. He was bare. It was a turn on. It all worked. The point of his ambition was standing tall.

"Slow down, Richard. You don't have a condom."

He fumbled for a condom like a football player trying to find a loose football. He couldn't put it on, because she was pulling him down. No condom, that was ok with her. Out of control he couldn't find time to get it right. The fantastic goodness was beyond his control. There was no retraction. The action was too quick. He was off the mark. She could feel him lose it. A premature release happened before her time.

She says, "You pulled away in time to release a shot. I've got to work with you. It's on my stomach. It's all over me."

After the experience she grabbed the camera and turned out the night light as she walked to the bathroom. He was falling asleep and she could feel the effect of his good time. She had some fun, but it went too fast to satisfy her. She wanted a deeper, longer lasting experience. He had his delight again. It clearly put his lights out.

She turned on the shower to clean off his semen. The partial happiness of her experience wasn't the way she wanted it to go. She wanted a greater lasting performance.

When she returned, he was in dream land. She wanted another shot, but was glad he was sleeping. She went upstairs to her own bedroom. The experiment was a misfire. She would have to give him another try. She had to figure out how to cool him down. At least she had the camera video to see where she went wrong. She plugged the camera into the TV.

"Where did I go wrong?" She whispered.

Her new approach had to keep him in check. The next time she would slow him down.

She thought about using ice cream to cool his momentum. Maybe she should stay dressed for a longer time. That might hold him off.

CHAPTER 26

DREAMING OF THE GREAT FIRE

ICHARD'S DREAM WASN'T of the workout they had during the evening and night. It was of a terrorist attack. It started this way.

He was talking in his sleep. *"Don't pick on us. They're up to something. They're going to burn the town. I saw them tampering with the gas valves."*

Small towns have a way of attracting big headlines, especially when crazy things happen. There were funerals and weddings that made local news. Gossip was a stretch in time to air out the laundry, maybe sugar coat a promising romance, or talk about the neighbor. Gossip was king among small towns like Fairport Harbor. Most folks had to say something about the weather, their high school team, or a criminal act like a drug bust. Fairport Harbor was no different. Little events were fashioned to make them seem bigger than they really were.

An exception was coming. This time the news in Fairport Harbor was going national. Because of the workout with Lindsay and the beer, he fell asleep.

It was cold outside as he fetched the paper. He read the newspaper headlines.

Broadcasters from across TV land from the East Coast to the West Coast were streaming into tiny harbor town. Fairport Harbor Burns.

Stern lived through the horrible event. He had his own version of the story to tell which he kept as a secret. He wasn't about to tell anyone what he had done the night before the great fire. She was a barroom pickup.

Stern was dreaming off and on. He fall asleep and the dream would start all over.

The big fuss was about the terrorist explosions. It wasn't an explosion at all. The enemy circumvented safety devices in the natural gas pipeline that was feeding natural gas to the town.

He woke up again and went to the refrigerator to grab a beer. He sat at the breakfast nook thinking about the great fire. He downed a second brew. After walking to the bathroom and back to his bed he fell into another trance.

Richard Stern was alerted early that Monday morning by a phone call. 'EVACUATE' the voice on the phone was excited, shouting, well certainly touting an imminent danger. Fairport Harbor was in the midst of a full scale evacuation order from the mayor.

The person said he had to get out of town. The town was on fire, many houses were burning. He said, "Get out now," and the person hung up.

Richard says, "Smoke, I smell smoke."

Stern dashed into the living room and looked out the window. An apartment was on fire across the street. It was a bad fire.

"This was bound to happen," said Stern to himself.

What Richard Stern was referring to was the fact that he suspected the terrorists had returned and he had enough fore warning of imminent danger. No one would believe a drunk. He saw them and so did this woman he was with. The FBI knew Stern could come up with some highly unusual circumstances.

The dream ended for a short time. It returned to the night before when he met a woman who was looking for friendship.

Stern tried to remember what happened the night before. He saw her sitting alone and introduced himself. Here he was talking to a pretty girl at a Mentor tavern.

The barmaid could see the conversation between the two was engaging and she offered to buy them a drink. He tipped the barmaid a five dollar bill. The couple had another beer even though it was getting late. It was almost last call.

Penny says, "Let's have one more. I'll buy."

Stern was surely not going to turn down a brew under the circumstances. They talked like they knew each other. She wanted to be his friend. They talked about friendships.

Stern says, "I'm glad I met you, Penny."

She already had plenty to drink. Stern wasn't exactly sober. He had one thing on his mind as most men do when they're intoxicated. Sex, that was on his mind as Penny reiterated her story of a failed marriage.

She went into some detail and Stern was all ears. His pledge to himself was to stay in line. He didn't want to ruin a friendship. It was fine to have one more brew and that was it. Of course, that was a pipedream and he knew it, especially since he was seated next to a woman who was more intelligent, younger and a totally attractive blond. He thought he knew her.

One thing led to another, an invitation was made to him to stop over to her apartment for a late night beer.

It was cold outside as they left. She only lived a couple blocks away. It was about 1:00AM in the morning.

They talked and drank more beer. Somewhere along the line Stern suggested she come to his house and she agreed. They could carry the conversation to Stern's house, because they liked each other. They were compatible.

The mystery about Stern was a story reoccurring. He dreamed and the dreams seem to turn into real events.

There was a natural attraction. It was happening again. He couldn't understand how the Lord placed him with attractive women. He had a choice. It was all about temptation.

He thought one thing first. She wanted to sleep with him. His mind kept going around when she suggested sleeping over.

She said, "You can sleep with me."

Now he was on the move. He wasn't turning her down as they kissed. He had been given the green light and a chance to score.

She was plenty drunk. He didn't want to take advantage of her condition. His second thought was a man's desire. She was a pretty woman. He thought about the devil as he unbuttoned her blouse. She was giving him the green light. He invited a pretty woman over to his house and started to undress her He could feel her ample breasts. Stern had second thoughts. Taking advantage of her wasn't right, but he was having trouble stopping. How could he handle this? This was the same way he entertained Agent Monica and seduced her.

He woke from the dream and went to the bathroom. He knew he had Penny or someone like her in his past. The question in his mind was one he couldn't answer.

The barmaid and Penny, he says, "They knew each other."

He walked back to the bedroom and thought; this is strange. Still, it was a dream. He fell asleep and the dream came roaring back.

They were back at the bar. The deserted bar, once called the Inferno, was a nice place to hide. Troubles could be left at the door. The name, Inferno, seemed fitting for the troubles that were coming.

He flashed to his house where he told Penny he couldn't take advantage of her. He took her to a bedroom next to his.

Penny protested, "Come on, let's do it."

She removed her blouse, off went her bra. Tapping on the bed, she invited him to lay with her. He started to unfasten his belt. All was moving fast. She succeeded in taking off his pants.

Richard says, "Wait, I have to pee."

Richard walked to his bathroom and jumped in the shower.

He yelled, "I want to be clean if we're going to have sex"

After he showered and brushed his teeth. He was ready. He only had a towel around his waist as he opened the bedroom door.

"This is a first for us; I want it to go right. I'll only be a few minutes before we get going. I have to find a condom. Just remember, I'll be back."

After a quick search in his bedroom he found a condom. He walked into her bedroom. The condom was lubricated and Stern lost control and it fell to the floor. He fumbled around trying to get it on. Penny started to talk about her previous husband. She was out of it. In between a sentence she passed out while talking about her 'bastard husband.' It was someone from another state. He was so close. Unrolling the condom, he figured it could be used in the morning. He didn't try to wake her.

"Damn, I blew it." I wish she would have. Damn!"

It was a missed opportunity. He conceded one promise. Everything was in place to have fun in the morning.

He grabbed the underwear and put it on. Stern walked back to his bedroom. Disappointment was firmly imbedded in his mind. He thought, hopefully she'll want to do it in the morning. His body hit the bed like an apple falling to the ground. Sleep came quick for him.

Stern woke up from the dream. He could tell the dream was an arousing affair. His underwear was spotty wet.

It was a weird dream. He didn't understand all the implications. His body was tired and it couldn't stand at the moment. Then he fell asleep.

Somewhat foggy in his head from a night of over-indulging, he remembered the woman from the last night. Was she in the other bedroom? He looked into the adjacent bedroom. Penny was there. She was sleeping and half undressed. Her boobs were exposed.

The phone rang. Stern dashed to his bedroom to answer the phone in one ring. The person on the other end talked like a person in a state of panic.

"Get in your car and drive out of town. I don't know what's going on. The mayor has ordered everyone to leave town. Houses are on fire. Natural gas is leaking somewhere. That's all I know, move it. I mean right now. Just get out of town."

Stern recognized the voice. It was Seth Wood, a neighbor down the street.

He opened one eye. It was a wild dream. He had a slight idea who Penny was. He went to the bathroom. Then he returned to his bed. It didn't take long to fall asleep. The dream came back quickly.

Stern heard the sirens and could smell smoke.

He had to wake his new found friend. There she was, so inviting. He rousted Penny.

"Penny, wake up. Put your clothes on we have to get out of town. The mayor has ordered an evacuation of Fairport Harbor. There's a natural gas leak. You drive straight home."

The noise outside was from cars going by. That wasn't unusual, but they could hear other noises. Background sound, people talking, yelling, and there were sirens from afar. They were getting closer. Sirens could be heard in different areas of the town. Each echo had a different pitch. There was no doubt in Stern's mind. The fires were all over.

Penny asked, "Where am I?"

"You're at my house in Fairport Harbor. I'm Richard Stern. I'm in the phone book."

"Oh God!" She cried.

Richard says, "Put your clothes on. You have to go. I'm leaving town as soon as I get dressed. I don't know what's going on."

Stern couldn't find his pants. His car keys were in them.

Richard yells, "I can't find my pants."

Penny says, "Your pants are in this room."

Now she was trying to remember what they did. She couldn't remember. This was very troubling for her.

She had to get her clothes on. Fishing through the clothes she spotted the condom on the floor. Panic was setting her up to cry. She found her bra. Buttoning her blouse wasn't a problem.

The condom was scary. She was trying to remember what happened. She saw the bathroom door and relieved herself. Once in the bedroom to make one last look, she was out of the bedroom in a flash. Stern only had his underwear on and fast walked her to the attached garage where her car was parked. He was a little embarrassed. He could see the sigh of relief as she fumbled through her purse looking for her car keys. She was still half drunk.

Richard says, "Penny, I'm glad I met you."

She had to ask, "I saw the condom in the bedroom. Did we do it? Your pants were in my bedroom. I'd really like to know."

Richard said, "No, you fell asleep as I was putting it on. I went to my bedroom. Don't worry; we didn't do anything. We were too drunk to do it. There isn't anything to worry about."

Penny was as bad as him, because she could only remember bits and pieces of how they met. They made it to his house from her house. She wondered if they did it at her house. She kind of remembered taking his pants off. She remembered that much. She felt fine, not sore from being treated badly like her ex-husband would treat her.

The fire saved her from further embarrassment. The emergency vehicles were coming, so she started her car and started to back out of the garage. What way does she have to go? She was sort of glad he wasn't a jerk and didn't question his honesty. She was embarrassed for the fact that she wasn't sure about the whole night. This was a blackout moment for her. She had started the heavy drinking ever since she broke her first marriage.

Stern was in a panic. His pants were in her bedroom. He had one leg stuck in his pants as he fell onto her bed. He was glad to wake Penny and get her moving. He wasn't very sober.

He stumbled again, but got his pants and tee shirt on. He ran out to the sidewalk. Penny was stopped in the drive, because of traffic. Stern had to yell a few finishing words to her.

Stern knew Penny was in total disarray. She looked scared as she back out of the drive. Across the street she saw the apartment engulfed in flames. She rolled down the window.

Richard says, "Look, Penny, I'm pointing south. Go that way. You can take any left turn to get out of town. This is really crazy."

Penny says, "Hey, I'll call you later if the town is still here. I hope I can call you, bye."

Penny seemed to know the way out of the house. People were standing outside. There was a pungent odor in the air. It was natural gas.

The fire trucks were coming to battle the blaze. Sirens were blaring from afar. Stern could tell they were coming from out of town.

The stale beer was still on Stern's breath and his bedroom smelled like a barroom. That was one of the smells permeating the house. He cracked open another beer. In his condition it was troubling to figure out if something was wrong with his house. An odor of gas and smoke seemed to fill his nostrils.

Stern felt he had time to grab his black berry brandy. The fridge still had some beer in it. He downed a beer, checked for his car keys, and put on pants, socks and shoes.

It was time to hustle The fumes in the house were somewhat bad. The fumes and smoke were coming from the apartment fire across the street. He moved rapidly to the garage. He wasn't sure if he should push the button for the garage door opener for fear it might set off an explosion. It was a panic decision. He didn't hesitate that long. Pushing the garage door button worked, he could get out of town. Once in the Honda, he backed out. He pushed the button again. He could hear the motor close the door. It was time to leave. There wasn't a problem.

Penny was long gone. He looked across the street. Fire and smoke was billowing out of the apartment building's windows. It looked like everyone from the building was on the street corner. He saw Mel and Cindy. They lived in the apartment next to the one on fire.

Stern heard someone say 'thank God, we got out.' That meant much to Stern. He could see the town was in a state of panic. All of this turmoil fed his mind. It could be terrorism.

The huge fire across the street was now being battled by firemen from several fire departments. There were fire trucks on every street. He had to drive north and west down Second Street. Once he got to High Street he was blocked again. He had to go east down Seventh Street.

Stern had one thing on his mind.

"It's terrorist. They're here."

Richard woke and his tee shirt was sweaty. He was running a slight fever. The booze was leaving his body.

The thoughts running through his mind were of the next terrorist threat. The devils were working overtime. They had just attacked a running event. The Boston Marathon had bombs blow up spectators. This was the new threat that John Campbell and him were talking about. Homegrown terrorists were going to attack regular Americans.

Al Qaeda was located in every state. It was obvious. Terrorists were running all over the country and targeting the public at large events. All Americans had to be on alert watching for the enemy.

Al Qaeda could recruit and have their pick of many unemployed, disgruntled Americans. People had to have jobs and the enemy was quite willing to shell out large amount of cash to recruit homegrown anarchists. This thought set off Richard. He started talking to himself.

He says, "Provide the young men with women and cash, they'll do the devils work. This would be the perfect way to recruit new Muslims radicals with anti-American feelings."

At that point Lindsay walked to his bedroom. She could hear him talking to himself.

"Are you dreaming again? I heard you. You're talking to yourself."

"Lindsay, I had a crazy dream again. I'll always wonder if the great fire in Fairport Harbor was staged by Al Qaeda terrorists."

Stern had more on his mind than the great fire. He was worried about running into someone named Penny. He had to slow down on his drinking. When he looked at her, he knew Lindsay was giving him plenty of help. She was like the medicine he needed.

His dreams seemed to come true far too often. Lindsay pointed it out to him. The FBI had written about his strange ability to see beyond the horizon.

He could only remember one Penny. She was a blond. What would he do if the other Penny showed up? He didn't want Lindsay getting into a fracas with some girlfriend from the past. He knew Brenda would come calling one day. Stern was doing it again He was making a prophecy. This one would come true and it wouldn't be nice.

Lindsay says, "You have two habits. Drinking is one and the dreams, well they're something else. I'm telling you; you're not a weirdo, so don't worry about the first two habits."

I'll have to work with you and you'll get better."

Another trouble was homegrown terrorists. He was thinking about the next job they were setting up. There were too many foreign university students filled with hate in the country. They wanted an American education and had the ability to create horrific terror in the schools. Disgruntled college kids, they could easily be recruit.

Richard tells his campus theory that he and John Campbell spoke about in detail.

"Lindsay, I probably told you this. College campuses are a perfect breeding ground for Al Qaeda want-a-be terrorists. If they want new recruits, Al Qaeda leaders can easily pick out the bad apples that had a chip on their shoulder by just watching anti-American rallies."

Mr. Stern was right. The government was letting more young people into the country to attend universities. Many of these people were Muslim extremists. They get visas to stay in the country. When the visas expire, they choose to stay and nobody knows they're here.

CHAPTER 27

PICTURES ON THE LAKE

RICHARD ASKED LINDSAY to practice using his camera equipment. Taking pictures of Lake Erie boaters would help her develop photography techniques. With a fresh mind using his camera and video equipment her ideas might blossom. By picking out action photos she was about to move the camera with grace like a ballerina.

"Lindsay, work on your own style. Try using the video for moving targets. Just keep practicing and you'll be better at it than me."

With this suggestion in mind she took regular walks to the beach to snap pictures of boaters. Birds were everywhere. She walked to the Sunset Bar and Grill for an occasional water. From the outside patio she kept a watchful eye for unusual objects on Lake Erie. If Ronnie Curliss saw a submarine, there was no reason for it not to happen again.

The routine went on for a few weeks. Picture snapping was becoming a favorite pastime for Lindsay as she worked to refine her experience. Still pictures were her best work, but she could use the video function of the camera to capture moving action shots of power boats roaring across Lake Erie.

She still did her regular home secretarial work, but always managed to break away for a walk to the beach. Richard was improving by her approach to his problem.

After Richard came home from trips, he and Lindsay shared experiences especially when he returned from good investigative work. She had plenty of stored up adventures to tell him and didn't hold back when she related one such experience.

The conversation when this way. As she was snapping pictures from the beach, a large yacht passed by. The action shot she took was of particular interest. It was of a yacht moving toward Painesville Township Park. The interesting part of the picture she captured was of the cruiser yacht called Brother M. The ship had a large contingent of lightly clad women. The sun was quite warm that day and the ladies, some without bathing suit tops or bottoms were being chased by nude men. She switched to video to capture the entire scene. The men aboard the yacht seemed to be taking full advantage of the women. As she zoomed in on the deck of the yacht, it appeared the women were being held down against their will. She thought it was maybe an X rated movie. Her conscience told her different. It looked criminal. Lindsay thought the women were being raped.

She immediately called the US Coast Guard and reported what she was viewing. The coast guard sent out one of their fast action watercraft to inspect the situation. It took them twenty minutes to arrive at the starboard side of the Brother M. The Brother M captain was ordered to cut his engines and standby to be boarded.

In the interval of time before the coast guard craft arrived the ladies had put bathing suit on and the men did the same. The coastguardsmen boarded and inspected the yacht for safety equipment. When questioned by the coastguard officer, no irregularities were found. The women didn't protest or complain of mistreatment. It appeared the young people were enjoying the day of fun in the sun.

The captain of the Brother M was asked where he was heading. He told the officer they were going back to Sandusky to drop off their regular customers. The Brother M was only a tourist yacht and made regular trips to Fairport Harbor and back to the home port of Sandusky, Ohio. They would do the same trip twice a week, always with a large contingent of men and women. Everyone had to be at least twenty-one years old to make the trip.

Permission was granted to proceed as the coast guard officer found no grounds to halt their progress. He made a thorough report. The most interesting part of the report was the fact that the crew and tourist all seemed to be Middle Eastern men, maybe Muslim or people of European decent.

The coast guard officer called Lindsay on her cell phone and said they checked out the Brother M and found nothing unusual. They were permitted to proceed back to their home port in Sandusky. He told her she did the right thing by calling the coast guard.

When she got back to the office, she was excited. Lindsay told Richard that she thought one of the men was a regular visitor she had seen at the Oasis Club in Santee, California. The camera wasn't good enough to capture that fact. Still it stuck in her mind and she related the suspicion to him.

She says, "I'm not sure, but I think one of those men was a regular customer at the Oasis Club. He was there to visit Abdul Madhi. Maybe we better call the FBI now."

He says, "No, we don't have enough facts. This is all conjecture. You're not sure. The coast guard checked the ship. We can't tell the FBI we think we know someone on the ship. I mean you're old customer. What are we going to say? We think he's a terrorist. That isn't going to fly. What's that going to do for us? We don't have solid proof. The ship might be a floating prostitute ring."

Lindsay says, "We have to say something. I have pictures."

"Yes, I have to take a ride on that ship."

Lindsay almost fell over. She was shocked by that idea. She held back and didn't say anything for a minute. Then it all registered. The very idea of Richard going on that kind of ship was out of the question.

"You're not going on a ship with prostitutes. I'm making; I mean we're making good progress. No sir, you're not going on that boat."

"Maybe, I'll send a letter to Agent Ron Roman. It'll be a short letter letting him know we think we found a prostitution ring. I'll give him some details about the Brother M. I'll say we think it's a prostitute ship. I'll send him a copy of the video you captured. I don't want him to get it until we're back from Sandusky. We need to do some investigating."

Lindsay heard him say, 'when we're back from Sandusky.'

She asks, "What do you mean?"

"We can go together."

He continues, "If we find something out, then we'll be in the position to collect a reward, because we'll have the firsthand knowledge the FBI needs. We'll let Agent Roman decide at that point. Most likely, he'll call me. I can't tell his boss, Cliff Moses, he doesn't like me."

Richard didn't know that Agent Micovich had already tipped off Agent Roman about gun running on Lake Erie.

Richard wrote the letter addressing it to FBI Agent Roman that evening. He expressed what they knew about the Brother M. Lindsay proof read the letter.

"You told him about the coast guard," said Lindsay. "That was good. Send it in an Email. I'll feel better knowing the FBI has this information.

In the meantime Agent Roman was putting two and two together with the information Agent Micovich had sent him. Supervisor Moses called for a stakeout in Sandusky.

Lindsay was still wondering and a bit frightened about a ride on the tour boat.

Chapter 28

Botched Boat Ride

ALL THE INFORMATION Agent Micovich was leaving for Agent Ron Roman was blending into a gun running game that was moving north. Agent Nicole Swider and Kayla Jacobson worked with Agent Micovich to put together a purpose. There was reason to believe the underground syndicate was making big money off automatic weapons because of the government's idea to freeze the sale of semi-automatic weapons.

The agents knew the weapons were being transported in vans after the big bust. What they did know was heard from third party gossip. Nothing was solid, the evidence was still sketchy. Supervisor Moses requested additional help. He was granted one new agent, a recruit that was learning. Moses met Agent Marisa Ross and immediately placed her with Agent Micovich. Agent Ross came on board because of the gun running developments. Agent Micovich told her they would be visiting marinas as sightseers.

'Operation Moving North' was the new maneuver. FBI and ATF only netted one shipment. There had to be others. The FBI didn't have an exact location. The south shore of Lake Erie had many marinas. Agent Monica and Agent Marisa Ross traveled to various marinas one by one. Each time they spent a day watching for suspicious activity. It was a new experience for Agent Ross and

Monica. Monica was working with a new recruit and training her at the same time. They in turn relayed the information to Agent Roman, although nothing worthwhile.

Agent Roman had new information to share with his boss. He told Supervisor Moses of the development. He showed a picture of the Brother M, which was supplied by Richard Stern. That hit a nerve with Moses.

Roman says, "It's a tourist ship. The coast guard checked it out. Supposedly, it leaves twice a week to Fairport Harbor and Ashtabula. There might be something illegal going on. Stern says something about a prostitution ring."

Supervisor Moses says, "If Mr. Stern has anything to do with this investigation, it'll turn out to be a fiasco."

Agent Roman explained the situations that Agent Micovich told him. They only found one van that was carrying weapons. The operation around El Paso was finished for the time being. It was likely the Mexican cartel just moved their base of operation. Gun running was still moving north and likely heading to Sandusky based on information from an Indian agent.

Supervisor Moses thought about the tie between the Brother M and gun running to Ashtabula. He decided to arrange a stakeout. He ordered Roman and Wright to take charge and watch the Brother M. Moses wanted his most experienced men on this stakeout.

Stern had his own idea. He was going to pay for a ride on the Brother M. He told Lindsay the best way to find out what's going is to get into the action. Lindsay protested. For one thing she didn't want him hooking up with prostitutes.

Lindsay says, "I don't like this idea. You and I can stay a good match, but going on a prostitute ship is really off the chart. I'd be worried the entire time you're on that tour boat. How am I going to control you with all those girls running around?"

Richard says, "Lindsay, you're the most beautiful person I know."

"You can't control yourself, Richard. At least not yet, I mean. You'll start drinking. If you start drinking and these bathing suit babes attempt to seduce you, I see trouble. Now I know how you get into jams. I understand how you operate. You're a hell or high water guy. I'll come right to the point. I don't like this idea at all. One big worry is catching some venereal disease, if you were going alone and that isn't going to happen."

He says, "You'll be with me. We're just going to be tourists. I want you to change your identity. Wear makeup that changes your features."

Lindsay thought about that idea. With a nod she agreed. She would go with him to make sure he doesn't do something stupid. She read how he had gotten into trouble.

She says, 'Yep, I have to go with you. We'll go for a boat ride, but I don't like it."

Richard made the arrangements for them by offering twice the money for a boat ride. The Brother M tourist rep would allow them to make a half trip. The trip to Fairport Harbor would end for them at the federal prior. The Captain of the Brother M approved. He would drop them off at that point in the tour. It would cost them $800.00 dollars each.

They could play blackjack and party with the ladies if they wanted to have some extra fun, but that would cost another $500.00 each.

The captain explained his operation was a full service luxury tour. Private gambling was allowed. The girls, called chaperones would do almost 'anything' for a nice tip. The girls were also show girls that provided entertainment at a variety of levels. Stern agreed and paid the upfront fee. Absolutely no cameras were allowed. Stern arranged for a bus to take them to Sandusky.

Richard told Lindsay this boat tour would help them cash in. If he could prove good on something Agent Micovich sent him, they would surely be in the money.

"Lindsay, we have to be careful. Remember, you might know one of the guys on board. If they suspect we're up to something, which would ruin their operation, I'm afraid we would be in trouble. You bring your weapon. I don't want this tour to be like taking LSD, a bad trip. Keep your gun loaded. We'll stay in the back of the boat. I'm going to carry two small inflatable life preservers. If we have to jump off the boat, we'll have life preservers. I should have asked. Can you swim?"

Lindsay says, "I lived near the Pacific Ocean. Of course I can swim. I'll be armed and loaded. I'm a little scared, but I'm not letting you go by yourself. I can see how dangerous this job can be. If I'm going with you, this .357 magnum will provide both of us with protection."

Richard says, "I'll have my own pistol."

The bus dropped them off near the marina in Sandusky on the morning of the trip. The day was going to be a little breezy. The captain of the Brother M was there to greet the guests. He said to expect a little choppy water on Lake Erie. There would be forty customers with two being dropped off in Fairport Harbor.

Agent Ron Roman and Bill Wright were watching the boarding party from their vantage point. When Roman spotted Richard Stern his eyes bugged out of his head. He nudged Agent Wright and handed him the binoculars.

Agent Roman says, "Bill, look at the boarding party. Tell me that isn't Richard Stern."

"Holly crap, it's him alright. We have to stop this trip. Let's ask the captain for a boarding manifest of the passengers. This stakeout is screwed."

Agent Roman summoned the captain to the dock. He identified himself as an FBI agent and asked to see the boarding manifest.

Agent Roman says, "I suspect one member of your boarding party is wanted by the FBI. We saw that person board this vessel. Agent Roman pointed out Mr. Richard Stern as the one. Stern would have to disembark. The captain surrendered Mr. Stern and Lindsay went with him.

Agent Roman with quick, pointed words demanded an explanation from Mr. Stern. He was plenty mad that Stern had botched the investigation. Stern introduced Lindsay to Agent Roman and Agent Wright as a way of cooling off the hot-headed agent.

Richard says, "We're one step ahead of you guys. What's wrong with that? I sent you an email with the details. Lindsay and I are going on a cruise to dig up a little more information."

Lindsay says, "We haven't done anything wrong. I couldn't let him go by himself. Not on this kind of yacht."

Agent Roman says, "Miss Wagner, do you know who you're with?"

She says, "Yes I do, Richard Stern, my boyfriend. I work for him."

Roman says, "Jesus, I don't believe this."

Agent Wright walked closer to eyeball Lindsay's figure. She could tell by his wishful grin that he was a wolf. Wright thought Mr. Stern's girlfriend would be a wonderful bedmate. He was very impressed with Mr. Stern's choice of a girlfriend. She was very beautiful in his estimation. How could he land this woman?

Wright says, "You're a lucky man, Mr. Stern. I hope Miss Wagner is prepared for the sorrowful acts of Mr. Stern."

That comment got under her skin. Lindsay was starting to get steamed. She was Mr. Stern's new girlfriend and knew him to be a pretty nice guy. She had some control over him. The FBI wasn't going to tell her whom to see and where to go.

Richard explained to Roman his reasoning for taking a trip on the Brother M. It seemed to him: he was following the enemy. Lindsay jumped in and indicated she was doing her best to keep her man from getting into trouble. She realized that their job was dangerous. To help her man secure information about the enemy and snatch a reward, she was all in. She knew Richard could use her connection on this boat trip, because she believed she knew one of the men aboard the Brother M. That information might help them score a reward.

Agent Roman had some advice for Miss Wagner.

"Stern has a way of getting into trouble. I can't minimize this, Miss Wagner. You have to be careful when working with Richard Stern."

Lindsay's reaction was swift. She couldn't get over his reprimand. Stern never took advantage of her. In a short time she learned so much by working with Richard. He was her guy and she was going to protect him. She wasn't going to give up on her personal quest, the real secret in her life. The fact that she wanted a beautiful son or daughter was none of their business. Richard just might be the guy that could provide her that gift from God.

Agent Roman made a very blunt point. He went a bit out of bounds with his example.

"Stern has messed some people up and one of them is my friend. Agent Monica Micovich has a son. Stern is the father. She's back from El Paso now. She could tell you some pretty hairy stories about Richard Stern."

Lindsay knew that. She heard enough from the male chauvinist agents who were obviously biased. She was a loyal girlfriend and was done hearing slams against her guy. She didn't want to hear anything about Agent Monica Micovich. She already knew enough.

She says, "Don't you guys have work to do? Maybe you like harassing regular tourists."

She had read all the FBI paperwork on Richard Stern. He seemed to be much better about drinking with her and she was glad Agent Micovich wasn't with them.

Lindsay says, "Now that you ruined our boat trip it's time to say goodbye. You agents need to get back to your job and leave us alone. Richard and I will travel back to Fairport Harbor. We'll see if we can get a refund and take a bus back home. Thanks for nothing!"

Lindsay wasn't finished. She had a few more words to say.

"Sorry we tried to help you fight the enemy. We aren't done and we'll be collecting a reward. It won't be long. You FBI guys better get ready to write some big checks. And we have delicious sex all the time, Agent Wright, so if you're jealous, too bad."

Richard couldn't believe what she was saying to the agents. Lindsay was definitely a hot potato when she felt intimidated.

Richard says, "OK, guys, we'll be leaving. Lindsay is just mad about missing the boat ride. We didn't know you guys were here. Let's go Lindsay. I bought insurance on this trip. They have to refund our money."

The FBI agents probably saved their lives. If Lindsay was found out to be someone that could finger the terrorist on board, they might have been dumped overboard.

The stakeout and investigation was blown. Agent Roman and Wright reported back to Supervisor Moses. They filled him in. Moses kept his cool for some reason. He wasn't that surprised that Mr. Stern was on the same trail.

"Agent Micovich and I had a talk about Mr. Stern. She knows him pretty well. There are some questions in my mind that I'm trying to understand. I don't know what's going on between Monica and Stern, but it can't be good. Now, Stern is dragging a new woman into the picture."

Agent Wright says, "She's a foxy lady. We're going to see both of them again."

Moses says, "That's what bothers me. We're going to see them again."

CHAPTER 29

JIHADIST IN AMERICA

L INDSAY AND RICHARD were riding back to Fairport Harbor. At least they got their money back from the Captain of the Brother M. Actually the captain was quite grateful for finding out the FBI was monitoring the marina and his yacht.

The back of the bus was somewhat cozy. There were open seats. Most of the travels were just consumed by the ride, reading, or sleeping.

As they moved along, Richard carried a conversation about the country. He was getting worked up. Lindsay detected his agitation. She knew how to handle his condition, but held out to see where he was going.

He reiterated a variation of a biblical saying.

"You know 'When a man's hands are idle, he'll be working in the devil's workshop.'

He made this point when talking about all the jobless people in the country.

He says, "We have too many young Americans looking for something to do. No jobs, it means trouble for America. Our country is falling apart. The government is out of control. The IRS is after the TEA PARTY, religious groups, and conservatives. I know you like the president, but average citizens are getting the shaft. I'm telling you, Lindsay. I see riots coming."

Lindsay says, "My hands are idle. Am I in the Devil's work shop?"

She was being coy and staying in the conversation. At the same time she positioned herself for an advance to shift the conversation.

Lindsay doesn't quite agree, however, she is starting to believe that corruption in the White House or with White House staff is happening. She knew government officials were covering for the president. She didn't want to say more on the matter. If she added fuel to his line of thought, he might start drinking again and that would be her worst nightmare.

"Richard, you know I'm still a Democrat. I don't want you to get upset. Everything that's happening will eventually bring down the perpetrators. People that lie cannot hide forever."

She went on to talk about their laptop. She was honed in on the jihadist website.

"Look at this, Richard."

He looked to see what she was viewing. It was an article about anarchists.

The internet can give anarchist ideas to join a Muslim movement or they can go to a university and team up with likeminded students. Within a short time a jihadist and radical cell is formed. These people can live in America and never be detected.

Richard says, "You and I know this is happening. America's conservatives and I say the pirates in the White House are part of this problem. Someone high up in government is giving protection to the enemy. The other part of the problem is people don't care. They vote like you."

Lindsay was a little perturbed by that statement. She stayed on the sideline rather than start a rock throwing contest. As she read about anarchists, she turned to him with her beautiful blue eyes. Lindsay listened intently.

He was being hypnotized by her. Doing his best not to be distracted, he continued to talk.

She was starting to understand the meaning of pirates in the White House. China was stealing jobs, stealing technology, and interfering with our business interests to the point where they could disrupt communications.

Richard explained further, "We're bringing in foreign students that have a chip on their shoulder. I told you that before. They are using our universities to learn. The end result is they go back to their homeland and terrorist training camps. They learn how to make IEDs, pipe bombs, and hand grenades and come back to America with all the evil in their head to cause mayhem."

Lindsay says, "I get it, my man. It's obvious, these people are homegrown terrorists."

Richard says, "Lindsay, you're starting to see the big picture. If we don't secure the borders, people like Abdul Madhi get in. We let criminals go at the direction of the pirates in the White House. They're only interested in recruiting voters. We have to start electing true Americans, like Tea Party members that have the good of the country as their motivation for being in office. Voters have to elect first class citizens. We don't need many career politicians."

Lindsay says, "Well, I'm voting for you."

Richard was revved up. Lindsay changed the topic in quick order. Rubbing with her hand, she moved lower to distract him. It worked almost instantly. He could feel her working at his belt buckle. He reached under her tee shirt and found the nipple. The distraction was moving fast. She initiated the charge, which changed her man's features. She could easily work him over at the moment, but decided to talk a little more and keep him pumped. He was plenty distracted at this point.

Lindsay asks, "What would happen if we could only have seven rounds of ammunition in our guns? Wouldn't that be crazy?"

"Lindsay, I can't talk with you right now. I'm trying to hold my fire. It isn't working.

She didn't stop her underhandedness until he was fully unloaded. She pulled out a handkerchief to clean up.

"Lindsay, you always know how to calm a man down."

She says, "Yeah, I know. That didn't take much effort. Go back to the police weapons. You were saying something about magazines and guns when you shot me in the hand. Didn't you know your gun was loaded?

"I could feel your fingers on the trigger."

"I guess I made you shoot."

"That was a sneak attack, my lady."

Richard wanted to return the favor, but the setting wasn't as easy. She would have to wait until they got home.

He says, "Ask not what Lindsay can do for me, ask when I will do double to her."

She says, "You can do it when we get back. Now, about those huge magazines, what did you want to say?"

They continued their talk about police, weapons, terrorists and the tour boat. The terrorists were arming up. On the other hand the government wants to take guns and lower the number of rounds that can be loaded in a gun. It didn't make sense.

Richard says, "I'll bet the police have huge magazines with thirty shot clips. All Americans should be armed to the teeth. We are at war with the jihadists. Homegrown terrorist cells are being recruited in every state. I can tell you there are many radical Muslims in this country. They are raising money to use against our way of life. I don't mean every Muslim. We have good people of all religions in this country. I would never want to surrender my guns or limit the size of a magazine. We need all the fire power we can carry."

Lindsay says, "I've learned a lot since I've been with you. I don't think they'll quit trying to kill us. They're nuts. They hate they're country and come here to sow their hate."

He says, "It's called jihad or a holy war against unbelievers. I guess if you're not a Muslim then you might be a non-believer. Like mosquitoes, Muslim radicals are all over this country. They will try to kill and injure anyone who doesn't believe in Islam. I said it, they're called jihadists. Just look at the two brothers that killed and maimed children and adults at the Boston Marathon. I would say that's a perfect example of jihadists."

Lindsay says, "I remember my college days. Some of those kids weren't friendly. I didn't understand some of them, but now when I look back, some professors are teaching the radicals to be more radical."

"Lindsay, from what I gather by listening to radio talk shows, colleges have changed. They're run by progressives. That's a code for lefty Democrats. Not you; you're a middle thinker. We have a whole new class of homegrown radicals being brainwashed. Uncle Bill O. Wildly would say the same thing on TV. We're being overrun by foreigners. Abortion is ok, free birth control for all. I listen. I'm a Rush baby for the past fifteen years. I go to his free school almost every day."

"Richard, I know. You make me turn on the radio just after the noon news. I'll admit he does get a Democrat like me to start thinking about the next generation."

She makes her first attempt to tell him the facts of life.

"I'd never have an abortion if I got pregnant. I want to have a son or daughter. Wouldn't that be cool?"

Their conversation was broken when an email set off a cell phone. The email came across Lindsay's phone that said ATF agents intercepted arms heading north on Interstate 77.

Agent Micovich's message was filled with detail. A van was full of automatic weapons. She went on to say agents had a stakeout at a truck stop and watched men loading trunks into a black and white van. Agent Kayla Jacobson and Nicole Swider followed them to Independence, Ohio. They assisted ATF agents with the arrest.

ATF officers stopped each van. They held the drivers until justice department attorneys could follow up with a search warrant.

Using a judge's order, the ATF officers made the drivers unload and open their load. The trunks were filled with automatic weapons. The drivers couldn't speak English. ATF officers had to wait for a Spanish speaking officer to read the drivers their Miranda rights.

Lindsay was more concerned about Agent Micovich. She just had a feeling that Miss Micovich wanted Richard to get close to her again. She was sending some pretty detailed messages to Richard.

Richard says, "We are under attack. I'm telling you this entire country is being assaulted by Al Qaeda cells. We have to do our part. This is why we have to keep our eyes open on Lake Erie. There are too many things going on around here to think something isn't going to happen. I think Al Qaeda is going to try to hit the power plant again. We have to be vigilant, Lindsay."

She says, "If they're using the Brother M to make money, maybe they have more ships out there. I saw a box in your closet that said 'high power telescope.' Let's set up a tripod with a high power lens to watch for other ships."

He says, "That's a good idea. You're right. I have a high power lens just for this purpose. I haven't used it in a long time. We can learn together. This could be our big break if we find something out. We have a lot of work to do, so let's go back home and see if we can get some sleep. Well, you won't have a problem sleeping, after I get through with you."

Lindsay says, "I'm all for that, but you have to learn how to relax without booze."

Richard says, "I try. I know I'll have trouble sleeping again. If we workout, maybe I won't need a few beers to calm down. We see when we get home."

She says, "You know I'll help you calm down. I have a way to help wear you down. You won't need any beer after a get done with you. That's going to be the rule today and tonight."

Stern could just feel the weight of her and her statement. She probably weighed 120 pounds, but her statement weighted a ton. The next trick was his to make. Putting her over the edge was a commitment that was due. Of course, he was prepared to let her use her charm and body. She said she had a multitude of ideas that hadn't been tried yet.

She says, 'We have to work on new positions. I'll let you arrest me tonight as an American jihadist. You can tie me up and hold me down. Just remember you'll have to read me my rights. I'm sure I'll plead for mercy and I'll do anything you ask."

CHAPTER 30

THE FROLIC AND THE FIND

L INDSAY PUT ON her nightgown and was completely naked underneath. She told him it would stop if he had anything to drink except water. She wanted him to be completely sober and clean. She told him to take a shower before they do anything. As he was in the shower she found some yarn to add a little fun to the upcoming experience.

When he went to her bedroom she was under the covers. See didn't want him to see what she had on. He was already in an upright fashion, because of the anticipation. She didn't want him to go over the cliff too fast as he did the last time.

Lindsay says, 'Stop, listen, and slow down. You have to read me my rights."

Richard says, "OK, I'll try."

"I mean it. Slow down Detective Stern. Remember the have to treat the fugitive with respect. Besides that we have all night to play. She gave him the yarn and asked him to tie her up. At that point the fun began. They played for a time before knighting each other as a reward for keeping the tempo on a slow and even course. Lindsay thought she had made great progress this time. He held himself in check. It had to be the fact that he was sober. She felt wonderful when all the shockwaves shook her body. The yarn idea didn't last long as she broke free after a few minutes. Her nails scratched his back. The pleasure was slow motion at first and built like a house of cards until the entire card house dumped inside. He was on fire humping at a feverous pace. She had goose bump running wild. He was learning. They held each other for a time before she made her way to the shower. She was quite happy with the way it happened.

She returned to see a man all smiles.

"Richard, I can see you had fun. Tomorrow, I get to make you satisfy me again. You can sleep up here. Here's a warning. If you wake up, I'll have to knock you out again. I'm going to keep you straight all week.

The next morning she didn't give him a chance to wake. Even though she worked him over again, she would get her piece of the pie. This time she took charge.

She says, "Have control."

The ride on top was a semi-fast action rodeo. She halted the ride before he lost control and resume her fun. She was starting to get better at giving him lessons.

After the action they showered together. It was time to halt the play.

She partially dressed and he went downstairs to his bedroom to finish dressing. It was time to put a business plan together. He gathered up the high power lens and camera apparatus. The assembly didn't take that long, but they had to practice.

The weather wasn't perfect. A fog was on the lake so the pictures didn't take very well. On their second attempt which was just before the afternoon sun came out they took more pictures. Then the sun burned off the fog. Their third attempt worked nicely. They went home to inspect the pictures of the ship that was well beyond the east break wall. There was some focus problems on the second group of pictures. Inspecting the third group of pictures produced a jackpot. The best of those pictures revealed the name of the ship. It was the fairly large cruise ship called the Green Whale.

The ship had what appeared to be a front hatch that was partially open. Another picture had a smaller vessel moving toward the Green

Whale. It was fashioned like a mini submarine. Stern thought about his experience in Oregon and started to piece together ideas. Like a man working a puzzle he thought they had just come across the action that Ronnie Curliss had saw from the Sunset Harbor Restaurant. He said he saw a submarine.

Richard tells his theory. "Lindsay, I think we have the next terrorist plot on camera."

She asks, "What do you mean?"

"The ship is called Green Whale, not Green Lake. The terrorist are working with a submersible. It's a small submarine."

She gasps, "Wow!"

"Hold your tongue. We have more work to do. I think they were working in the fog and didn't realize we were capturing this operation on our camera. They were pretty far out from the east wall. This could be our big break. Overhead planes or drones couldn't see through the fog. We got the master picture."

She asks, "What are we going to do?"

He says, "We're going back to the house. We need to follow that ship. It looks like their heading toward Perry. They're too far out on the lake to do anything to the power plant, but they might be testing something. I don't know for sure, but we're on to something big. Let's go get the car and follow that ship.

By the time they walked home and drove to Painesville Township Park the ship had vanished. Lindsay scanned the horizon.

"I don't see it, Richard."

Richard drove toward Perry Park but they still didn't see the ship. He went as far as Dock Road in Madison and the ship was out of sight. He drove down Chapel Road heading west.

"Lindsay, I think they moved way out to the shipping lane. We're going to drive back to Blackmore Road in Perry. I'll let you scan the horizon. Your eyesight is better than mine."

Lindsay agreed with that idea. She had the high power lens fixed and ready to scan the far out area of the lake. The landscape was changed. It was too high for them to see the lake.

"We're going back to Hardy Road. We'll get a better look at the lake from Painesville Township Park. We can get a picture from Lake Road. Lake Road was mostly washed away from erosion. Most of it fell into Lake Erie years ago. It's a dead end road to Lake Erie now."

By the time they got to the park it was three in the afternoon. Lindsay scanned in both directions. The ship was gone.

She says, 'They must have gone north toward Canada."

Richard says, "We're going to do this all week. Every morning we'll walk to the beach with the high power lens on the camera. We can have lunch at the Sunset Harbor Bar and Grill to break away from time to time."

She commands, "No drinking! You've been very good. You don't need that stuff. We got plenty of work to do."

Richard agreed and he was having a classic time with Lindsay. She suggested they try an afternoon delight, if they don't spot the ship.

"Lindsay, an afternoon delight would be wonderful."

Each day she worked with him. Keeping him off the sauce wasn't that difficult. She had a real weapon to use and wasn't afraid to tell him, 'no sex if you're drinking.'

CHAPTER 31

TRY DOING AA

SHE WAS HINTING for a week to give it a try. She gave him a good reason to try an AA meeting with her. The program had much success for many alcoholics.

She said, "David Skytta called and wanted to know how you're doing. I saw his profile in your personal file. He's been sober for a long time."

Richard knew him well. He was always asking him to attend AA. Stern made a few half-way attempts at becoming a member. A counselor from the Willoughby mental hospital told him, 'half measures don't work.'

"I'm a disappointment when it comes to meetings. They're all drunks. Dave will tell you that. I'm a dry drunk now. He'd tell you that. Dave Skytta has a million and one stories to tell."

Lindsay says, "We should try it. You do an examination on how you became an alcoholic. You think about it. Why do you end up in the hospital all the time? Trust me, ok. This can be our first date. We'll be together and we'll be sober."

There was no question in his mind he could stay sober. Lindsay was part of that reason, but he had to make the right choice. He could see she was right and good for him, so he agreed to give it a try.

What she was doing was working to free him. She had Richard under her spell. She was falling in love with him and that was a good feeling. Another feeling she had was a mother's feeling. Nature was telling her something was coming in the future. That was just fine with her. She was worried about saying anything that would distract him.

The unhappy ending of her first marriage was so difficult. She didn't want to travel that road again. Her tune was changing about marriage. She wanted to be with a guy. If she couldn't, she promised to just get pregnant and carry on with her child. She felt kind of guilty for setting Richard up to be a father again. They were taking chances like a good Catholics couple.

She knew something was up when she woke up a few times feeling nauseous. Suspicion mounted. She was afraid to check or say anything.

Lindsay and Richard drove to the Friday AA meeting to give him an extra boost in the right direction. It wasn't an easy sell for her.

As he drove along Richmond Street to the Painesville Church near the park square he saw a commercial sign on the back of a Lake Tran bus. Homeland Security—TSA Jobs in Cleveland.

Richard went into a silent trance. The advertisement set off a chain of thoughts. Returning to the memory lobe in Stern's brain was a comment made by the Cleveland TSA agent. Now it was quite memorable.

Stern recalled the agent's oversized wrinkled shirt that didn't seem to fit properly around the waist. He looked as if he just fought with a criminal or worse with a terrorist. If the shirt was properly tucked in, maybe he would look better.

The agent's name rang a bell, Winn Sally On the breast pocket was a gold name plate and TSA badge with a number. Their eyes met. Stern didn't like being on the receiving end of a profiling security guard. What brought Stern into scrutiny? It was the two paperback books Stern was carrying. The maroon cover and title of one book was, Terror by Invasion. It set off an alarm in the agents mind. The expression on the officer's face was a tip. Stern knew he was going to be pulled out of the line.

"What books do you read, mister?"

Stern stopped in his tracks and stepped towards the officer. Richard knew he shouldn't be advertising anything to do with terrorism at the airport, especially a subject that was so inflammatory.

Richard replies, "Books about terrorists, sir." It wasn't exactly a gold metal subject.

"I'm going to be a famous author one of these days."

Mr. Sally gave Stern the once over and seemed to know Stern wasn't any threat.

"Tell me your name and birthday, Mr. Future Author," commanded the agent. He did as instructed. The fact that he was carrying books about terrorism was enough to order a full scale search. The Transportation Security Officer Winn Sally told Richard the books he was carrying looked suspicious.

"We're hearing about people moving guns. Put this in your book. Gun runners are moving to the Great Lakes. We just had a meeting about gun runners. I've heard that marinas are under an FBI watch."

Mr. Sally had a smile on his face as he told Stern to move along. His last statement was a genuinely friendly bark that had some bite.

"Maybe you'll find some terrorists in Oregon, Mr. Stern."

Stern stopped and turned around. He looked at Mr. Sally and gave him last words.

"Been there and done that, Mr. Sally."

Stern should have known from this information that the Sandusky marina was under the radar screen. He forgot about the Cleveland Hopkins TSA agent.

Lindsay removed his trance with a wakeup call.

"Hey, are you watching the traffic lights?"

"Gees Lindsay, "I forgot about something that happened at Hopkins Airport. I should have known we were going to be watched by the FBI in Sandusky."

"Why," she asked.

"It's over now. I had a tip when I was going to Oregon. A TSA security guy stopped me at the airport and told me the FBI was watching marinas for gun runners. We walked right into their dragnet."

She says, "You actually knew in advance."

Lindsay thought about their experiences. She had met a man that was up to his eyeballs in all kinds of stuff. He was truly an adventurer. She adored the feeling of tracking down the enemy, although having the enemy chase her wasn't contemplated.

When they pulled into the church parking lot, she had a few encouraging words to say. She was forthright and honest. She was glad he would at least try a meeting. She couldn't do it for him. She told him so as did Sharon. Even when they were having fun in bed, he could later turn to booze and that would send him careening out of control. Sex was her method of managing his sleeping disorder and maybe helping with the drinking problem. He could give her a good feeling, sometimes that is. She still had to train him on special female techniques.

The skull session was about to begin where each person around the table had their chance to explain their life style. Mostly it was about their drinking habits.

Richard whispered to her. "When it's our turn don't tell them what you're doing to me. I mean the sex. Just say, I don't know. You think of something. You're the college trained beauty. You know what to say."

Richard was fearful. Lindsay could speak her mind. He watched her in action with the FBI agents.

She whispers back, "I've probably done this a hundred times. I attended meetings with my ex-husband. He wasn't going to stop even when ordered to stop by the judge. He didn't care about me. You're not that way, thank God. I think I have a little control."

"You're right, Lindsay. Others have tried with little success. I'm stupid.

Richard wasn't stupid. He couldn't accept the fact that he had a hereditary disease. Love was an answer and she wanted to use all the tools to get him to stop. He treated her far better than the ex-husband. He wanted them to share in life. He wanted to be a decent boyfriend and maybe take another chance at marriage. With all this in mind he knew the bounty hunting would have to end before he finds out he isn't lucky.

The small group started with a prayer and then the conversation took off. Some people were fresh out of jail and that was the reason they were there. Judges ordered the DUI offenders and wife beaters to attend AA meetings on a regular schedule. It was a mixture of alcoholics from all walks of life.

They discussed late night partying, finding new hookups, parents and grandparents that passed on the drinking habit to the offspring. AA meetings could be called a lonely hearts club, but it didn't have to be that way. In reality AA was a safe haven for many alcoholics. That was the message of the meeting.

In Richard Stern's turn to comment on life's histories, he wouldn't describe or divulge much. He said Lindsay was more responsible for him being at the meeting. He had a temptation to say he chases terrorists and that was the reason he drinks. Secrets to him were too personal. For all he knew there could be a spy or radical Muslim at the table. He wasn't going to open up to strangers. A jihadist could be sitting at the table and that would surely open a can of worms.

In closing he said everyone in his family drank. Mostly it was the men. He was a cop cat. He had the disease and it was that simple. He passed to Lindsay.

She said coming to an AA meeting with her friend was a way to help him. She hoped everyone in the room would learn from each other. She passed to the next man. He said he was sober for 14 years and still attended meetings for extra courage.

All took an oath in the AA meeting to never reiterate the conversations of the meeting.

At the end of the meeting the secretary voiced an AA pledge.

"What is said in AA stays among the members of AA."

To a certain extent that was true. However, everyone knows the alcoholic is a liar, so is the drug addict. How many times did Richard

Stern say the lie? 'I'll never drink again.' His thought at the time was probably honest, but the creep of alcoholism, conning and baffling, only waits for the right moment to resume the dishonesty.

Dave Skytta told him a dozen times, 'a beer is waiting for you somewhere.'

So many times did Richard Stern promise to remain sober; he couldn't count the times. Even when kneeing in front of Father Pete, he prayed that God would lift the burden. The religious redemption took place for a time, but Stern's lack of commitment reduced his chances of recovery. Richard read and heard the words at the AA meeting. 'Rarely do we fail, if we are honest.' He thought about the words. That was his problem.

Lindsay had a good feeling when she left with Richard. She had her own secret to tell, but didn't want to say anything that would detract from a nice Friday night.

As they walked out, Lindsay says, "How many marriages run the same course? They get ruined by the booze."

She felt like she did some good. It was like a Friday night date. He attended a meeting to discuss a topic that she suggested the week before. He did it. Maybe there was hope. There was hope. Richard did his part. The question that remained was perplexing. How does he jump of the tracks? She was determined to find out the answer.

He had a reward coming when they got home.

Lindsay says, "You've been a good boy. You strip and I'll take care of the rest."

CHAPTER 32

MONICA AND LINDSAY MEET

UPERVISOR CLIFF MOSES was glad to hear Agent Micovich, Agent Swider, and Agent Jacobson made a perfect triumphant to help bring down criminal gun-runners across state lines from Texas to Ohio. The fact that they were the top agents on the case made him feel great.

Moses knew Monica would make a serious turnaround. She was always a top performer. Her slips began by meeting Richard Stern and getting too close to him. Moses blamed himself for Agent Paula Gavalia's tragic death and Monica Micovich's fall. They both worked late hours. It was their tenacity and dedication that was a true inspiration to all the people that knew them.

Monica was in a redemption mode as far as Supervisor Moses was concerned. He wasn't sure if she was ready to come back to Cleveland as a permanent agent. Cases she was working on became stagnant, because she was away. Having her back working on the old cases would put a feather in his cap and make the Cleveland FBI a premier unit again.

For Moses first things first, Agent Micovich was given the responsibility of training Agent Marisa Ross. They seemed like the perfect fit to act like sunbathers at marinas from Mentor to Toledo. Agent Ross was learning from one of the best FBI agents.

Moses had Agents Swider and Jacobson return to Cleveland. They would track any tips about gun-running. They would go to gun shows and gun stores to examine their record keeping.

He wanted Monica to do well, although he was optimistic and reluctant. If she started another shindig with Agent Wright, that would dash his hope. Additionally, Mr. Stern wasn't far off. He could easily unplug her redemption. She could get side tracked with that bozo. With all this on his shoulders, Moses thought about retiring. He didn't want to have a heart attack because of all the tension, but he wanted Monica to take his job as supervisor.

He had asked the bureau to approve a temporary transfer for Monica to Cleveland. The object of his recall was to let her finish the jobs she was doing in Cleveland and Detroit, but Agent Ross and Micovich had a greater mission to follow. Moses suspected guns were moving by boats on Lake Erie. Also, he didn't have to worry about Agent Wright since Monica was with Marisa. They would snoop around all the marinas on the south side of Lake Erie. More attention would be given to Sandusky and Toledo.

Moses had to make a private call to Monica to personally express his gratitude for all the work she had done.

Moses says, "Monica, it's your old or new boss, Cliff. Don't think I gave you a shit job training Agent Ross. Hold off and don't blast me after I say this. You and the other agents have done well. I'm glad you're helping Agent Ross adjust to undercover surveillance. I'm trying to keep Nicole and Kayla as a team and I'm asking for your cooperation. What I mean is this. Keep Agent Ross away from Agent Wright. I have Wright and Roman in Toledo for the next week.

"Wow, Cliff, you don't waste any time getting that out in the open. She'll be fine with me. You know; I liked it in El Paso, but I did miss you guys."

Moses says, "The 'Fast and Furious' case, that's still a Department of Justice situation in Washington. I don't think they want you on the case. Let me say it this way. Heads of state in our government worry about their jobs. You had them in a panic."

Agent Micovich says, "Cliff, I think we know something is wrong in Washington."

He says, "We need you to stay up here. I'm requesting a permanent transfer as long as you and Agent Wright don't screw things up. I hope you understand."

"Thanks, Cliff; I'd like Michael to visit with his father and go to school here. He's six years old now and growing like a weed."

Cliff says, "Well, I think that would be nice as long as Stern is in line. Agent Roman and Wright ran into Stern and his secretary or girlfriend. I'm not sure of their relationship, but Wright said she's a nice looking woman. You know Wright. Anyhow, maybe the bureau will approve your permanent transfer."

"Cliff, I'm sorry about the last year. I'm on track now. You tell Wright to stay away from Agent Ross."

He says, "He has an order from me. I'll send him to Siberia if he starts something. And yes, you are definitely on track. Take care. I think you two agent will be a team. Bye, Monica."

"Good bye, Cliff."

Supervisor Cliff Moses was opening up. His great desire to have his most trusted agent back overshadowed good sense, but he had an inner feeling she was focused again. Moses, while intentionally making the transfer happen for Agent Monica, was ordering a dose of trouble.

Monica was thrilled to hear a temporary transfer was changing. The new request by Supervisor Moses would help her settle. Michael was always moving to new neighborhoods. She didn't like it. Michael didn't understand, but he was growing up. She wanted him to have a base. A permanent home for her son was the best thing she could offer. She and Cliff were good friends even if he was the boss. When they parted, it was most troubling to both. They had shared so much pain and victory together. She had to stay in line, but it was difficult for her to ignore Agent Wright. The loving feeling was still there.

Monica had two good reasons to come back to Northeast Ohio other than work. She wanted Michael to see his real father.

Another important reason was supplied by Cliff. It was the news about Richard's secretary. She wasn't just a secretary. The hussy was moving in for the kill. This new was most troubling for Monica.

Monica sent an Email message to Richard which was intercepted by Lindsay. In the message Monica said she might be returning to the Cleveland FBI office for a long time. She indicated a desire to bring Michael over. Maybe even the three could go out for lunch. She would call before coming over.

Lindsay really didn't want Agent Monica coming over to Richard's house. With Richard away at a sport's game, Lindsay decided to reply to the message in her own words. Since she was far from pleased by the news, her response would set the facts on the table.

Lunch with Monica was out of the question. If Monica brought his son over that was another issue and she didn't want to interfere with Richard and his son. In either case she was uncomfortable. Call it a woman's intuition; Lindsay had a reason for her caution because of the Email. Richard was still in recovery mode. She didn't want Monica investigating Richard.

She needed to reply in a way to let Monica know about Richard's relationship with her. It was time for Secretary Wagner to let Miss Micovich know she was Richard's girlfriend. There wasn't any need for them to go out for lunch. If that was to happen, she would be with them.

Her reply was frank.

> Richard and I would be happy to take Michael, even for an overnight stay. I'm sure we could all have lunch together. I want to meet you and Michael. Richard and I have been sharing his house and we work and play as if we're married.
>
> Please call before you come over. Sometimes we're busy, but Richard and I will be so happy to see his son. Have a nice day,
>
> Lindsay Wagner

CHAPTER 33

I SAW THE GUN

MEXICAN AUTHORITIES CONVEYED a message to Washington that an FBI agent was harming their good relationship. Agent Monica Micovich had stepped on some toes in and around El Paso. The Washington pirates in the White House had a scull session. From the meeting they insisted the DOJ keep Agent Micovich out of El Paso. She should be working on other matters. With that overture assistance from Washington DC's FBI Bureau made quick work of Agent Micovich's permanent transfer.

Two weeks had passed since the last Email from Monica to Richard, which Lindsay intercepted. Just when the world seemed to stop, Agent Micovich was surprised by the news she received from her supervisor. She was ordered to permanently transfer to Cleveland.

Monica called Richard to say she would be in Cleveland early Thursday morning. She could leave Michael for the afternoon around 2:00PM and pick him up in the evening at 8:00PM. She told Richard she was now approved for a permanent transfer.

Monica arrived at 2:00PM on the dot. Richard saw her pull into his drive on the monitor and quickly was out the door to meet them. Monica got out of her rented Cadillac. Michael charged to his dad and Monica walked over to give Richard a firm hug. This came as a bit of a shock to him. He smiled at her.

Richard says, "We're almost one happy family."

Monica says, "We are Richard! I'm happy to be back. Michael is so happy to see you. So am I. I mean you've been doing so well. I can tell by looking at you. You look so healthy."

Butch, the softball assigner, had called him to umpire a last minute softball game.

Richard was ready. He was in his uniform. Fortunately the game wasn't far away.

He says, "I've got a game to work, fast-pitch softball. Lindsay is coming back from the beach. She's practicing with my camera equipment. She'll bring Michael to the game at Painesville City Park. I'd like Michael to watch his dad umpire. These games only last one or two hours. We'll have dinner after the game. She's a great cook, but we'll probably go to the Pizza Parlor."

Monica says, "That's nice. I hope they get along."

Richard says, "Well now that you said that, I think I better drive all of us to the game. We'll be together as an ice breaker. Michael and Lindsay will have a chance to interact."

Monica agreed with that idea. She could see she was up against another woman. This time it wasn't her colleagues. Monica could tell Lindsay had her nails dug into him. There had to be a way to work with Richard, maybe pull them apart. Monica wanted to get back to the point of being in control of Richard.

She says, "Michael will be attending 1st grade at Wickliffe elementary school. This will be his first time in a public school."

"Richard says, "That's great. Look, Lindsay is back."

Monica looked and she was disheartened. Lindsay wasn't fat, old, or homely. They were about the same age. That was the most troubling factor. Richard was much older than her. That was one of the reasons Monica held against Richard. Now here is another woman her age having a ball with him. Monica, resentful, thought one thing. She had to thwart this union.

Lindsay says, "Hey, who's that handsome boy."

Michael was a bit shy, moving to his mother. He didn't stay that way as Lindsay greeted Richard with a kiss.

They introduced each other in a business manner. There was coolness between Monica and Lindsay. Richard detected negatively charged women. His first thought was of physics. Like charges avoid each other and his first impression was going to be totally correct. The two female knights were going to square off.

Monica left and Richard, Lindsay and Michael went to the Painesville ball fields. The game was a quick one. The score was lopsided and finished in five innings with the Harvey girls going ahead by ten runs to end the game by a run rule.

The three hopped in the car and drove to the Pizza Parlor. Richard explained to Michael that Lindsay worked at the jail across the street.

Lindsay says, "Now I work for your dad, Michael. He's the boss. She winked at Richard.

Michael liked that comment. He was adjusting to Lindsay. He wanted to know what she did at the jail.

"Well, before I left to work with your dad, I ordered the food for the prisoners. I made sure everything was clean. Your dad and I met over there in that parking lot. My car had a flat tire and he fixed it for me. Your dad is my hero. I really got lucky when your dad came to my rescue. We came here to this restaurant and he asked me to work with him as his helper."

The waitress, Dawn, came over to take their order. It was a pleasant surprise for all of them. Lindsay was happy to introduce Dawn to Michael. Joy, the cook, came over to say hello.

Dawn says, "The Loparos aren't here. Joy and I are holding down the fort."

Michael tells Dawn, "I'm going to be a FBI agent and a detective like my mom."

Dawn says, "That's a very good ambition, Michael."

She took their order and the conversation took a turn. Michael voiced a thought that caught them by surprise. He didn't hold back.

Michael says, "Mom told me dad gets into trouble. She had to help him a few times. That's why he isn't with us. Was he in jail?"

Lindsay says, "No, Michael, your dad is a good man."

Michael asks Lindsay. "Don't you want to be a detective?"

Lindsay says, "No, I had to leave the county jail, because they said they didn't need me anymore. Now I work for your dad and it is the best thing that happened to me. I don't have to deal with prisoners.

Richard says, "Michael, you need to stay away from people that get in trouble."

Michael says, "Mom doesn't. She captures them. That's what I'm going to do."

They finished supper and left the Pizza Parlor. By the time they got home it was almost eight o'clock. Richard knew Monica would be back on time. She was. Monica didn't say much. After a short conversation about dad's game, Michael and Monica left. Richard and Lindsay stood outside and waved good bye.

Monica beeped the horn and Michael waved.

"Monica doesn't like me, but I think your son does."

On the way back to the motel Michael unloaded a secret to his mom. One thing about Michael, he was very observant and voiced his opinion. Monica asked a simple question.

"Michael, what do you think of Lindsay?"

Michael says, "Well Mom, I think she's a detective. Lindsay said she worked at the jail. Now she works with dad. Why is she carrying a gun?"

Monica says, "How do you know that, Michael?

"I saw it, mom. I saw it when she opened her purse. I think she's a detective."

Agent Monica made a quick assumption. Lindsay has a license to carry. She could prove that by checking the FBI files.

She didn't automatically think this was a concern. Although she had to give Richard specific orders not to let the weapons get in Michael's hands. She was mostly concerned about Miss Wagner. Maybe she didn't understand the inquisitive nature of a young boy.

Michael was at that age where he could remove the gun from her purse.

Monica had to order Michael to never touch a gun. She explained to him the safely all big people choose to protect themselves.

"Michael, do you understand, guns are for adults, not for you or your friends. You're going to make new friends when school starts. You tell me if your friends ever play with a gun. Mom says never touch a gun. We don't want anyone getting hurt. Do you understand?"

"Ok, mom, I'm going to be like you when I grow up. Then I can carry a gun."

CHAPTER 34

PICTURES ON LAKE ERIE

DOING HER NORMAL routine like a good employee, Lindsay checked for phone messages and reviewed Emails. The phone rang a few times. Most of the calls amounted to nothing. Richard left early in the morning. The Sandusky marina, where Brother M moored, was the target. He called just before noon and would call again after five o'clock to report on his finding.

Dock workers reported seeing good looking chicks boarding the Brother M before she sailed. The workers made a point of watching for the girls. He was going to wait at the marina to see what other crafts docked there besides the Brother M, which wasn't there.

When the clock hit twelve noon, Lindsay's next step was to walk down East Street to the shore of Lake Erie. She had Richard's high power lens on the camera which was becoming easier to operate. Far away images came into focus much faster for her. The terrific features of the camera helped to steady moving objects. Also, the camera could take up to four hundred pictures in high definition.

There were plenty of landscape pictures to view, but she focused on Lake Erie and the surrounding shoreline.

Lake Erie was a shallow lake compare to the other Great Lakes. Winds could whip up waves in a hurry. Boaters had to be careful and know the oncoming weather events or be caught off guard. This day was relatively calm.

Lake Erie's white lake birds were flying overhead in search of food. The nuclear power plant towers were standing tall eight miles to the east. The breeze moved the steam coming out of the cooling towers in a curl into the blue sky.

To the west were the US Coast Guard Station, the federal pier, and the port authority boat launch. The beach was starting to fill with tan buffs and swimmers.

Pointing the camera northwest, she saw the west break wall and old lighthouse. Out of the harbor came a rather large yacht. She was leaving Grand River in a lazy pace as it approached the lighthouse. Lindsay zoomed in on the light cruiser. Another craft with sails in full bloom passed by which block the name of the yacht. Although her view was blocked, she believed this large yacht was similar to the Brother M. Lindsay raced down the beach to get a better look. Brother M was just like this yacht. Fortunately, it turned left heading toward Cleveland. She swung the camera and snapped a picture of the watercraft as it left the harbor. In bold letters Brother M was painted on the aft back board.

Talking to herself, she said, "I'll get back to you, later. This is a big deal. I'm calling, Richard."

They talked about the sighting of the Brother M. It was strange that it turned west.

Richard says, "I'll stay in Sandusky and see if the yacht comes this way. I may have to stay overnight."

Lindsay gripes, "Alone, oh, that's no fun. I want to stay with you."

"You keep watching for the other ship. We're going to cash in on this threat. I think they're going to strike the power plant soon. I'm sending an Email to Agent Roman about our investigation. I think it's time to blow the case wide open. You be careful, honey."

Always joking, Lindsay says, "I will, Mr. Stern."

Lindsay was being truthful. She wasn't too worried about being alone. She had her equalizer only a step away from the computer. It was hidden in her purse. Only time would change her condition from calm to calamity.

Lindsay resumed her scan. The entire break wall to the west was in good condition. Green foliage had grown over the wall as it met Headlands Beach. Headlands State Park had no protection like the block walls that protected Fairport Harbor. The old lighthouse seated on the west wall kept ships safe, when the fog settled on Lake Erie.

The blinking light and foghorn helped many ships navigate to the harbor entrance before GPS instrumentation became the norm. The harbor was a safe haven for small watercraft when the mighty west wind erupted. Because of the west break wall, the Village of Fairport Harbor had a beach of natural sand. The beach was spared the punishing gale winds and waves of the Northwest.

Directly in front of Fairport Harbor was the north wall which ran perpendicular to the shoreline. Its eastern section had a partially sunken mass of rock. The sunken rectangular chunks jutted up out of the water at the far eastern end. The wall of huge stone blocks ran west to form the harbor entrance. It was here that her camera focused.

She called Richard again and asked if he wanted her to follow the yacht.

"No, it may double back towards you. Stick around for a short time and then get back to the office. You stay home and guard the house. Remember, the enemy saw me at the library. We're zeroing in on this operation. I don't want any miscues. We're going in for the kill."

Richard had no idea his statement was close to being true. The victim was someone he never envisioned. Lindsay did have reason to fear, but she couldn't see into the future.

Lindsay answered, OK. She shrugged her shoulders and figured he knew what's best. With that she resumed her work.

She figured the power plant cooling towers were the most interesting landscape feature, so she pointed and clicked the button. The Lake Erie water only had a slight ripple. In the afternoon the wind could kick up and be relatively calm in the evening or before a storm.

Lindsay continued to scan the horizon from West to East. When she was finished, she walked home. She walked at a fast pace, wanting to download the pictures and be near the phone in case an important call came in. She felt the operation was heading for a conclusion.

The doorbell rang which was a bit unnerving. She ran to the living room and looked out the window.

CHAPTER 35

WOMEN FIGHT FOR STERN

A GENT MONICA TOLD Agent Ross that she was on her own for the afternoon because Michael had seen a gun that Richard Stern's secretary was carrying. She wanted to discuss the issue before it got out of hand.

It took a little over a half hour to get to Stern's house. Monica rang the doorbell.

Lindsay spied outside to see who it could be. The answer was a Cadillac parked across the street. It was Agent Monica Micovich.

Lindsay opened the door for her and expressed surprise. Monica didn't call to say she was coming over.

Agent Monica asks, "Hi, Lindsay, is Richard still home?"

"Sorry, Monica, he's gone."

She told Lindsay her abrupt stop was prompted by an Email she received from Richard. He said he was planning a trip to Sandusky. Monica wanted to know the reasons for his investigation in Sandusky. She wanted to catch him before he left. Besides, if he did leave, she would know exactly where he is.

The handgun was on her mind, but she held off being up that discussion. That would be the last topic to discuss.

Monica was worried for Richard too. Based on past experience she knew his tendencies. Knowing that gun runners had been detected and moving to Sandusky was painting a worrisome picture. His past history was reason enough for Agent Micovich to get involved without going through her supervisor. She figured it would be better to bypass Moses because he would surely nix the idea of investigating Stern.

Lindsay had to think fast.

"He's on the road, traveling as usual."

She didn't want to say much. Her only thought was to be cordial and brush off Monica as fast as she could.

Monica asks, "Well, where is he heading?"

"I think he said west, yeah, he's heading west."

Monica says, "He's going to Sandusky. Isn't that right?"

Lindsay didn't like the way she was coming across. She wasn't going to be interrogated.

Monica was pressing the issue. She wanted to pin-point his exact location.

Lindsay was evasive. "Maybe, he is. Why do you want to know?"

Lindsay was becoming distressed by the questioning.

Monica replied, "You're his secretary. I would think he'd tell you exactly where he is. So tell me where is he. Just to let you know, I'm going to Sandusky, Lindsay. I think I know where he's going. Maybe I can help him, if he gets in trouble."

Lindsay was becoming alarmed by the tone of her voice. Her thought was explicit. Agent Monica was after him and it wasn't for FBI business. The temptation to say something contemptuous was overwhelming. The thought of both of them meeting at some motel or hotel flashed in her head. She had no alternative.

Lindsay exploded. "I know you want him, Monica. It won't work. Sorry, he's my boyfriend. I love him."

Agent Monica recoiled, "This is official FBI business. Don't start with that crap. You listen, secretary. Why didn't you say he was going to Sandusky?"

"I told you; I'm his girlfriend. Don't you get it? We live together. I'm sleeping with him. Get that through your envious head and stay away from him. I know what you're thinking. You don't know how to keep a guy. You're going to try and take him from me."

Monica didn't like the accusation. The fur on the cats was standing tall. She was starting to fume. The next words from Lindsay really lit the fuse.

"I read the file. You had a one night stand with him, got pregnant, and now you want him back. Here is the point, girl. He's mine."

Lindsay was pointing a finger at her and Monica was boiling. From a female's point of view the accusations were pretty much on target. She wasn't going to let Lindsay have the last word. She slapped Lindsay's arm away almost in a violent way.

Lindsay thought quickly. She had to have an equalizer and turned to fetch her purse which was near the computer. Although her pistol was in the purse, she wanted the mace defender and was going to use it.

Monica watched for a moment and sprung like a cat as Lindsay moved for her purse.

All Monica could think was the comment that Michael made to her. 'I saw the gun, mom. It was in her purse.'

Monica pursued her to the point of attack. She made an offensive move before Lindsay could pull the gun from her purse. Her first upright kick landed square on Lindsay's wrist. The snap of a bone and cry from Lindsay was loud and clear enough to draw attention from the lady neighbor. Lindsay dropped the purse strap and held her wrist. Monica's second kick hit Lindsay in the midsection which doubled her up. The pain was terrible and she fell forward striking the side of her head on an end table near the computer.

The fight was over in seconds. Lindsay didn't stand a chance against a martial arts expert. Lindsay was motionless on the floor next to the computer table. Monica went to her aid. She felt for her pulse. It was there; Lindsay was breathing, but unconscious.

She found her pulse and looked inside. Then she immediately called 911. The dispatcher took down the information and within minutes the Fairport Harbor rescue ambulance was on the scene with a police squad car reporting at the same time.

This wasn't an unusual run for the ambulance. They had been at Mr. Stern's house before. This time it was serious and Mr. Stern wasn't the casualty.

Agent Monica Micovich identified herself as an FBI agent on official business.

She reported to police. "I had to subdue her. She was reaching for a weapon. It's in her purse."

The EMT's asked Agent Monica to move away. After an immediate evaluation, Lindsay was placed on a stretcher. Her condition was serious. The ambulance took off with lights flashing and headed to Tri-Point medical center. She was now semi-conscious from the fight. Holding her midsection she complained.

"My baby!

The paramedics looked at each other and concluded she could have internal injuries.

They called the ER staff and reported her condition.

The police knew Agent Micovich. Monica didn't have to pull out her badge, but did so anyway. She was considerably upset over the fight.

She said, "I didn't mean to use as much force as I did. She went for the handgun."

In her own mind Monica thought her action was a bit beyond normal. The first kick rendered Lindsay defenseless. The second kick was clearly meant to punish her adversary.

Her conscience was in doubt. To justify her action she said the fight just got out of control when Lindsay made a dash for her purse.

A small plastic mace canister was found in the purse and the pistol. Monica told officers that her son had seen a pistol in her purse. All this information was recorded. Monica reiterated the fact that she was on official duty when the fight broke out.

She explained the circumstance in the order that it occurred. Lake County Sheriff's deputies came to Stern's house to help out with the investigation. They found the story to be plausible and the evidence at the scene was corroborated. They released Agent Micovich.

EMT's kept monitoring Lindsay Wagner vitals until they reached the hospital. She complained about her baby. She put her good hand on her stomach. Paramedics had splinted the broken wrist and tried to keep her calm.

"My baby, I'm pregnant."

The team of rescue officers had radioed her status. Lindsay was rushed into emergency surgery after being examined. There was internal bleeding. The unborn, eight week old fetus died from blunt force trauma.

The mother was semi-conscious with a concussion. Her broken wrist was secondary to the operation that saved the mother's life. All safety measures were taken to safe guard Lindsay's life. She was beat up physically, but the emotional aspect was a greater concern.

The loss of the unborn was a terrible blow. She wanted the baby, so bad. She told the nurse that the father didn't know.

She asked the nurse. "Please call him."

A nurse called Mr. Stern to report on Lindsay's condition. The call came as a total shock. He dropped his surveillance operation and drove to the hospital in a maddening rush.

ONE DAY LATER

By this time Richard cooled down. He was allowed to stay with Lindsay through the night. He was told to relax and rest; they would monitor her condition throughout the night. She was sedated and they both needed to rest. The doctor's advice was comforting just for the fact that Lindsay would recover and she should be able to conceive again. He didn't give any more details other than to say she would likely experience great emotional confliction.

"The loss of a child even this early in development is very troubling for a mother. You'll need to be reassuring that she will get better. Give her comfort, give her space, she'll need you and you will have to understand the emotional turmoil that she will undergo."

When Agent Monica found out, she was speechless and heartbroken. The news hit her hard. Her heavy handed attack was the reason Lindsay lost her child. Monica called Richard to explain. The confession didn't help. She was drenched in guilt.

Richard didn't want to hear her confession. He knew Monica could whip him in a fight.

"I don't have anything to say, Monica. This is really bad. You could kill a man twice your size with one kick."

The Lake County Sheriff's department with assistance from Fairport Harbor police turned in their investigation. An independent attorney was called in to review the findings. A Lake County lawyer, Dave Farren, was asked to make his conclusion based on the police report. His report was explicit. It was self-defense. Even though Agent Micovich had the extraordinary training to subdue an adversary, she acted in accordance with the rules of engagement.

Supervisor Cliff Moses was confounded. Based on the sheriff's report Monica was within her legal rights, but the damage done was far and away over the top. In his view Agent Micovich acted vigorously to end a threat, however, he was astonished by the fact that Miss Wagner was so beat up.

"Why, Monica?" He asked.

She told most of the truth.

"I wanted to protect Richard and there was the issue of the handgun. I didn't want Michael around her if she was carrying a weapon."

Cliff Moses shook his head. "I gave you another chance and this damages everything."

CHAPTER 36

TRAGIC LOSS OF LIFE

THE LOOK ON Moses' face was enough to signal bad news. Monica prepared for the worst.

Moses says, "I'm not saying it could have been avoided. This is really messy. The bureau has completed their review of your service, Monica. I can't help feeling sorry for all that you've been through. Stern was involved in this again; only this time he wasn't there."

Monica responds, "Mr. Stern didn't do anything. Get to the point, chief. There's no sense in lathering up bad news. It's written on your face."

"We want to keep you, Monica. You are one of our main go to persons when we need a tough job done."

Monica stops Moses.

She says, "But, we can't have a woman getting involved with an FBI informer and defending herself in self-defense. She had a gun, chief. She was going for the gun."

Moses says, "Yes, they see it that way, but with one caveat. Extreme force is what they say. It's messy. The woman was pregnant. Now and then I get mad. I know a kangaroo court verdict, when I see it. They say, 'endangering the public, acting without orders.' They say, 'Excessive force is an obstacle to justice.' I read the report and all the other bull-shit the bureau has scraped up. They look at the overall record. A woman loses a baby. It's bad. In the past you stepped on some political toes. I know you're good at what you do. I know the Washington DC folks were laying for you. There is going to be a second review. They may rule in your favor."

Monica asks, "Is that it?"

Moses moved close to her.

"Maybe they're trying to protect you. I asked them to give you some time off before a final decision is reached," says Moses as he looks in her eyes.

The emotions were running high. The pain each felt was real. He was under the gun. He couldn't fire her as they suggested.

Instinctively, Monica reaches into her blazer and hands Moses her ID badge and pistol. Monica was serious. She ended a life. The whole affair was too much for her to endure.

She says, "Tell them to—no I'll write a letter of resignation."

Moses says, "No, you're not doing this. You take some time off. Please, go talk to Father Pete. Everything that happened was done in self-defense. You can't throw away your career with the FBI, because of an accident."

Moses was her mentor. This was not the way he saw the end.

Moses says, "It was an accident, Monica. You didn't know. I can tell you this. God didn't want this to happen. Go talk with the Catholic priest. Father Pete has helped you in the past."

He handed her the gun and badge. Take this back. Go Agent Micovich. You'll pull through this. I know you. You're not a quitter. She looked at him and could see the determination. She took the gun and ID badge and placed the gun in her holster and the ID badge in her blazer pocket.

Without another word she walked out of the office.

Moses called Father Pete at his parish house in Fairport Harbor and told him the full story. He said Monica was extremely troubled by the accident and was about to quit the FBI.

"Father Pete, this is Agent Monica Micovich's supervisor with the Cleveland FBI, Cliff Moses. I'm sure you read about the accident.

Father Pete says, "I have and I said a prayer for all of them."

"I asked Monica to call you. I'm sure you have the words of wisdom that will help her deal with this tragedy."

Father Pete says, "You know I'll help her."

Moses adds, "The newspapers made the accident seem like Monica's actions were over the top. The woman had a gun and was reaching for it. Monica used her martial arts training to subdue the woman. She delivered a kick to her midsection. The body blow cause trauma to the fetus. The woman lost the unborn. It was a self-defense accident that ended in a tragic loss. She was about eight weeks into her pregnancy. Richard Stern was the father."

"Supervisor Moses, you know Monica has been through three years of torment. She still prays for Richard Stern. I'm sure this incident just adds to her misery. The good news is this. She has a strong faith in God. That will pull her through this temporary calamity."

The tragic event that caused Lindsay to lose her baby was ruled an accident. After Moses delivered a recommendation to give Agent Monica Micovich more time to heal emotionally, it was granted. The FBI Bureau in Washington DC had an ax to grind because of pressure exerted by the Department of Justice. The FBI agency wasn't going to be bullied. A second review of the case made their decision a slap on the wrist. They decided to dry dock Agent Micovich for three months with pay and have her undergo a mental evaluation. After that she was to report to Erie, Pennsylvania.

Monica did as Moses instructed. She called Father Pete. He gave her a pep talk, so she could resolve the emotional fallout. He had chosen the right words to help her stand again.

Richard worked with Lindsay everyday helping her recover a broken spirit. This was the toughest job he ever had to do. Something as bad as this usually caused him to retreat to booze. Willpower scotched that temptation. She had been the best part of his life. He was going to nurse her back to her old self even if it took forever.

Monica recovered from the mental trauma. She used the loss of her partner, Agent Paula Gavalia, as an inspiration. Paula left her with willpower. The three months passed by quickly. She didn't let the grass grow under her feet. Instead, she moved on with her life, because she had Michael. She had to uproot him again, but he needed her and she needed him.

At times the loss of Agent Paula Gavalia was enough to send tears streaming down Monica's face. The two agents had a vision of the future. They would always team up spiritually. Monica believed that Paula was still at her side. On these occasions she remembered Father Pete's words of wisdom 'take care of your son and job. Believe in God and all His love for mankind.' It provided her the strength to overcome tragedy.

Each time, when she was down, she remembered Paula's power. Monica had the determination and willpower. She would not let Paula down.

Monica continued to provide information to Richard Stern, so he could net another reward. It was partially done, so she could help with the doctor's bills for Lindsay. She still thought Richard would be a good dad. It was important for her to keep the dialogue open with him. She wanted forgiveness for being so offensive. She tried over and over to express her sadness and sorrow. She knew the last kick wasn't necessary.

Stern wasn't sitting on his hands. He had put together a second file of evidence. It was the money trail. Lindsay was his partner and had to get back to normal. He knew Lindsay had to be hypnotized after she recovered. She held something in her mind. The financier that was still in America was tied to Abdul Madhi. He or they had to be found.

The FBI had some information on the source of money to finance the attack on the power plant and recruit homegrown terrorists, because of Agent Paula Gavalia and Agent Micovich's previous work.

Many questions were still unanswered about gun running, the IRS, and many other issues. Top secret information was being leaked from top officials in Washington. A secret search of phone calls was being done by DOJ investigators. The National Security Agency was gathering plenty of data on US citizens.

The pirates in Washington DC were withholding some information. Some congressional figures thought a cover up was going full throttle. Vital persons that knew secrets were kept under the cloak of secrecy. Tracking down the enemy was becoming impossible because of the stonewalling. It was assumed that the details not released were labeled top secret or were classified as presidential privilege.

Supervisor Cliff Moses said he was sure the people up the ladder were involved in a cover up. He might have to submit his comments as an alias or he would be labeled a whistleblower. The way the government was operating no one was safe from DOJ intervention.

Lindsay and Richard had the potential to receive some serious reward money, since Richard disclosed the submarine plot. Expose the enemy to the FBI turned the table on the enemy.

The next step was quite freaky. Richard and Lindsay didn't have to do anything. It was God that had the final say in how to deal with terrorists.

CHAPTER 37

IN GOD WE TRUST

STERN HAD LET the cat out of the bag. He told Lindsay time would tell if we stop the enemy. The FBI had the information that helped to fill in the blanks and it came in the nick of time. He sent in the photographs of the mother ship, Green Whale and the enemy submarine.

Richard explains, "Lindsay, I sent in our photos. Watch how thing move now. We are going to hear of some US Coast Guard action.

The enemy was in position to launch a strike on the Perry Nuclear Power Plant. The Department of Homeland Security was put on alert. A showdown was imminent. An enemy was planning to use the submersible watercraft to attack under dead of night.

The Cleveland FBI provided the US Ninth Coast Guard District with a red alert. The Rear Admiral Marty Marks in Cleveland who was in charge of all the Great Lakes made a decision to dispatch additional cutters from Detroit to help patrol the islands near Sandusky. He shifted his forces to protect and defend the nuclear plants.

He ordered an increase in aircraft patrols. Somehow the cruiser Green Whale stayed out of site. It was a combination of luck and a crafty captain that kept them off the watchful eye of the US Coast Guard. Captain Amjad Walliki on the Green Whale used the Canadian border as his launch site. He changed the features of Green

Whale using paint, fake sails, fake furniture, and costumed terrorists. They looked like tourists. The sub would have to travel many miles underwater to reach the target.

The captain said, "Don't break radio silence. They can't see us with bad weather moving in. This is the best time to launch an attack. The shore units are moving into position. It'll be dark in a few hours. We must strike when they are blind. A storm will be our best friend."

Although shallow, Lake Erie is a large body of water with many types of watercraft on the move. Planes and drones were watching for Green Whale and enemy activity on land. They concentrated their surveillance near the shoreline. The change in weather grounded most of the aircraft through the evening. The weather wasn't expected to improve until late afternoon the next day.

Green Whale's captain had complete control of the terrorist's mission. The plan was well conceived. He could launch an attack at any time, but chose a dubious time to strike. He waited for the storm coming from the west. Heading straight onto Lake Erie, the storm was a monster covering three states.

The frogmen in the sub were well trained and could strike in the dead of night no matter what the weather.

Preliminary steps had to be in place. First, the attack submarine would drop the saboteurs. They had to be in place to blow the transmission lines after receiving an order by the assault commander. Second, the guard house would be assaulted. The few guards on duty could be surrounded and drugged without a shot being fired. The enemy would change into their clothes. Once that was accomplished the assault commander would order power plant employees to be kidnapped as they arrived at the main gate. Their identity badges would provide clearance to pass through interior check points.

Enemy commandos would make their way to the nerve center of the nuclear power plant and order technicians to override safety systems and put cooling controls in manual operation. The cooling water to the reactors would be cut off by timed explosive charges installed by the frogmen in the sub. Once the power plant's water system was cutoff the control center would be disabled. Some safety devises would be tricked to misread just like the natural gas system in Fairport Harbor. The nuclear reactors would overheat and a Chernobyl event would eventually happen. The radiation would spread for hundreds of miles.

Two terrorist helicopters would extract the frogmen and team leaders. One helicopter was to travel to the Green Whale and drop the frogmen in Canadian water. Green Whale would pick them up. She would stay in Canadian waters and wait for the sub to return.

The other helicopter was to take team leaders to a mosque in Toronto, Canada. Other lesser value terrorists would go to Salem, Ohio in vans. They would leave Salem in exchanged vehicles and travel to Sharon, Pennsylvania. After a rest period, they would head to El Paso, Texas and finally Mexico.

The submarine extraction would be the tricky part of the plan. It had to make its way to berth with the mother ship in a timely manner even in a Lake Erie storm. The Green Whale would sail to Detroit and berth at a marina owned by a banker.

It was an act of nature or God's hand that changed the enemy's operation. A storm was brewing southwest of Indiana and was moving rapidly toward the Northeast. This fast developing weather event complicated a well thought out plan. Captain Amjad Walliki was well aware of the storm. He wants the cover of a storm to blanket his attack. It was a risky decision to move ahead with the plan. Captain Walliki could see how vicious the storm had grown. He wasted no time explaining the problem. The enemy forces on land were told to standby and hold their position. The assault commander told his men to retreat rather than take control of the main gate. The plan was not going as intended.

When the submarine was released from Green Whale all systems were working. The storm was bearing down on Ohio. As the weather report came in Captain Walliki had to worry. The sub couldn't break radio silence.

The captain had a good idea how bad it was going to be. He could remember the plight of the Edmund Fitzgerald. Gale winds were expected and the captain had to abort the mission when he heard the assault commander order his men to retreat.

Engine trouble aboard the submersible caused slow propulsion. The sub was in trouble. Captain Walliki realized he was at the mercy of Mother Nature by being way out in the center of Lake Erie. The sub could be lost in time. With the storm moving in fast, the crew on board the sub decided to stay underwater. They had no chance of working in gale winds. It was safer to be underwater until fair weather returned. The experience was harrowing. The timing of the super storm couldn't be worse for the submarine terrorists.

Green Whale headed into the wind. His best option was to head for Fairport Harbor. The storm was merciless. In time he decided to drop anchor. The sub had to ride out the storm on its own. The crew of four on the sub wasn't used to such a terrible turn of events. The terrorists on land had abandoned all plans. Their commander didn't hesitate. They were ordered to stand down and return to safe houses any way they could. The operation was in complete disarray.

Blowing across Lake Erie, the waves were as bad on top of the water as below. The sub rocked violently like an amusement ride. The men worried the sub would break apart. If this was a reenactment of World War II submariners being bombed by depth charges, it was totally surreal. It certainly felt similar to quakes when the enemy dropped depth charges. The concussion of the waves rendered the sub completely off course.

Lightning struck the Green Whale and her communication was disabled. Now the storm was in control of the mission on the mother ship. The sub wasn't supposed to communicate, but tried to anyway.

The submarine was being blown off course by 40 to 50 miles. The men on board surmised the peril of the situation. It seemed the storm would cease, but another gale came roaring back, but it was less intense and only lasted an hour. The God in heaven had the angels flapping their wings.

They tried several time during the next day to communicate with the Green Whale. They waited two days before surfacing. The captain ordered them to dive immediately when he opened the hatch. Reasonable calm was back, but the captain's face was white like a ghost.

He ordered, "Prepare to raise the periscope."

As he spied on the surroundings, his eyes pressed against the view finder. The lens gave a clear outline of the beach. The distance to land was about one mile as he zoomed in.

"Oh, no, no, something is wrong."

He knew they were well east of the Perry site. His GPS coordinates malfunctioned. He believed he should be off the coast of Conneaut, Ohio.

When he lowered and raised the periscope again and viewed the surrounding area, a shocked look froze his face like celery dipped in dry ice. He looked at his watch to see the time and date. He wondered if the storm had driven them into a time warp.

In his Arabic language he explained to the men on board.

"We're in a time warp. The German army is on land. I see an invasion. The Americans are landing."

He looked at his watch again. His fear worsened. He retracted the periscope.

"Normandy, June 6, 1944."

The men thought he hit his head or was hallucinating because of the storm.

"Captain, what's wrong. You're sick."

The crew members could sense something was definitely wrong. The captain again had a white face, like a ghost.

He tried his best to gather himself. He told the crew what he saw.

"We're in the past. I saw Germans, Nazi army soldiers and the Americans are landing. I don't know where we are. It's like the Bermuda Triangle. Am I dreaming?"

The second in command told the captain to look again.

"Sorry, I will not. You look, Madhi."

Abdul Madhi raised the periscope to look. Almost dumbfounded, he had the same sensation as the captain. They were both seeing a pitched battle.

The captain ordered him to look at his watch.

The sub captain explained, "Look at the date, man! Look at the date! We're not in the same time zone. The storm, it knocked us out. We're in something called the Bermuda Triangle."

The frogman looked to see the date on his watch.

"Captain, I don't know. The watch isn't working."

The captain screamed "No, Allah had taken over!"

The terrorists could not harm anyone. Mystery surrounded the frightened terrorist.

Richard Stern's team was involved and would play a pivotal role, but God took over, not Allah. God controls Mother Nature. He caused the outcome. Fate played a part in Conneaut, Ohio. The World War II battle was twisting the captain's mind. The people in Conneaut always put on a show depicting an invasion at Normandy in 1944.

Abdul Madhi was able to repair the subs propulsion system. When they made it back to the shipping channel, which was five miles east of Fairport Harbor. They saw the mother ship.

The captain was relieved.

Madhi shouted to the Green Whale captain.

"The storm had interfered with the operation of the sub."

The Green Whale captain ordered them off the submarine. All the men scrambled out of the sub. Abdul Madhi stood close to the hatch.

Captain Walliki balked, "I'm disappointed, like my deceased friend, Mr. Bigg. When he was alive, he told me how to end a mission when it turns sour. We have to kill the cancer. Your ship didn't perform, Abdul Madhi. You told me; you're ready. We had to abort this mission, because of your submarine. Now a US plane has spotted us. I fear the US Coast Guard will be here soon. I'll have to explain your research craft was lost at sea, because of the storm. We have to sink the sub and make a run for it."

Abdul Madhi protested. He wanted a chance to escape in the sub. After all, the sub was seaworthy. He was being defiant.

"No, the sub won't make it to Canada on its own. It's too slow."

Madhi says, "I'll take it there myself."

Captain Walliki says, "All of you, get in the water and swim here."

They jumped in as the captain ordered, except Abdul Madhi. The crew of the submarine started swimming to the Green Whale. Madhi refused.

Captain Walliki yells, "You're all fools, sink the sub with Abdul Madhi. Fire, shoot the captain and his crew."

The volley of fire was merciless. Madhi scrambled inside the sub before being hit. He quickly closed the hatch. He could hear the gunfire. The bullets weren't effective as they ricocheted off the subs armored outer skin. He dropped below the surface of Lake Erie as the submarine sank out of sight. It vanished in a hail of bullets that seemed to sink the submarine.

The sharpshooter said, "We got him, captain."

The men swimming in the water made a case to be spared a similar fate.

"Captain, rescue us. We followed your orders." The men in the water cried for mercy.

The captain ordered, "Shoot them again and again! Shoot them until they can't float." They died by bullets and drowned.

"They have failed. We'll make a run for Canada."

He ordered, "Full speed ahead!"

Within an hour the US Coast Guard and Canadian Coast Guard sailors had them stopped. Captain Walliki saw the futility of a fight and surrendered. He ordered his crew to drop their weapons and allow the coast guard sailors to come aboard.

The US Coast Guardsmen boarded the Green Whale without incident. The Chief Petty Officer in charge placed the captain under arrest along with the entire crew.

The large terrorist cruiser was towed to the US Coast Guard station in Fairport Harbor where the FBI was waiting. Agent Ron

Roman impressed Captain Walliki with photos of the murderous gunfire that killed the men in the water.

Agent Roman made his point quickly. "You see Captain Walliki, we have a drone in the air taking photos. Surprise, you're men are on candid camera. Aren't you the one who gave the order to kill those helpless sailors?"

"You must provide me with a lawyer," said Captain Walliki.

Drone photographs proved the crew of the submarine was mercilessly shot to death. A search of the area only recovered three crew members of the sub. Signed confessions helped steer some rational that the sub was sunk by the Green Whale crew under orders from Captain Walliki. A search for the submarine didn't produce any results.

The drone was placed in the right area by a tip from a pair of bounty hunters. The Green Whale was identified by Richard Stern and Lindsay Wagner using their photos that were sent to FBI Agent Ron Roman.

The coast guard commander concluded the sub was lost, but it was never verified. Agent Ron Roman said he had a concern that one mastermind was still on the loose. He told his boss, Supervisor Moses, that Stern and his girlfriend were tracking the terrorists from Santee, California to Portland, Oregon to Ohio.

"Looks to me like they earn another reward for the evidence they supplied."

Moses replies, "That bastard does this all the time. I'll support your findings, Agent Roman. Both of them will likely earn a hefty check from Uncle Sam."

CHAPTER 38

EVERYONE ON BOARD

CAPTAIN WALLIKI AND his crew were charged with murder. The crew pleaded and fingered the captain as the man in charge of the terrorist mission. He thought his crew was subordinate, but they fell like dominos when asked to become witnesses. With the photographs from Lindsay and Richard plus the video from the drone, everyone on board was accused of murder. The crew was spared from the death penalty.

The captain was found guilty of murder. He didn't last long. He was found hanged and it was assumed the crew may have finished the captain stay on earth.

Agent Monica Micovich didn't give up on Richard Stern. She was sure Lindsay would leave him once he started drinking.

Agent Monica Micovich and Michael didn't live in Erie, Pennsylvania. They moved to Dock Road in Madison, Ohio. She no longer had to travel in heavy traffic. Basically she split the difference between Cleveland and Erie, Pennsylvania. Dock Road had many amenities that suited Michael's development. Michael was going to school, making friends, and he wasn't far from Dad's home. Michael was start out right, exploring, learning how to be a detective and a bounty hunter. Richard would pick him up on the weekends. Lindsay and Richard would take him outdoors to Indian Point, the Cleveland

Zoo, and enjoy Lake Erie. All the seasons transitioned naturally unlike El Paso, Texas.

Lindsay made a full recovery. By being with Michael she had a youngster to recondition her emotional stability. She was afraid to get pregnant again, but her doctor said she was healthy and could have a baby. Mr. Stern knew this and he was prepared for the news, because Lindsay was back to her young self. She wasn't afraid to take him down.

Supervisor Cliff Moses was reluctant to retire, but father time had got the best of him. With Agent Micovich gone, he no longer had the passion to find a replacement. Plus, he was through writing reports that filled Mr. Stern's pocket with Uncle Sam's money.

Agent Ron Roman and Bill Wright were always on the go. If they weren't fishing together, they were hunting down the bad guys.

Agent Roman made a suspicious, forward looking statement to his partner as they were unloading his boat at the Fairport Harbor Port Authority boat ramp.

"Bill, I'm afraid to say this, but I think one of the terrorists got away. The sub was never recovered. That man might still be out there."

ATF Agent Dana Bohatch met Agent Micovich while the two were investigating the same gun running case. The chance meeting was greeted with glee as the two realize they worked in the same building. They became close friends. Monica even suggested Dana transfer to the FBI, Division of Homeland Security.

Dana said she had a great assignment in Kingsville, Ohio, but she thought about the suggestion for a time. She ended up stopping over Monica's house after work. They arranged a visit on the weekend. The two found common interest which helped Monica overcome the loss of her best friend and partner, Agent Paula Gavalia. Agent Bohatch had a great husband and terrific family that also weighed heavily on Monica's disposition.

Agent Marisa Ross had to avoid the advances from Agent Wright. Wright wasn't one to back off. He was coy. The new relationship would become office gossip.

Chapter 39

Recovery

THE DOCTORS TOLD Lindsay to take things slow for a while. Understanding the meaning was clearly understood. She surely didn't want Stern to falter in his quest to control his disease. Without question he didn't want to resume a bad habit, one that could kill him.

Her desire to be loved and express joy was difficult. Her loss was extremely troubling. The unborn baby was no different than a full term baby. She expressed this to Richard and he understood. She had to hold on to her man. Certainly, she wasn't ready for action, the type she used to control her guy.

Mr. Stern was given guidelines to follow in order to help her recover. He told the doctors most of the facts. He sheepishly ignored the help Lindsay had provided for him. It was most important for him to hold Lindsay and say 'I love you.'

To say it was a fact, to live it was reality.

Richard turned to the doctor to express his thanks for saving Lindsay's life.

"We're a team, doc. I need her for so many reasons. She has given me strength to continue my quest to help defend America against the jihadists. I could go into other reasons, but having a companion that understands life's trials is so important."

The psychiatrist walked in as the MD was leaving. They briefly conversed about her physical condition.

Doctor Feldstein talked with Mr. Stern in private as Lindsay slept.

He says, "Her mental struggle with loss will be something you need to watch. Do call me, if she has periods of difficultly dealing with emotional strain."

Richard thanked the doctor for his advice. He gave the doctor a hint that she helped him straighten out his own shortcomings.

"She has some control over me, doc. I can't lose her over this. I don't want to fall apart."

The doctor went to see Lindsay the next day. He kind of signaled the happiness of two people working for a similar cause in life.

Lindsay says, "He's supposed to hypnotize me. What do you think about that, Doctor Feldstein. Maybe we have more to do."

"Lindsay, you received a serious concussion. Your brain is still reverberating and in recovery. The child you were carrying is in the hands of God. Your significant other should allow you plenty of time to rest. Absolutely, no hypnotic attempts at all, I'll let Mr. Stern know this. This is not the time for exercising the brain."

Richard visited Lindsay daily. He had much news to tell her, but held back. He didn't want to talk about terrorists and his communication with the FBI.

The FBI had concluded the team of bounty hunters, Richard Stern and Lindsay Wagner, had provided information that prevented a serious terrorist operation. The work they had done was beyond what FBI agents had uncovered.

Several weeks past, Lindsay was out of the hospital. She was feeling much better. The big picture unfolded for both of them. Stern received a special delivery notice. In the correspondence was the answer he was anticipating. It was good news.

Richard says, "Lindsay, I think we're going to get a check in the mail. This has happened to me before and it looks like history is about to repeat. I think we're going to get a check."

Lindsay says, "That is good news, if it happens, but I'm still not ready to jump for joy."

He says, "I know you're not. You need more time to heal. We can make life again. Happiness will come back. I'm asking you to just take life slow."

Lindsay jokes, "You need to understand the word, slow. Do you get it?"

Richard had a partner that wasn't going to fall apart. She was starting to crack a smile. This was a sign for him. She was coming back to live life again. God was shining a light on her.

Another week passed. The folder came by special delivery. The delivery man requested a signature for the mail. Richard sort of knew it was the reward. He handed it to Lindsay.

"Lindsay, you better open this. Maybe the government is after us. I bet you know the Pirates in the White House have been reading our emails. Maybe they saw one of our saucy videos. The IRS has been socking it to Tea Party members. I'm probably under investigation."

Lindsay says, "OK, I'll see if you're under investigation. That won't surprise me."

She carefully opened the letter as if it was a letter bomb.

She says, "I hope this doesn't explode or contain some toxic powder."

Richard says, "No, they already screened it; look inside."

A smile broke across her face. It was a letter of congratulation. She couldn't believe it. They had successfully helped deter the enemy of the United States. A reward check was included for the apprehension of numerous terrorist wanted by the Department of Homeland Security.

Lindsay exclaimed! "We did it, Richard. They gave us a whopper check."

She held the folder and hugged her guy. The joy of winning was stunning. She held him tightly. She kissed him and he kissed her. His joy was the fact that she felt some of her torture had subsided. They were coming back together like husband and wife.

Richard says, "My reward is being with you. This hug and kiss are the best. Just hold me, Lindsay. Don't tell me how much. I want to treasure this moment with you."

Lindsay says, "You're going to get a double reward tonight."

Richard says, "After we cash it, maybe we can move to the next step."

She asks, "What's the next step? Are we going to watch our homemade movies?"

"We're going to make a new movie, called SLOW."

Lindsay says, "Oh my God, are you sure, I'm ready?"

Richard says, "We'll let the doctors give us the green light."

"If I get the green light, you're going to have a smile on your face that I can't remove."

Richard confesses, "I want to feel you bounce up and down."

Lindsay says, "I can tell; I know how you are. It's going to feel like the first time and that wasn't slow, my man."

He says, "Lindsay, I didn't tell you this, but I think you were causing incredible dreams."

She has some fun with him. "You know, Mr. Stern; I'm not a quitter. I'll take you down pretty soon. You'll really be dreaming after that. I have a feeling we're heading for another adventure. One thing for sure, I'm not done doing it in ways you never dreamed possible."

He says, "That, my girl will signal the start of the next mission. I think we better celebrate this occasion with a coffee and dinner."

Just as he finished talking, the doorbell rang.

Richard asked, "Who could that be?"

Almost by a stroke of luck and a touch of kindness Mike and Mary Leinniger were passing by and saw his car in the driveway. They decided to stop and wish Lindsay a speedy recovery after hearing she was recovering at home.

Richard shouted to Lindsay, "Mike and Mary Leinniger came to visit. Come on in folks. Lindsay is feeling much better."

Mary Leinniger says, "We wanted to express our hope that Lindsay is feeling better. You two made the news. We read it in the newspaper. FBI rewards Fairport Harbor couple."

Lindsay says, "Thank you, Mary we aren't done yet. My guy is ready to dream again and his dreams come true."

Richard says, "Lindsay makes me dream."

Lindsay says, "We were thinking about going out to have a nice quiet dinner to celebrate."

Mike says, "We're heading to the Sunset Harbor Bar and Grill. Why don't you join us? Ronnie Curliss and his sister, Sherry, will be there. You know them."

Lindsay says, "Oh my God, this is how it all started."

THE END